The
HEAT OF
THE SUN

'*The Heat of the Sun* is by turns wildly colourful and straitlaced, witty and rueful, reserved and operatic'

Andrew Solomon, author of *The Noonday Demon*

'David Rain is far too young to be writing this exquisitely'

The Booklog

'This book captures the gaiety and tumult of a troubled age. But it is ultimately a novel of friendship, of love, and of lives'

Irish Examiner

'Rain's novel is a touching, often searing tale of friendship, betrayal and love. His flawed characters are staggering beneath the weight of the past, which they carry like burdens even beyond the book's chilling, operatic conclusion'

kpage

The

HEAT OF THE SUN

◆

DAVID RAIN

Atlantic Books

LONDON

First published in Great Britain in 2012 by Atlantic Books,
an imprint of Atlantic Books Ltd.
This paperback edition published in Great Britain in 2013
by Atlantic Books.

1 2 3 4 5 6 7 8 9

A CIP catalogue record for this book is available from the British Library.

Paperback ISBN: 978-0-85789-205-8
E-book ISBN: 978-0-85789-800-5

Printed in Great Britain by CPI Group (UK) Ltd, Croydon, CR0 4YY

Atlantic Books
An imprint of Atlantic Books Ltd
Ormond House
26–27 Boswell Street
London
WC1N 3JZ

www.atlantic-books.co.uk

For Antony, who asked:
'What happened to that boy?'

PROGRAMME

Overture 11

Act One: A Boy Called Trouble 21

Act Two: Telemachus, Stay 67

Between the Acts 133

Act Three: After Tokugawa 143

Act Four: The Gravity of Americans 185

Curtain 271

ON THE GRAVITY OF AMERICANS AND WHY IT DOES NOT
PREVENT THEM FROM ACTING RASHLY

Chapter title from Alexis de Tocqueville's
Democracy in America

Overture

In Havana before the revolution, I sat one afternoon on a hotel terrace, playing chess with an elderly gentleman who had struck up my acquaintance. Something about him was familiar. He was the type of American who seems almost British: leisured, with a patrician voice and perfect manners. A cravat, red as blood, burgeoned at his neck; his suit was crisp, immaculately white, and he studied the board with eyes blue and gleaming as the tropical sea. He said he had lived in the hotel for ten years. He called himself an exile. Fondly, he spoke of New York City and asked me what had changed. Imagining some sorrow of the heart had compelled him to leave, I hoped to hear his story, but he would not be drawn. Only later did I realize he was a financier, known in his glory days as the Emperor of Wall Street, who had perpetrated a fraud that had ruined thousands of investors. I wondered if he really thought he could never go home. He had served his sentence, paid his debts: the face that had sold a million newspapers would be anonymous now. Only a species of vanity kept him in his Cuban fastness, dreaming of Carnegie Hall and the Palm Court at the Plaza.

Some years ago in San Francisco I attended a production of Puccini's *Tartarin*. The opera, you will recall, is based on a novel by Alphonse Daudet. In the figure of Tartarin, the provincial braggart who is Don Quixote and Sancho Panza united in a single man, there is an allegory of the clash between fantasy and reality and the comedy that results from their irreconcilable claims. In a neighbouring box sat a divorcée (long neck nobly poised) who had been notorious not so long before. She caused no sensation; those around her were blithe, as was she, while the young man who accompanied her might never have known that her name had been a byword for womanly corruption.

Scandal seldom endures. In the days when I still took on journalism, I covered a trial in Hong Kong. A Chinese houseboy had murdered his lover, but this was no commonplace affair, given that the lover had been male, English, a nephew of the Assistant Colonial Secretary and betrothed to the Governor's daughter. Inevitably, the boy was condemned to hang. Flashbulbs blazed; the judge's gavel pounded; the governor's daughter broke into hysterical execration; but even this crime of passion, I reflected, would soon mean little to the world at large. Ours is an age of amnesia. This is a mercy. Yet certain scandals refuse to vanish.

For a time I believed that the Pinkerton affair would be forgotten. Its day had been dazzling: I had illumined it myself. Perhaps in used bookstores you may still turn up *Benjamin Franklin Pinkerton: A Life* by Woodley A. Sharpless (New York: Harper & Row, 1947). It is not a good book. That my first essay in the biographer's art should have been so rushed and dishonest a production has been a source of regret to me, although, of course, in those days the full story could never have been told. Whitewash was wanted, and whitewash I provided: I was too good a publicist to be a good writer.

Unfortunately, my distortions found their way into subsequent accounts. With *Pinkerton: Enigma and Truth* by Marius Brander (London: Gollancz, 1953), we need not concern ourselves. Promising much and delivering little, the book is a cut-and-paste from contemporary press reports, not to mention the work of a certain Woodley A. Sharpless.

Miriam Riley Vetch's biography of Kate Pinkerton, *Senator's Wife* (Boston: Houghton Mifflin, 1961), caused outrage in Democrat circles. That Kate Pinkerton encouraged the suicide of her husband's Japanese lover seems unlikely to me, nor can I believe that she acted as procuress for her admittedly promiscuous husband. The case against Mrs Vetch may be stated succinctly if I declare that she would never have been permitted to set foot in Kate Pinkerton's drawing room. Mrs Vetch, however, was fortunate in her publicists. For a year she lectured coast to coast on the woman she insisted on calling, appallingly, 'Kate'; there was talk of a movie (Yardley Urban was to play the lead), but the danger was averted, the public lost interest, and Mrs Vetch moved on to her next project, a life of Julia Ward Howe that promised startling revelations.

No threat came from Webster M. Cullen's *Pinkerton, Japan, and the War in the Pacific* (Chapel Hill: University of North Carolina Press, 1968). Cullen is the college professor par excellence, substituting theory for fact, copiousness for judgement, and jargon for good English. His readers were few.

When I checked the school history books, I was relieved to see that the Pinkerton affair rated a cryptic mention, if any: hardly a story for the eyes of youth. By now I thought of it as my story, and was by no means keen for it to be sniffed at and snickered over by those who could never understand it as I did. The whole business seemed buried as deep as the Teapot Dome scandal (that catastrophic blight on the reputation of President Harding), the Kellogg–Briand Pact or the Smoot–Hawley Tariff Act.

Then came Burl Blakey's novel *The Senator* (New York: Viking, 1974). Of a piece with Mr Blakey's other productions, this *roman-à-clef* of sex and corruption amongst America's ruling classes was a Book-of-the-Month Club main selection and *New York Times* number one bestseller. There is little point in castigating Mr Blakey. He is a force of nature: one is only surprised that in his several careers as gambler, deep-sea fisherman, and lover of starlets and models, he should find time to produce his eight-hundred-page epics. The movie, starring Hayden Granger, Rosalind Magenta, and a floppy-haired Curtis Kincaid, Jr (complete with purplish contact lenses) as the half-Japanese B. F. Pinkerton II, became the decade's biggest box office draw.

Today, there can be no hope that the Pinkerton affair will be forgotten. Perhaps there never was. When a man in high office dies we are always a little alarmed, as if we had expected death to tread lightly around those elevated above the common fray. When his death is violent and trailing skeins of scandal, our alarm becomes excitement and can hardly be held in check. Had Benjamin Franklin Pinkerton been an obscure figure his fate would have been shocking enough, but that so bleak a destiny should envelop a man so eminent lifted it to proportions of classical tragedy. What was the senator but the Great Man, brought low by his fatal flaw? A textbook case, out of A. C. Bradley!

He could have been president. Three times he put himself forward for the Democratic nomination: in 1920, when he lost, by a whisker, to James M. Cox; in 1928, when he lost (to the party's later regret) to Alfred E. Smith; in 1932, when he lost, decisively this time, to Franklin D. Roosevelt. There were those who said that the senator never fulfilled his potential, and yet, while failing to attain the highest office, still he became a significant architect of national affairs. In the Wilson years it was Senator Pinkerton who laid the foundations for American policy in the Philippines; during the Republican hegemony of Harding, Coolidge, and Hoover, he remained a prominent figure; but it was under Roosevelt that he came into his own, playing a key role in foreign policy as America moved towards the Second World War. Many remember Senator Pinkerton advocating internment of Japanese Americans. The part he played in the Manhattan Project has been documented extensively. By the end he was one of President Truman's closest advisers, and in the view of many it was the senator, more than any other man, who swayed Truman towards dropping atomic bombs on Hiroshima and Nagasaki.

The Pinkerton affair could be considered under many angles. The Manville connection was a story in itself. Benjamin Franklin Pinkerton, son of an hotelier from Atlantic City, hardly seemed cut out for his exalted station. That he owed it to a fortunate marriage was never in doubt. The world might never have heard of B. F. Pinkerton had it not been for his father-in-law, the long-serving Senator Cassius Cornelius Manville (Democrat, New York), who saw in the handsome naval officer a substitute for the son he had lost in the Cuban campaign of 1898. The Manvilles, that great East Coast political family, hardly knew what a viper they took to their breasts in the young lieutenant from the USS *Abraham Lincoln*. Later, many would ask what sort of woman Kate Pinkerton (née Manville) must have been: a woman not only apprised from the first of her husband's dubious past, but one who connived for so long to conceal it, even taking the child of his previous union as her own. Later, she must have wondered if the boy's Japanese mother achieved in death the victory she had been denied in life.

But I fear I slip into the tones of Mrs Vetch.

Naturally, much coverage was devoted to the provenance and peculiar history of Benjamin Franklin Pinkerton II. 'Trouble', as he was known, was a figure shocking enough, considering only his crimes; when, added to these, came the truth about his birth, the mixture was explosive. Condemnation, like buckshot, spluttered in all directions. Some directed their greatest outrage at B. F. Pinkerton; others, at B. F. Pinkerton II. Conservatives declared that a traitor was a traitor – what more was there to be said? Liberals asked: What was the son but the victim of the father? What chance had the boy? With his blond American looks, Trouble could hardly have known he was half Japanese, the son of a geisha girl who had killed herself for love of his faithless father. The truth might have devastated him at any time; in the event, it was kept from him for so long that, when he learned it, he could hardly help going a little mad.

To others, the victim was neither Pinkerton II nor the hapless Japanese girl; the one to be pitied was the young Lieutenant Pinkerton, drawn into the seductive lure of the Orient. The Pinkerton affair, in this view, was a sort of moral Pearl Harbor: Yellow Peril striking again, with Pinkerton II a fitting symbol that East is East, West is West, and never the twain should meet.

Next year, to my astonishment, marks an anniversary: forty years since my story's end. It is time to begin. I am an old man, and tired; sometimes I wish I could surge free of the past, like a Saturn V rocket, shedding stages on its way out of the atmosphere. Perhaps, in setting down my story, I will achieve some freedom from it. For years I refused to talk about the Pinkertons. But history cannot be left to Mr Burl Blakey. This book will appear only after my death. I shall paint no monsters. I shall level no blame. My purpose is simply to tell the story: not the definitive story (for where is that to be found?), but the story as it appeared to me, from my first meeting with Trouble to the end of my association with his family, many years later. Perhaps the story is not mine to tell. In the lives of the Pinkertons, I was, I suppose, a bystander, but one well placed on more than one occasion to witness the unfolding of their story.

It is the saddest story I know. The ending is so out of proportion with the beginning. Yet for me that ending is implicit in every step that precedes it: that eternal moment when the atomic cloud, one summer's morning, bloomed above the port of Nagasaki, where, many years before, a young man had dallied with a girl known as Butterfly.

ACT ONE

A Boy Called Trouble

'You're sure this is worth it?'

He twisted around. 'Trust me.'

The hill was low, a gentle incline, but I sweated and my heart beat hard. Grimly, I leaned on my ashplant and said it wasn't easy; Le Vol replied that nothing worthwhile ever was.

Winter in Vermont, I thought, was going to be cold. The days were drawing in. All the way up from the playing fields, the trees beside the lane had cast down their leaves: topaz and bronze, ochre and vermilion, saffron and scarlet and burnt orange. They filled me with a strange, exultant despair. They stuck to my shoes, to the end of my ashplant.

I had been surprised when Le Vol asked me to the place he called Nirvana. In my first days at Blaze he had hardly spoken to me, even though he slept in the cubicle next to mine. On the day I arrived I stepped towards him nervously, holding out my hand; but when I told him my name he only grunted, flopped down on his cot with a squeak of springs, and buried his face in a book that he produced from a pocket of his jacket like a magician's cards.

Why he had warmed towards me I was never quite certain. Perhaps he saw that I was unsuited, like him, to the boisterous world of Blaze. On Wednesday afternoons, when there were no classes and the fields were clamorous with football, hockey, and baseball, Le Vol and I had exemptions: I, for my ashplant; Le Vol, for the sickness that had laid him up the year before and still left him weak. We were expected to remain in the library, stiff-backed before the elderly lady librarian, but the lady, ever-reliably, always fell asleep.

The cries from the playing fields had faded and the ground had grown level. Le Vol beckoned me around a clump of trees. Quivering in the tawny light lay a graveyard. I was puzzled. Nirvana, I had imagined, would be a hut or, perhaps, a forest bower.

The graveyard looked abandoned, a remnant of early settlers. Weeds grew riotously. I peered at green, cracked headstones. Born Lincolnshire. Born Sussex. Born Warwickshire. And died in Vermont, long ago. I pictured flickering ghosts. I had thought of America as new, raw, but, even in America, history tugged implacably beneath the crust of the present day.

I said to Le Vol: 'Why do you call it Nirvana?'

'Don't be silly. This isn't Nirvana.' He strode towards a curtain of vines that seethed, thick and prickly, between the trees. Leaning down, he parted the way. 'A tunnel, I'm afraid. You'll have to crawl.'

'You don't seem to appreciate I'm a cripple.'

Bent double, I pushed my way after Le Vol through a low, dense darkness. We emerged into a vault, a grey, cobwebbed cell with two heavy-slabbed tombs jammed against opposing walls and a narrow walkway between them, carpeted with crunching leaves. A rusted lantern hung from the ceiling. Part of the back wall had crumbled, leaving a jagged slot of window that disclosed a view down the hill, across the many-coloured trees, towards the school buildings.

'The perfect lookout,' said Le Vol.

'For what?' Gingerly, I eased myself into position on a tomb. 'This place stinks.'

'Only mould.' He pushed back his coily red hair. A long-limbed, untidy fellow, he was inky-fingered, bitten-nailed, and his clothes did not quite fit him.

'*And* it's cold,' I said.

'But I couldn't keep Nirvana from you until next summer.' Le Vol, on the tomb opposite mine, drew forth a pouch of tobacco. My nerves were piano strings, waiting to be struck. I told myself I must act like other fellows: all I had to do was act like the others.

Several sets of initials, a penis, and a libellous statement about President McKinley had been scratched into the stone. 'Who else knows about this place?' I said.

'No one.'

'Lately, you mean.'

Firing up his pipe, Le Vol furrowed his brow with a contemplative air, and I asked him how he had found Nirvana.

'I was running away, actually. From Hunter.'

'You're not in trouble with Scranway?'

Eddie Scranway, I had learned soon enough, was the bully of Blaze Academy. Three years our senior, he was a ruthless fellow, feared by all, and had a golden retriever called Hunter. Only Scranway, whose father headed the school's Board of Trustees, was allowed to keep a dog.

'It was last week. He was on the rampage – you know,' said Le Vol.

I didn't really: not yet. 'And you pressed yourself into the foliage?'

'And found myself in a magic world.' He passed the pipe to me. His hands, long and veined, hung between parted, updrawn knees. How many others, I wondered, had he brought to Nirvana? I leaned against the cold wall. Puffing the pipe, I coughed a little, but only at first. Birdsong and intermittent gusts of breeze were all that disturbed the silence.

'So how long have you had that stick?' Le Vol asked.

'I told you, I'm a cripple. I've always had it.' Easier to lie. Why think of Paris? Why think of a green boxy sedan slamming into me on the Champs-Elysées? That I had once been different was of no account: I was who I was now, and time would not turn back.

Le Vol mused: 'At least you've had some advantages. Just think, going around the world! And there's me, who'd appreciate it, buried in the provinces.' He was a minister's son from St Paul, Minnesota. 'Then they send me here. Damn my father! You've no family at all?'

'Just my aunt. She's all that's left.'

'You're lucky. Family's a terrible thing.'

'Only people who *have* families say that.' My deepest wish was to see my father alive again.

Le Vol was eager to hear about my travels. This embarrassed me: what had I been but my father's passenger? Through the jagged window, Blaze Hall flared in the failing light. The main block of the school was a fine red-brick mansion, an English country house spirited across the ocean.

'Have you thought about this war?' Le Vol gestured with the pipe, as if, of a sudden, the war were all around us. We could have been in a lookout somewhere, with the front advancing rapidly. I strained for sounds of shelling, for the stuttering clack of machine-gun fire.

A dog barked in the distance.

'I don't get it,' I said. 'It's as if everything changed as soon as I left France. I think about it all, Notre Dame and the Boulevard Saint Michel and the Arc de Triomphe, and don't understand how there can be a war. Not in France.'

'Ever heard of Agincourt? Ever heard of Waterloo? Nothing lasts, Sharpless. Things get made. Then they fall apart.'

'You've been reading Mr Adams again,' I said.

'Mr Adams, Mr Wells.' Le Vol patted a pocket and drew forth a book: *The World Set Free*. He leafed through the pages. 'Don't rely on anything, that's the lesson of our lives. Maybe one day there'll be a world government, bringing peace to all. More likely, there'll be bombs that kill everything, raining down from the air. The end of the world as we know it. Ever wonder what you'll do when they let you out of here, Sharpless?'

'When I'm grown up? Why, what will you be?'

'I'm going to travel. See the world. While it's still there.'

'That's a thing to do, not to be,' I said.

'You could come with me – hoboes, how about it? See America, boxcar by boxcar!' I thought he was mocking me, but I made no protest. 'Last year in St Paul, when I had rheumatic fever, I used to lie in a window seat in the afternoons. I was so bored I wanted to die. Horses went by, and trolley cars and automobiles, and I thought: Take me with you. If only they'd take me wherever they were going. I don't want to be sick. I don't want to be weak. And I won't be. Nor should you. One day you'll throw away that walking stick.'

The pipe passed between us, back and forth. Blue-grey smoke swirled around us in the shadowy, chill space, and I wondered if Le Vol could really like me. I had never been friends with another boy. Cold seeped through my flannels and I thought of the body in the tomb beneath me; of course, it would be nothing now but a cage of bones.

Le Vol let down his drawn-up knees, kicking his heels against mossy stone. He yawned and stretched, knitting together his fingers; his jacket hung open and his bony ribs strained beneath the tautened whiteness of his shirt. Time thickened and slowed. I looked away: at the rusted, hanging door of the vault; at the leaf-scattered floor; at Le Vol again, his face curiously blank, his lips a little parted.

27

I had known this would happen. What moved me was not desire, but inevitability. I stood between the tombs; Le Vol shifted his hips. Lightly, I touched his shoulders, his chest, and felt for a moment a welling power, as if I could have all the things I wanted, as if all I wished would come to pass. We were about to do what other fellows did. Would we speak of it when it was over? I let my hand descend, feeling the hardness beneath his grey flannels. I tugged at his fly buttons. Again, closer, came the barking of the dog, and I wondered if Le Vol had heard it too.

There was a sound of running, of raised, excited voices. Le Vol pushed me away.

Somebody screamed.

'Get him! Get him!' We knew the voices.

'Pussy in the well! Pussy in the well!' Tramplings came from the graveyard: hard, insistent. A scuffle, blows.

'Damn, he bit me!' (Who bit? Hunter? No, not Hunter.)

'Quick, the rope, you idiot!'

How close they were! Hunter was frantic.

The scream again: a terrified wail.

'No… don't!' When I grabbed Le Vol's shoulder he had not yet moved; now, hunching low, he blundered back through vegetable darkness. Standing, swaying, alone in the stony cell, I could hear all that happened, picture it too: Le Vol erupting, dishevelled, from the vines; Scranway turning, eyes gleaming, as his henchmen, Quibble and Kane, readied the victim for the sacrifice.

'Leave him. What's he done?' – This from Le Vol.

'Why,' demanded Quibble, 'are you lurking, Le Vol?'

'Lurker Le Vol… Lurker Le Vol!' What a fool was Kane!

Quibble cursed. 'Keep hold of him. Stop squirming, Billy Billicay!'

Billicay: I knew the name – a skinny fellow with porcupine hair and little round spectacles. I had seen him often, looking lost, and wondered how such a boy could survive at Blaze.

'Leave him, I said!' – Le Vol again.

A crunch, a crack. Hunter barked.

Too late, I knew what I must do. Knuckles whitening on my ashplant, I lowered myself to my knees and painfully left Nirvana, digging my way through stalky dark obstructions. Burrs pricked me, leaves slapped my face; then came a pain that seared my right leg, in all the six places where it had shattered. I sank down, gripping my shin as if to hold it together. From outside came no sounds of struggle any more, only a whimpering, then laughter.

I had heard about the game called Pussy in the Well. Somewhere in the grounds of Blaze was the real well down which the 'pussy' had once been dangled. It had been covered over years ago, after one too many broken bodies had been hauled up from the bottom. But if no well was available, there were always pussies, and other fellows could improvise.

Through screening undergrowth, this is what I saw: Le Vol, unmoving, prone between two leaning, mossy headstones; Quibble, high in the branches of a yew, rope at the ready, fixing it in place; Kane, when the rope dropped, looping it under the armpits of the terrified Billy Billicay.

Quibble leaped from the branches. He tugged at the end of the rope. How gleefully they cried out – bullet-headed Quibble, knife-nosed Kane – as little Billy Billicay rose in the air!

And standing by, watching almost indifferently, Scranway only smiled and held Hunter's lead. Not for Eddie Scranway the sordid exigencies of bullying, the raised voices, the grappling, the blows; his role was to direct, to inspire, and, when appropriate, to administer urbanely the *coup de grâce*.

Edward F. Scranway, Jr was the handsomest fellow at Blaze, his uniform always immaculate, his nails neatly manicured, his patent-leather hair never in need of brushing. A man already, he shaved with casual ostentation every morning in the dorm bathroom, towel tucked around tight torso, muscles rippling in his bent right arm. One thought of Scranway and imagined a gleaming blade travelling smoothly over an uptilted, moist jaw.

When he let Hunter go, I thought the dog would bound forward, leaping up, snapping at Billy Billicay's heels. Instead, Scranway, with a raised finger, commanded Hunter to stay, and Hunter stayed.

Quibble and Kane stepped back respectfully as their master advanced upon the strung-up victim. Billy Billicay – shoulders hunched, jacket rucked up around the rope – was too afraid to do more than snivel. His spectacles flashed; his feet, unkicking, hung at the height of Scranway's chest as Scranway took in hand first one little shoe, then the other, unknotting the laces with the air of a fond father tending a beloved child. After plucking off the shoes and peeling off the socks, he handed the items to Kane, who received them gravely, like a manservant.

The final touch was accomplished with adroitness still more admirable. Reaching up, Scranway fondled at the fastenings of Billy Billicay's trousers, tugged them down, underwear and all, and tossed them inside out to Quibble, who slung them over his shoulder. The trousers – that was an essential part of Pussy in the Well: should Billy Billicay find his way down from the tree, there must be no easy end to his humiliation.

The little party stood surveying their handiwork. A delighted Kane chanted, 'Pussy in the well! Pussy in the well!' and Quibble cawed, but Scranway hushed them – as if, at this pinnacle of accomplishment, there could be no place for vulgarity. Dread filled me as I gazed upon Billy Billicay's hairless, pale thighs. A child: just a child.

With a curt laugh, Scranway tapped the little boy's hip, setting him swaying like a pendulum; then, as if he were bored, he turned on his heels and strode off through the crunching leaves.

Hunter padded obediently behind; Quibble too. Kane leaped up on a mossy slab and danced. As he shuffled, his head swayed from side to side and his nose seemed more than usually like the point of a knife, cleaving the air with thoughtless strokes. Kane was a scarecrow of a fellow, quite without the lumpy bulk of Quibble.

Only after Kane followed the others did I pull myself from the graveyard jungle. I had torn my jacket; there was a scratch on my cheek; I felt the wetness of flowing blood. Floundering, I made my way to Le Vol. Almost sobbing, I shook him and told him he was a fool.

His eyes opened. 'Damn Quibble. His fist's like a rock.'

We did our best to save Billy Billicay. There was no need to cut him down from the tree. His arms, pushed upwards by the tautened rope, slipped from harness of their own accord, and down he dropped. I reached him first. His spectacles were smashed. I took off my jacket and tied it like an apron around his naked thighs. Le Vol lifted him in his arms and carried him. Billy Billicay was light, but the journey was long. 'It's all right, Billy,' and 'Not long, Billy,' and 'We'll protect you, Billy,' we said, but Billy Billicay was silent all the way.

By the time we got back it was dark, and the others were in the dining hall. Furtively, Le Vol and I took Billy Billicay up to the dorm and put him to bed. With the unspoken, steady conviction of schoolboys, we would say nothing of what Scranway had done: it was our secret, as if we were ashamed.

We could not have saved Billy Billicay. I smoothed his chill forehead. In stripy pyjamas, he lay back on his pillow. Without his spectacles, his eyes were haunted, hollow, as if already he had left life behind. No one knew much about Billy Billicay. He was a person of no importance, one of those destined to pass through the world like a phantom, leaving no mark.

The day after, Billy Billicay rose as if nothing had happened, sat in the dining hall in his usual silence, and slipped crabwise down the corridors, eyes averted. The day after that, he cut classes in the afternoon. No one knew where he had gone; it was some time, indeed, before the alarm was raised. Later, we heard that they had found him in the graveyard.

The rope, secured by Quibble, still hung from the tree.

McManus II, the dorm room where I slept at Blaze, was a long, high-ceilinged chamber, partitioned in parallel lines. The partitions, evidently, had been put in place to afford us some protection against violence and immorality; in truth, they fostered both. The construction was of the flimsiest. No doors were provided, only curtains; cubicles were open at the top, and fellows could easily scale the dividing walls. In many places, partitions had been punched through; spyholes had been gouged and stuck up with chewing gum. Each cubicle contained an army-style cot, usually rickety, with a cabinet beside it that could not be locked. In the daytime, the place was merely drab, cheerless; at night, when moonlight slanted through the windows and spilled over the tops of the partitions, it became a place of fear. Many times I lay awake, listening to the creakings of the wind, the hootings of an owl, and, closer at hand, the whisperings and suppressed laughter, the furtive rockings, the gasps and sometimes thumpings and shouts that ended abruptly with a dazzle of light and a master's angry cries.

One afternoon, soon after Billy Billicay's death, I asked to be excused from class, saying I was unwell. It was not a lie: a febrile nervousness had afflicted me since that day at Nirvana. I went up to the dorm. The light was a filmy grey. How strange they seemed, these lines of cubicles!

Mine was number twelve. I pulled back the curtain on its rattling pole. I sat on the cot and it squeaked, sagged. Pictures – a horse, an actress, an automobile – had been pasted to the partitions by fellows in the past; pasted up, torn away, and pasted over again, leaving a palimpsest of ragged colours and shapes. I thought of the evening ahead: hobbies hour, dinner, study hall, prayers. I thought of the day to come, with its unwanted lessons: Literature, History, Latin. I thought of Billy Billicay, of what a fool he had been. How little imagination, to think that his life could never change! – as if all he had been or ever could be was Pussy in the Well, dangling from the tree, while the elegant, rough inquisitor ripped his trousers down.

I thought about my father. He told me once that in the life of every man there was one great good fortune and one misfortune of equal force. What these were in his case he never went on to tell me, but my good fortune, if I had one, was to be his son. Addison Sharpless was a man of no particular gifts – he was difficult to love, moody, dissolute, but it is to him that I owe my peripatetic life and that outsider's angle that (I like to think) has made me a writer. He was a Southerner. Born in Georgia after the Civil War, he was the heir of a ruined family, remnants of an *ancien régime* clinging to the tatters of old ways. As a boy, roaming their shabby plantation, he dreamed of a life unburdened by the past, and, after quarrelling with my grandfather, lighted out for wilder regions of plains, mountains, deserts: Oklahoma, Colorado, Utah. Successively he became a saddle-maker's assistant, a dry-goods merchant, a traveller in patent medicines. In San Francisco he found himself in charge of the customs house, and it was there, in 1900, at the age of thirty-four, that he married the harbour-master's daughter. I was born a year later.

My father took up a consular posting and we sailed to Nagasaki. The posting was the first of many. Whether he was determined to proceed ever westwards, perpetually in flight from his origins, I cannot say, but by the time I was eight years old I found myself in Paris. There was much I could barely remember: not Japan, where I had lived in the obliviousness of infancy; not Indochine, where Mama had died, sinking beneath a feverish burden while I lay in my little bed, unknowing, and the tin roofs drummed with monsoonal rains. There was Ceylon: what was Ceylon? Green, interminable terraced hills watched from the window of a climbing train. Turkey: what was Turkey? A man in a fez, a bubbling pipe, the weird high wailings of Mohammedan calls to prayer.

Only France flamed out with the vividness of life. Fondly, I recalled my father on honey-coloured boulevards, a portly figure in a frock coat, with moustache neatly waxed and the cane that he liked to carry, spinning it sometimes in a white-gloved hand. He referred to this gentlemanly affectation as his 'ashplant': a knobbly sapling of iron-tough wood, lacquered darkly black. How settled he seemed, how magnificently middle-aged! He kept a mistress in the Latin Quarter, a buxom, high-coloured girl from Dieppe with a delightful kindly laugh.

In Paris, I barely thought of myself as American. America was a dream: America was photographs, sepia images in a crackly-backed book. What had they to do with me, this tumbledown house in a place called Georgia, this beautiful unremembered Mama, this Addison Sharpless from another life, strangely slender, in a straw boater by a boardwalk rail? Slipped between leaves was a postcard of San Francisco; visible in the picture, indicated by an arrow, was the low, long apartment house, glaring white as a monastery, where Woodley Addison Sharpless made his entrance into the world. His American life had been brief. Days later, we left the white apartment house for the ship that waited to bear us away, across the blue Pacific and out into the world.

My misfortune, which for many years would outweigh my sense of good fortune, happened in Paris, one afternoon on the Pont Saint Michel. My father was taking me to tea with his mistress when suddenly he collapsed. His ashplant clattered into the gutter; his trilby rolled across the cobblestones and he clutched his heart, convulsing. A woman screamed, and I cried out and kicked as strangers, milling forward, shouldered me aside, bearing me away from my dying father. Two days later, on the Champs-Elysées, I ran into traffic and almost died. How could I know where I was going? Tears blinded me.

I had tried before, and failed, to write about this in my journal. I tried again now and had barely begun my entry when noises in the dormitory interrupted me. I was alarmed. If I were sick, I should have gone to the infirmary; to be in dorms in daytime was forbidden. First came a footstep. Then a shuffle. Next, a creak, followed to my amazement by raucous music, horns squealing with brassy impertinence. I peered down the aisle. Billy Billicay's cubicle lay at the far end: number thirty. It had been empty since he died. The sounds, I felt certain, were from there.

Riding over the music came a brazen, mocking voice – whether male or female, it was hard to tell – that first chanted some nonsensical recitative about sweethearts, love, and love lost, before bellowing out how you'd miss me, honey, miss my huggin', miss my kissin', some of these days when I was far away.

At Billy Billicay's cubicle, the curtain was open, and inside, busying himself with unpacking, was a new fellow. The first thing I remarked was his thick, unusually blond hair. He wore it a little long but not at all raggedly; it shone out even in the dusky gloom. Fellows at Blaze, Scranway aside, were shabby; this fellow was neat. His uniform, as he moved, seemed barely to crumple, as if made of a special fabric denied to the rest of us. A ring flashed on a finger. Bending down, averted from me, he retrieved a rolled-up sock from the floor.

Only after he stood again did the fellow see me watching him. He smiled. His mouth was wide, full-lipped, the teeth white and regular. Playfully he tapped me on the arm with the sock and said, 'I just *adore* Sophie, don't you?'

He had to raise his voice above the music.

'Sophie Tucker.' He indicated the phonograph; frilly-horned, it perched perilously on the cabinet beside the cot.

The fellow's eyes were extraordinary: deep, penetrating, an invitation into a darkness at once alarming and warm. Often, in times to come, I would wonder how to describe those eyes, so peculiar, so immoderate, beneath the blond sweep of hair. They were not blue, not black: they were violet.

On the cot, over the scratchy military blankets, the fellow had laid a silken quilt; on the partitions, he had tacked up colourful prints.

'A Braque,' I said, surprised. In those days, Americans knew nothing of modern art.

The fellow tossed the sock up high and plucked it from the air. 'Funny, isn't it? What do you think it's meant to be?'

'Houses on a hillside.' I had seen the picture in Paris.

'Do you know, I believe you're right.' Leaning forward, the fellow inspected the flat, block-like shapes. Gracefully, the pale nape of his neck stretched from his collar, and I feared for him, as if a neck so slender might easily be snapped. Should I tell him not to display these fineries? This was Blaze: all, I was certain, would be soiled and broken soon. Yet there was something about the fellow that belied his fey appearance: a tensile strength.

He held out a hand to me. 'They call me Trouble. Don't ask me why. I'm Pinkerton – Ben Pinkerton.'

Trouble, or Pinkerton, was shorter than I, a good head shorter, but perfectly proportioned, a little man. Whether he was younger than I or older, it was hard to tell. His hand, as I shook it, was dry and sleek, a delicate glove; there was a shock of cold from the ring. I wondered if he knew he would be sleeping in a dead boy's bed. Others, I supposed, would tell him soon enough.

The next time I saw Trouble was at dinner. He had found himself at a table far from mine, with fellows I did not know. I was worried for him. I struggled to listen while Le Vol told me something funny that had happened that afternoon in Literature with Mr Gregg. Often I glanced towards that distant table. How would others take to Trouble?

There was one clue, and it puzzled me: laughter, sudden and sharp, loud enough to ride across the clamour all around – and then the applause of eager hands. Trouble tilted back his chair. He grinned and someone slapped him between the shoulder blades.

Le Vol said irritably, 'Who's the new guy?'

Across the table from us a fellow called Elmsley, tight-collared with an acned neck, leaned forward and informed us in a low voice, as if it were a secret, that he had seen Trouble arrive that afternoon. 'In a big automobile – black, with windows all dark at the back. But you know who he *is*, don't you?'

I had disliked Elmsley from the first. The pustules on his neck were yellow half globes, buried in circles of reddened flesh; his teeth were brownish and sharp, like a rodent's fangs, and there was something rodenty, too, in his tapering nose, which wrinkled as he said: 'Pinkerton. The senator's son.'

Le Vol slammed his knife against his plate. For a moment I thought he might leap up, denunciations at the ready, and rush to Trouble's table. Dimly, I remembered a harangue he had delivered one night in the dorm upon the subject of a certain Senator B. F. Pinkerton (Democrat, New York) and the wickedness of his policy on the Philippines.

Elmsley sniggered, 'He looks like a sissy. A preening sissy.' And, as if to illustrate his own unlikely manliness, he speared a roast potato on his fork and stuffed it, whole, into his mouth. Chewing rapidly, cheeks ballooning, Elmsley resembled more than ever a hairless, pustular rat.

Things moved fast for Trouble after that. Soon he was surrounded by a circle of admirers. In the dining hall, his table was uproarious. Laughter exploded repeatedly; pellets of moistened bread flew back and forth. In the dorm before lights out, and sometimes even afterwards, he played his phonograph. How well we came to know the oeuvre of Sophie Tucker!

There was no stopping Trouble. Many were the tales of smoking, drinking, midnight expeditions out of bounds. There was one story, a myth perhaps, of Trouble and the Townsend twins returning in the back of a farmer's truck, on a Sunday morning, all the way from Burlington, reclining on hay. When Trouble was punished, it made no difference. Neither threats nor the swish of a master's cane deterred him. Never had a nickname seemed so apt. He said he had been tossed out of another school; that was why he had arrived at Blaze so late.

My sympathy for Trouble withered as his popularity grew. Le Vol professed himself disgusted with Trouble, and I agreed. Springs would judder as Le Vol, in the cubicle next to mine, shifted restlessly on his cot, struggling to read Mr Wells or Mr Adams as Sophie Tucker boomed out. One night he strode to Trouble's cubicle and shouted, halfway through 'Nobody Loves a Fat Girl, But Oh How a Fat Girl Can Love', that Senator B. F. Pinkerton (Democrat, New York) was a capitalist lackey, a criminal, and a liar.

Acolytes clustered in Trouble's cubicle: crushed together on the trunk or cross-legged on the floor. I pictured them – the Townsend twins, Earl Pritchard, Ralph Rex, Jr – twisting their necks towards their idol in unison as he clapped his hands, whooped, and declared that Le Vol had to be his friend: 'You hate the senator? Marvellous! But so do I.'

Defeated, Le Vol stalked away.

'What I don't get,' he said to me later, 'is the Scranway angle.'

'What angle?' I said.

'On Trouble.'

Le Vol often brought up Trouble: I never did. We hunched, bored, across a library table, hearing cries from the playing fields. The sky outside glimmered like steel. There could be no prospect of Nirvana, even had we been willing to go there again. Something, it seemed, had ended for us, or had never really begun.

'Scranway hasn't done a thing,' Le Vol went on. 'It's odd. Trouble's a prime candidate for Pussy in the Well.'

'Somehow,' I said, 'I can't see it. He's no Billy Billicay.'

'Don't believe it. Scranway's biding his time.'

Those last weeks of that fall term were Trouble's season, his time of greatness. The trick with eccentricity is to carry it off with brusque elan, as if unaware of it as eccentricity at all. Trouble was the type who, in his admirable self-absorption, his superlative egotism, simply acted as he wished to act, and found that weaker types fell in with him avidly.

No doubt his father had shown him the way. Curious, I studied the papers in the library, searching for news of the great man. I found it frequently. Week after week, Senator B. F. Pinkerton (Democrat, New York) fulminated on the floor of the Senate, urging America to join the war in Europe. His reasons interested me little; what intrigued me was the respect, the awe in which the world appeared to hold him. A large, florid man with a stern centre parting, pince-nez and a carefully cultivated moustache, he resembled his son only in his look of formidable self-possession. He pictured himself, I imagined, as a statesman in the Roman mould – not as the bluff, blustering walrus in a starched collar that I saw.

Likewise, B. F. Pinkerton II never acknowledged what was, to others, his defining characteristic: his size. He was uncommonly small. Perhaps that was why he had made himself into an athlete of formidable prowess. Often he was seen going to and from the gym, a pair of boxing gloves dangling from his neck. Strange to think of him slamming at a punching bag, even swinging a fist at a heavy opponent!

From a window in the library, I could see the tennis courts, crisscrossed through a mesh of wiry fences. Once I watched as

Trouble slammed through set after set with a willowy fellow from Iowa called 'Hoppy' Hopkins. When Trouble served, he propelled the ball across the net with a force that suggested it was an enemy to be vanquished; when Hoppy sent a shot back high, Trouble leaped explosively and his shirt rode up, exposing the hollow of his barely fleshed belly, the hard downward arch of his ribs.

Picture Trouble at an impromptu game of baseball: hunched forward, feet shifting, bat prodding the air behind his shoulders, tongue stuck in a corner of his mouth in a parody of concentration. When Earl Pritchard rockets the ball towards him, Trouble strikes at it like an uncommonly graceful lumberjack, connects with an explosive crack, and pelts from base to base as if he is flying. Always, when I think of Trouble in those days, it is of a little man in motion: clattering downstairs, no hand on the banister; darting across the quadrangle, hailing an acolyte; on the lawns, running against the wind on a windy day.

Trouble's greatness came to a head on the night before we left for Christmas vacation. We had stayed up late in McManus II, freed already from the constraints of term. Fellows played cards, wrestled, roared with laughter. Some sang dirty songs. Some smoked. Some took turns on the landing, watching for masters, but no one really cared if we were caught.

I found myself in Le Vol's cubicle, where Le Vol, in his element, argued politics with a bellicose Elmsley and a lumbering fellow from Texas called Joe Boyd, who prodded the air with a knobbly index finger. I only pretended to listen. From time to time others joined us, then drifted away, shaking their heads.

One thing was odd. Sophie Tucker was silent. 'Where's Trouble?' I heard it said, and 'What can Trouble be up to?' That he was *up* to something was clear. The Townsend twins had also gone missing; so had Ralph Rex, Jr.

The mystery would be explained, but not before a master came clumping up the stairs, yelled for order, and lights were extinguished at last.

I had drifted asleep when a hand shook me. I sat up sharply. Above the cubicles, snow flurried against high windows, fracturing the light of a gibbous moon.

Le Vol, eyes excited, held a finger to his lips. 'Trouble's sent word. Something's up.'

'What are you talking about?'

'Quick! Get dressed. We're going. All of us.'

He held out my trousers, coat, boots. Dazed, I pulled them over winter pyjamas. Icy gusts skirled between the cubicles. By the far wall a window yawned wide. Outside, a ladder stood against the sill. In hushed eagerness, fellows clambered down into the snowy yard.

Joe Boyd disappeared from view. Le Vol and I were the last ones left.

'You go,' I said. 'I can't – my leg.'

'I'll hold the ladder for you. Give me that.' He grabbed my ashplant and tossed it from the window.

From the ladder, he called back: 'Now, follow, you hear?'

'But you *hate* Trouble,' I said.

'Sharpless, this is rebellion – the Boston Tea Party!'

Doubtfully, I watched as Le Vol descended. The ladder shook as I made my way after him, swinging out my damaged leg numbly between rungs. Snowflakes stung my face. I shouted to Le Vol to hold the ladder steady.

'Not so loud,' he shouted back.

When I reached the ground, Joe Boyd raced towards us. He had stolen the wheelbarrow from the gardener's shed.

42

'The cripple-carrier! In you get, Sharpless!' he cried, and rammed the clumsy vehicle into my calves.

With a gasp, I collapsed into its depths and we were off, charging across the fields and up the hill. Snow churned beneath the single wheel; several times the barrow lurched, and I almost found myself pitched to the ground.

Laughter sounded, and raised voices, before the graveyard came into view. Through barren trees appeared an orange incandescence, shivering and crackling against the night.

We rounded a corner. Between tomb-slabs was a mighty bonfire, and circling it, uproarious, were perhaps forty fellows. All seemed ecstatic. I saw Elmsley, arm-wrestling with Hoppy Hopkins; the Townsend twins; Earl Pritchard; Ralph Rex, Jr; Quibble and Kane – Quibble, in a cap with woolly earflaps, a drunken grin on his face; Kane, swaying dangerously, knife-nose red at the tip. Cigarettes glowed in gloved hands; beer foamed from brown, glinting bottles; and on the other side of the fire Trouble had clambered up to the top of a vault and gazed down benevolently on the revels he had commanded. Weirdly, he appeared to hover above the flames, and I found myself wondering if he was angel or demon.

Somebody thrust a beer bottle into my hand. Le Vol had gone, vanishing into the crowd. A dog barked and the Townsend twins, tuneless in unison, caterwauled a song by Sophie Tucker.

Then I saw the effigy hanging from the yew. A scarecrow draped in a school jacket, it swayed from a rope around its neck. I gasped, and did not think now that Trouble might be an angel.

In the firelight, all of us were demonic.

Elmsley appeared beside me. He was shorter than I, and his rodenty face nuzzled close to mine in a parody of affection. 'The Billy Billicay Memorial Service!' he cried. 'The scarecrow was my suggestion. But I don't think it pays to stand out too much, do you?'

'At Blaze, you mean?' I said.

'Let's say someone might be in trouble soon – get it?'

Turning, I saw a figure deep in shadow, withdrawn amongst the trees. It was Scranway, his overcoat shrouding him like a cloak. Unmoving, he held Hunter's lead; it was as if, late as it was, he had just happened to be taking his dog for a walk and paused, with idle interest, upon this unexpected scene.

Blaze was bleak when term resumed, a place of clanking pipes, of overshoes in heaps inside entrance halls, of icicles on gutters and frost on glass, of the doggy, stale smell of snow-spattered coats drying on lines of verdigris hooks. Classrooms were stifling; leaning forward, head on arms, I stared from steamy windows, watching the crisscross flurryings of snow. At night I huddled under my blankets in my dressing gown. Everything I did – bathing, buttoning my shirt – was awkward, as if my fingers were twice their normal size. Quadrangles and courtyards were slippery, slushy. Snowballs whizzed by and exploded into powder against backs, chests, and walls, to the accompaniment of delighted or anguished cries.

We were in Literature with Mr Gregg when the bad things began. Striding up and down between desks, slapping a fellow on the head from time to time, Mr Gregg was discoursing on Shakespeare's late romances and the difficulties critics encounter with a form that dares to mingle comedy and tragedy, realism and fantasy. Often he wrote quotations, names or dates for us to copy down, squealing out rapid-fire curlicues of chalky, illegible handwriting. When he informed us of Dr Johnson's negative judgement of *Cymbeline* – '*Unresisting imbecility*... so like the minds of most in this room' – he charged to the board to record it for us.

Classrooms at Blaze had twin blackboards that slid up and down like sash windows. That day, both boards in the room had been left in the upper position. Impatiently, Mr Gregg reached for the pole with a hook in the end that stood behind his desk. As the outer board thudded into position, he seized a stub of chalk, scrawling up s. JOHNSON (1709–84), followed by the quotation in full.

None of us copied it down. Intent upon his task, Mr Gregg had not noticed the other blackboard that now stood revealed, looming over the class from on high. But at once, every fellow had eyes for nothing else.

First there was silence, then explosive laughter.

Mr Gregg reeled around. Every face, he realized, was fixed upon the board above, where the question was posed in handwriting of a clarity he could never have emulated:

WHY WAS B. F. PINKERTON II

EXPELLED FROM MILITARY SCHOOL?

Underneath, a crude drawing suggested the answer.

Trouble sat diagonally across from me, three seats ahead. I could not see his face, but the flush that spread up his neck stood out clearly enough. As turmoil reigned around him, he seemed suspended in place: but only for a moment.

He rushed from the room.

'Mr Pinkerton!' Mr Gregg cried, lunging to the door, and called again down the corridor: 'Mr Pinkerton!'

* * *

45

Soon the charges were known all over Blaze. Joe Boyd told us the story that evening at dinner; he had heard it from Hoppy Hopkins, who had heard it from a fellow in Form C.

This was the story. Before Trouble came to Blaze, he had been at naval school in Maryland, where (so it was said) he had proved himself unusually inept. With his shabby gear, his supercilious quips, his inability to stand to attention, the penalties he incurred for his classmates were legion. None of them liked him; or rather, only one did. This was Scotty Ridgeway, the handsome, popular son of an admiral who had distinguished himself in the Spanish–American War. Scotty Ridgeway, like his father, was a model of seamanly prowess, but Scotty's academic work was not up to much. All he wanted was naval glory. Bad grades would not only deprive him of his place as an officer cadet, but disgrace him in his father's eyes. Quietly, he grew desperate: but Trouble was on hand. When an important test loomed, Trouble broke into the school office, stealing the papers to give to his friend.

Soon the crime was traced, but worse was to come when a diary discovered in Trouble's desk revealed crimes still darker. Trouble, it appeared, had been at the centre of a circle of corruption. Scotty Ridgeway was the first of his victims; later, the two of them initiated others into the vilest depravities.

The scandal rocked the school. Only the most stringent efforts kept it from the public prints. Admiral Ridgeway, at all costs, had to be prevented from knowing the charges; Senator Pinkerton, defending his son, threatened legal action. In the end, Scotty Ridgeway was saved, while B. F. Pinkerton II was compelled to leave and was banned from ever serving in the US Navy.

'Quite a story.' Elmsley winked at me from across the table.

'It's the biggest secret – the biggest ever,' said Joe Boyd, awed.

'Not much of a secret,' said Le Vol, 'if all of us know it. Who found this out, anyway?'

'Someone,' said Elmsley, 'who's not fond of Trouble.'

Trouble's glory departed as swiftly as it had arrived. He had no peace. In corridors, fellows shouldered roughly past him. Towels flicked at him in the bathroom. One day, several fellows held his head down a toilet bowl and pulled the chain. His smallness became a curse to him. He was tripped up, pushed into walls; the stairs, which he had taken so confidently before, became places of danger where a mischievous hand, a malevolent foot, might seek him out. More than once he stumbled and fell. 'Watch it, little boy!' and 'Get away from me!' came the wails of outrage as he cannoned into fellows further down.

Cubicle number thirty was desecrated. First the silken quilt was hacked with knives, set alight, pissed on, then flung from a window. Obscene additions covered the colourful pictures. Jubilantly, fellows flung Trouble's phonograph records like discuses up and down the corridors, inundating the brown linoleum with a jagged sea of black.

They smashed the phonograph too.

In study hall and at dinner, Trouble sat alone. Of the acolytes, none remained. True, some had lingered – the Townsend twins had been the last to hold out – but the burden of conformity was too much. To take Trouble's part was to invite assault, derision, the vilest accusations. For a few days fellows shook their heads, wondering how Trouble had taken us all in; then none spoke of the past any more. Trouble might never have enchanted any of us.

The masters did not know what was going on. The world of the boys, like the secret lives of animals, unfolded beneath their awareness. If Mr Gregg thought again of the incident with the blackboard, he must have seen it as an isolated outrage, not the first in an evil chain. In class, Trouble betrayed little, sitting in silent dignity. The stares, the whispered jokes, the compasses stabbing his buttocks, came only when the master's back was turned.

One afternoon, as snow fell thickly, Mr Gregg made us read aloud from *Cymbeline*. The scene was a long one and the class soon grew restless; besides, Mr Gregg had assigned a part to Trouble. Guffaws, barely suppressed, accompanied every speech that Guiderius delivered.

In the scene, Guiderius and Arviragus, the king's disguised sons, conduct a burial service in the woods for Imogen, whom they falsely believe to be dead as well as a boy; that she is their sister is also unknown to them. Neither the pathos nor the absurdity of the situation infused our reading. Trouble was dutiful, his voice clipped and passionless; Elmsley, as Arviragus, sounded uncommonly nervous, stumbling often, as if in the mere act of playing a scene with Trouble he had compromised himself.

Trouble intoned:

> Why, he but sleeps:
> If he be gone, he'll make his grave a bed;
> With female fairies will his tomb be haunted,
> And worms will not come to thee.

The snorts were loud. Mr Gregg looked up from his book. Elmsley replied, stumblingly:

With fairest flowers,
Whilst summer lasts, and I live here, Fidele,
I'll sweeten thy sad grave.

Eight fellows had speaking parts. I was one of them, and we all had to stand. I resented this; I was the Soothsayer, who speaks only when the scene is almost over. Outside, glaring whitely under the pale sun, snow covered the playing fields like an intimation of death.

We had reached the part where Guiderius and Arviragus sing their famous funeral song. Trouble had the first verse. At the direction *Song* he paused. Someone stifled a shriek.

'Just read it, Mr Pinkerton,' said Mr Gregg.

Suddenly I was alarmed. Trouble faced the class. In fascinated, confused longing, we all gazed back at him. From the first I had sensed his magic; now, as if all along he had been biding his time, waiting for his moment, the magic reached out to touch us all.

Mr Gregg looked puzzled. Then Trouble began to sing:

Fear no more the heat o' th' sun,
    Nor the furious winter's rages;
Thou thy worldly task hast done,
    Home art gone and ta'en thy wages.
Golden lads and girls all must,
As chimney-sweepers, come to dust.

On the first lines, Trouble's voice wavered; after that, the tone became assured. I slumped into my seat, pinned down as if by oppressive gravity, yet something in me struggled to escape, like a bird that flurries at the bars of its cage. Trouble delivered the song slowly, giving each word its due in a clear, soaring tenor. The song, in all its melancholy beauty, might have been a summation of all that life could hold. The setting, I realized later, was the one by Sir Hubert Parry: I would come to know it well.

The second verse was for Arviragus; then the two had alternating lines. Elmsley looked about him. Terror flashed in his face, and he dissolved into the resignation of the damned as Trouble pushed aside an empty desk, advanced upon him, and draped an arm across his shoulder. Elmsley could barely move his lips; it was Trouble who sang his parts, with Elmsley propped beside him like a ventriloquist's dummy:

> Fear no more the lightning-flash,
> > Nor the all-dreaded thunder-stone;
> Fear not slander, censure rash;
> > Thou hast finish'd joy and moan.
> All lovers young, all lovers must
> Consign to thee and come to dust.

When the song was over, there was silence, and I wondered what it meant. Time, it seemed, was stranded in its flight, as if a pendulum had swung high, hovered, and refused to sweep down. We had been lifted out of ourselves. The fellow who had sung was no schoolboy victim, fresh from being tripped up on the stairs; the fellows who had listened were not the tormentors they had been and would be again.

Then came the applause. Who began it I cannot say; first one pair of hands struck softly, slowly together, then another and another, until the sound surged across the room like thunder, sweeping us all into its startling grip.

That evening it was my turn to be chapel monitor, readying the chapel for morning service. All except the most pious fellows resented this task. It was worst in winter. Situated apart from other buildings at the bottom of a sloping lawn, the chapel was cold enough to make me shiver even as I swept the aisles, polished the brass, changed the candles, and adjusted the hymnals in scarf, gloves, and overcoat.

I was anything but thorough. There were meant to be two monitors: Trouble had been rostered with me that evening, and I had not been able to find him. I was angry. I had left my tasks too late and it was time for dinner.

Only as I was about to leave did I pause, slumping exhaustedly on the front pew. And what, I wondered, had become of Trouble? When the bell had rung and Mr Gregg's class had spilled into the corridor there had been jokes, jostlings, but feeble ones; Trouble strode away, and not a single fellow tried to hold him back.

Still his song disturbed me. In the chapel, the melody came back to me, its strange beauty burning into me like a brand. I gazed up at the lectern, at the crucifix, at the high windows. Fugitive sunset flashed through stained glass and, resting my chin on my ashplant, I felt myself slipping into violet eyes, into a dark brightness where questions hovered over me like imponderable hanging fruit.

I had hauled myself to my feet and was about to trudge back down the aisle when I heard a groan. At first I thought it was the wind, but the groan came again, and I swivelled towards the altar. Perhaps someone waited there, watching me, setting me up for some cruel joke, but I stumped in that direction all the same. Carpet, thick and blood-red, sank beneath my boots. White linen concealed the table, dropping at the corners in papery folds.

For a third time I heard the groan, a sound of pain. I paced around the table. Oh, but I had not been thorough!

Trouble lay on his side, doubled over.

I prodded him with my ashplant. 'Can you hear me?'

'Damn, I must have passed out.' He raised his head, wincing. 'Who are you?'

I reminded him of my name.

'Leave me alone.' He shivered violently. He wore no coat, no hat; his attackers must have set upon him in another building, then carried him out to the chapel and left him here.

'You're blue with cold,' I said. 'Can you stand?'

'Leave me,' he said again, and coughed.

'You'll have to go to the infirmary. I'll get help.'

'No!' He reached up, grabbing the edge of the table; I thought he would pull down the cloth, candles and all, and I flustered about him, but he waved me away. Like a drunkard, he staggered down the steps and crashed into the railing before the first pew. He stood swaying, holding it tightly.

'You'll catch your death.' I tugged away my scarf, struggled out of my coat. 'Here, let me help you.'

Had Trouble shouted at me, I should not have been surprised; but he turned, pliantly enough. Bundling him into my outdoor things, I realized anew how small he was. Blood glistened darkly against his blond hair.

In the chapel porch, we paused. The snow had stopped falling and lay beneath the moonlight in pillowy drifts. From the dining hall, across an upward slope of whiteness, vertical strips of light shone through cracks in the curtains. The infirmary was further still: across a quadrangle, two flights up.

'Careful on the steps,' I said. 'It's a bit of a way.'

He said to me suddenly: 'Who are you? Who are you, really?'

'Come on, you're light-headed. Infirmary!'

'No, no infirmary.' He strode towards the dining hall, and all I could do was try to keep up. In the vestibule, he paused. Before us stood a set of swinging doors with portholes in the upper halves,

52

like twin cheery faces. The clamour of voices, the clatter and scrape of cutlery, sounded from within.

He pushed through the doors. A clear, wide track led to the dais at the end of the hall, where masters and senior fellows, Scranway included, dined together at the high table. Trouble progressed slowly, my too-long coat dragging on the floor behind him like a cape.

Silence fell. Under sickly electric light, the dishevelled, bloodied Trouble was an apparition: Banquo's ghost.

At the foot of the dais, Trouble stopped. He stretched out an arm and pointed. His voice, when he spoke, was steady.

'Fight me,' he said. 'Fight me yourself.'

He dropped his arm, swayed, and crumpled to the floor. Cries broke out. Frantically the headmaster tried to quell the uproar, as Mr Gregg rushed towards the prone boy.

They kept Trouble in the infirmary for three days. The cut on his forehead was long, but not deep; his ribs were bruised, but none was cracked, and he had caught a chill. On the afternoon of the second day, I visited him. I found him sitting up against pillows. Circling his temples was a white bandage. He held a pen and resting on his thighs was a portable escritoire, with a sheet of paper at the ready.

'A visitor. Isn't that dangerous?' he said.

'For anyone else, perhaps.'

'Compassion for the cripple? I wouldn't bet on it. How's Eddie Scranway?'

'The masters wondered why you pointed at him,' I said. 'Scranway was in class all that afternoon.'

'I *was* light-headed. You said so.'

The infirmary occupied an attic under the eaves, with creamy walls sloping between dormer windows. I thought of the hospital ward where I had lain for weeks in Paris. I hated hospitals. I hated sickrooms. I never wanted to be in a sickroom again. 'They must have asked who did it, didn't they?'

'Do you think they want to know?'

There were five other beds, four of them empty, pillows crisp as untrodden snow. A mousy boy slept in the bed next to Trouble's; disturbingly, he reminded me of Billy Billicay. Under the window gleamed a spindly hoop-backed chair. I perched on the end of Trouble's bed. 'I don't know how you stand it,' I said. 'How *can* you stand what they've done to you?'

'Don't you think I deserve it? You've heard the stories.'

'Stories are stories.'

'Oh, the test paper, that's true. Maybe it was stupid of me, but it seemed so unfair, Scotty being kept out of officer training, all for the sake of some silly set of questions. But the diary? Come on! Let's just say there are people who hate the senator. They'll do anything to disgrace him.'

'They failed, though. It wasn't in the papers.'

'But the story's spreading.' Cries, like birdcalls, echoed from the playing fields. The boy in the next bed shifted, murmuring; he must have been dreaming. Trouble reached for a handkerchief, sneezing into it lustily. The bed squeaked and shook, and I asked, too urgently, how the story could have spread. His nonchalance maddened me.

'At Navy school, there was a fellow from Kentucky or Tennessee, somewhere like that, who'd never seen the sea before. They called him Landlubber and ragged him about what sort of sailor he'd make. His real name was Elmsley – Dan Elmsley. Guess whose cousin he is?'

'I'll kill that little rodent.'

54

'Relax. It wasn't Elmsley. Not really.'

'What? Elmsley heard it from Cousin Dan.'

'Well, he might have let slip a few things. But he didn't do this.' Trouble sneezed again. 'Listen,' he went on, between wipings of his nose, 'there might be… a favour you can do for me. Would you like that?'

'Depends what it is, doesn't it?'

'One moment,' he said, and dipped his pen into the inkwell on the escritoire. As he wrote, a furrow appeared between his dark eyebrows; writing, I suspected, had never been easy for him.

'There.' He held up his paper and blew on it. 'I think the bulletin board in McManus Two would be best, don't you?'

I took the paper carefully. Trouble's handwriting was remarkably neat.

CHALLENGE

That BASTARD Eddie Scranway has terrified Blaze long enough. He is a COWARD, doing everything through his 'assistants'. On Monday afternoon, Douglas Quibble and Frank Kane jumped me, beat me up, and left me unconscious. THEY ACTED UNDER SCRANWAY'S ORDERS. For that reason, I, B. F. Pinkerton II, hereby challenge Eddie (COWARD) Scranway to fight me OPENLY, with BOXING GLOVES (Queensberry Rules), in the gym at ten o'clock (p.m.) on the last day of term. I will NOT fight Douglas Quibble or Frank Kane. I WILL fight Eddie Scranway. May the best man win.

Sincerely,

B. F. Pinkerton II

P.S. If Eddie Scranway does NOT accept this challenge, it is proof that he is a COWARD.

'You like it?' said Trouble.

'I love it. But think! So it was Quibble and Kane. How can you prove Scranway put them up to it?'

'You don't think he did?'

'He'll deny it.'

'To the masters? Let him! But you know and I know and Hunter the dog knows why Quibble and Kane do anything, ever. It's time to call Scranway's bluff.'

'Queensberry Rules? Trouble, even I know that boxers are matched according to weight. And you're tiny.'

'So I'll train. We've got three weeks.'

'We?' I said.

'It's a duel. I'll need a second.'

I laughed, but Trouble was in earnest. Solemnly then, I looked into his strange eyes, spat into my palm, and gripped his hand. I hated Blaze Academy: I hated all that it stood for. To champion Trouble would be to strike a blow against it. A blow for freedom. The boy in the next bed twisted, crying out faintly. Fever glistened on his forehead.

As I left, I asked Trouble: 'How did you know that song, anyway? The one in class.'

'Oh, Mama took me to the play once. Boring as all hell it was, but I liked the song and learned it. Funny, isn't it? *Golden lads and girls all must, as chimney-sweepers, come to dust…* Why must they? Didn't us golden lads have any other career options in those days?'

'Mr Gregg says it's not about children going up chimneys. A chimney-sweeper was a name for a dandelion – blow on it, and it's gone. And it's *as* for *like*. Golden lads, *like* dandelions, end up as dust.'

'Don't we all?' said Trouble. 'Even Eddie Scranway.'

* * *

'It's a prank, it has to be!'

'Talk about a massacre! Imagine it.'

'Did Trouble even write it? I can't believe it.'

'Three years younger, six years smaller!'

'He's in the infirmary. Who put up this notice?'

That evening, fellows clustered excitedly by the bulletin board in McManus II.

'Say, where's Scranway? Has he seen this?'

As if in answer, the door swung open and Scranway entered with Hunter loping behind. The fellows fell silent; nervously, some shuffled away from the bulletin board.

Scranway, taking in the situation at once, ripped the challenge from the wall. If I thought his face would change as he read it, I was wrong. Around us, voices sounded again, rising into a clamour:

'You'll wipe the floor with him, Scranway.'

'Trouble's crazy. You'll show him, Scranway.'

'Roll up, roll up for the fight of the century!'

Scranway held up a hand and silence fell. He crushed the paper into a ball. He tossed it into the air and caught it. He dropped it, kicked it like a football.

'Whoever posted that,' he said, 'can tell Trouble I'm calling his bluff. He wants a fight? He's on.'

Cheers erupted with volcanic force.

In my cubicle, I found Le Vol sitting on my cot. He sprang to his feet as I entered.

'What do you think you're playing at? It was you, wasn't it? You put up that challenge.'

'Haven't you always wanted a revolution?'

'I'm warning you, that's all. Trouble's trouble.'

'Maybe he's my kind of trouble.'

'Yes, if you want to get beaten to a pulp! It was bad enough, tagging after him in the dining hall when he put on his little show. People are talking. This is Trouble, remember – Trouble! Think what kind of person he is.'

'I have.' I slumped down on my cot. Le Vol's face had flushed and I looked away from him. How ugly he was, how gangly and grotesque, with his fiery hair and ill-fitting uniform!

'Give it up, Sharpless. I'm telling you as a friend.'

Later that night, on the way to the bathroom, I found a ball of paper on the floor. No one was looking, so I picked it up, uncrumpled it, and folded it neatly. The challenge might have been a holy relic, something vital I had to keep.

My duties as Trouble's 'second' began soon enough. Whether he was rising early to run around the grounds, performing sit-ups or push-ups between classes, jumping rope, touching toes, propelling himself along parallel bars, lifting dumb-bells or pummelling a punching bag, I was with him, counting laps, counting repetitions, counting time.

We were objects of derision, but neither of us cared. With peculiar exaltation I saw the sneers and heard the guffaws as we stood in assemblies side by side, as we made our way along corridors together, as we sat apart from others at meals, sequestered in our special world.

Fellows gathered to watch Trouble train. Some called him 'squirt' or 'little boy'; some called him worse things, but there came no greater torments. When I said to Trouble that their behaviour surprised me, he looked at me pityingly. Hadn't Scranway dictated their every move? Only Scranway, in the fight of the century, could deliver Trouble to his fate.

Elmsley liked to hint at what was coming. He had taken to following us, trailing after us, watching us from a distance, poking his rodenty nose from behind a pillar as we passed. When I warned him off, his ugly mouth smirked, teeth glimmering like a clutch of razor blades.

One afternoon, as winter gave way to spring, I sat on a bench in the changing room while Trouble showered. From behind a partition came the roar of water. I leaned back against the clammy wall. Smells of ammonia and smells of sweat mingled pungently with the thickening steam.

'You think you're his one true friend, I suppose?'

The voice startled me: Elmsley, sliding closer along the varnished bench.

'If you were his friend' – Elmsley spoke low – 'you'd make him give this up. But no, you have to have a tragedy, like *Cymbeline*.'

'That isn't a tragedy, it's a romance. It's different. Mr Gregg said so.' I thought of Trouble singing with Elmsley in class. And Trouble in the chapel, lying beaten. Understanding flowed through my awareness like a stain. Bitterly, I said: 'You told Scranway about the song and the applause. That's why he set Quibble and Kane on to Trouble.'

'I don't know what you're talking about,' said Elmsley.

'Just like you told him what your cousin said.'

My ashplant rested beside me. Elmsley gripped it, leaped up, and swung it playfully, too close to my face.

'Give that back.' I staggered to my feet.

He smirked. 'I thought we were pals, Sharpless.'

'You're a spy. Scranway's spy.'

'You know, I rather like this stick. How's about a bit of the old soft shoe?' He clicked his heels together, a song-and-dance man, slapping my ashplant to the tiled floor: one side, then the other.

59

I flung myself upon him. I was slow, but bigger, heavier. The floor was wet. He skidded backwards. I pinned him against the wall. He squirmed, squealed. A steamy mirror reflected us: the bulky earnest fool and this mischievous, mocking imp. I dug my nails into his hand, forcing my ashplant from his grip. I blundered back, almost falling.

He nursed his hand. 'You bastard, Sharpless!'

'Get out, Elmsley.'

His voice rose. 'Do you think anybody likes you? Fellows were sorry for you for a while, that's all. Pathetic cripple.'

'Shut up!' I swung back the ashplant.

Never in my life had I fought another boy. I felt strong and weak all at once. Already, it seemed, I could feel the heavy stick slam, with a sickening crunch, into his ribs. Yes, let him cry out, sinking to his knees, blood vomiting from his astonished mouth! I would kill him: kill him. An instant more and I would have done it: could have.

Then Trouble was there. He gripped my ashplant. Slowly, reluctantly, I lowered my arm. Tucked about Trouble's torso was a towel. His blond hair was dark and in tendrils, dripping steadily.

I said to him, 'Don't you know what he's done?'

'Everyone knows what he's done. Get out, Elmsley.'

Elmsley, like a rodent, scurried to the door, but turned back to Trouble with a sneer and said: 'Scranway's going to smash your teeth down your throat.'

My anger at Elmsley left me shaken. I was a bookish boy, and solitary. But I wanted so much to beat Elmsley that afterwards I half-regretted I had not done it. I told myself that Elmsley could bring out murderous passions in a saint. But dimly I realized another explanation for my fury. It was Trouble: Trouble

60

was dangerous. He had in him an excitability that had to go to extremes. And I wanted to go with him.

As the fight of the century drew near, I lived in a trance of longing. One day Mr Gregg asked me if anything was wrong.

'No, sir. Nothing.' I mumbled something about Elizabethan lyrics. After Trouble had sung the song from *Cymbeline*, I had enquired, shyly, of Mr Gregg where I could find more verses like that. My question delighted him, and he pushed into my hands a copy of *The Golden Pomp*, an anthology of sixteenth- and seventeenth-century verse edited by Sir Arthur Quiller-Couch. Now I was returning it, endeavouring to thank him.

He asked me if I had profited from it.

'Yes, sir. Oh, yes.' For weeks the little book had sailed beside me, enchanting me with its cargo of Shakespeare and Campion, Sidney and Fletcher, Spenser and Herrick and John Donne. In the rhythms of these pages, clanging like cymbals, exploding like fireworks, meandering like streams, I sensed a connection with Trouble's magic.

'This enthusiasm for verse is something *new*, Mr Sharpless?'

I said, before I could stop myself: 'I'm going to be a poet.'

'Dear me, it's as bad as that? Hmm… perhaps, then, this is the place to go next.' From a shelf behind his desk Mr Gregg brought down another book, larger this time. 'Sir Arthur again. But now the big picture – the whole story, as it were.'

The Oxford Book of English Verse was a volume considerably more substantial than *The Golden Pomp*. Both daunted and grateful, I riffled through the pages. Awkwardly, I thanked him.

I had reached the door when Mr Gregg called me back.

'Tell me, you seem to be thick with Mr Pinkerton these days.

Perhaps you could make him join the Glee Club? It's not as if they're overburdened with talent, and that performance of his in class was remarkable.'

He cleared his throat. Distractedly, he tidied some papers on his desk.

'You know, I've never believed this nonsense about being an all-rounder,' he went on. 'One should capitalize on one's areas of strength. A little chap like that will never make a pugilist, for example.'

'No, sir. I suppose not, sir.'

In Mr Gregg's eyes was both a certainty and a demand. I knew where he was leading. He had offered a way out, a release from the spell that bound me.

Fumbling, I reached into my jacket for the challenge. I held it out to him.

'Well,' he said, when he had read it. 'Well, well.'

We were in Geography the next morning when the message came for Trouble to report to the headmaster. Fellows exchanged glances. There were murmurs, raised eyebrows.

After the lesson I was making my way upstairs, lagging behind the others, when Trouble appeared on the landing. At once a group of fellows surrounded him, quizzing him. One pushed him in the chest. Several jeered. Only with difficulty did he break away.

I gripped his arm. 'What happened?'

'It was frightful. There was me, there was Scranway, there was the old boy glaring at us over that enormous ugly desk. And those ears of his, have you seen those ears up close?'

'What? What are you talking about?'

'The hairs! Huge sprouty tufts. Wouldn't you say it behooves a man of his age to remove the coarse hairs that grow from his nose and ears? I'd have said it was common courtesy.'

I almost shook him. 'Trouble!'

'Oh, we've got to call the whole thing off. Finished. Over. Or we're both out.'

'No! But how did he know?' I tried to sound shocked.

Trouble laughed. 'It was satisfying up to a point. *Mr Scranway, you ought to be ashamed of yourself.* Well, I've always thought *that*, but not that *I'm* an imbecile and irresponsible and a disruptive influence.' He kicked the banisters. 'Damn it. Damn it to hell!'

'Come on, it's not so bad, is it?' I said.

'Who squealed?'

'Obvious, isn't it? Scranway couldn't go through with it. A job cut out for Elmsley, wouldn't you say?'

Trouble grabbed my ashplant. Startled, I let it slip from me. With a yelp, he bounded down the stairs, three steps at a time, slashing at his imagined enemy as he went. The sun, bold with spring, spilled through the tall landing windows and struck his bright hair. In the hall below he pirouetted, bowed, and held my ashplant aloft before his face like a sacred sword.

I said, amazed: 'First a boxer! What now, a samurai?'

McManus II was subdued on the night before the Easter vacation. As I packed my trunk, I thought what a contrast this end of term made with the last: no uproar, no games, no devil-may-care escape into the night. The headmaster's interview with Trouble and Scranway had left its mark. Masters had been looking in regularly. There would be no slacking of discipline. Lights would be extinguished strictly at ten, just when all of us would have gathered in the gym, fervent for the fight of the century.

Trouble knocked on the wall of my partition. He mimed a punch, a swift uppercut.

'You're glad really, aren't you?' I asked him.

'What's to be glad about? Haven't you heard of David and Goliath?' He sat, bouncing a little, on my cot. He wore silk pyjamas and a dressing gown that might have been a smoking jacket. Looking at him, I wondered how much I had really come to know him.

Sometimes I still thought he was a stranger.

'Hey, Trouble.' Ralph Rex, Jr passed by.

'Hey, Rex.' Slowly, shyly at first, Trouble's acolytes were drifting back. That night Earl Pritchard had joined us at dinner; lately, the Townsend twins looked wistfully in our direction. Had Trouble still possessed his phonograph, he could easily have summoned them back to cubicle number thirty: all it would take was Sophie Tucker's siren songs sounding out again.

A shout, almost a scream, came from near the door.

'*Who did this?*' It was Scranway.

By the time we got there a crowd had formed. Slumped to the floor, almost sobbing, Scranway cradled in his arms the inert form of Hunter.

Voices buzzed all around us.

'What's happened? Is Hunter dead?'

'I saw it all. Scranway was about to take him out for his walk. Hunter couldn't get up.'

'Then he was sick.'

'There's a steak next to his basket – half chewed!'

'Someone's poisoned Hunter? Who'd do that?'

Wildly, Scranway looked about him. Fellows stepped back.

Scranway rose. He was still in all his clothes, with an overcoat on top. For once, he was not immaculate; his hair was dishevelled and his eyes burned. He pushed through the crowd. He pointed at Trouble. 'You. *You.*'

Trouble looked astonished. 'No.'

I stepped forward. 'It's true. Leave him alone.'

Scranway shoved me aside. My legs buckled beneath me; I thudded to the floor and could only look on, helpless, as he grabbed Trouble, shaking him, slapping him. Trouble stumbled back. He held up his fists, assumed a boxer's stance, but Scranway had no time for Queensberry Rules.

They slammed against one partition, then another. Trouble was lithe, fast on his feet, but Scranway, with his superior bulk, grappled him to the floor.

They punched, kicked, pummelled.

I gripped my leg, wincing at the pain, as my gaze ricocheted between the battle on the floor and the onlookers hunkered above. Murderous delight flared in every face. Some bellowed their support for Scranway – then Trouble – then Scranway.

'Thrilling, isn't it? Eddie just loves that dog.'The voice insinuated itself into my ear. 'Well, *loved.*'

'Get away from me, Elmsley.' He leaned over me like a secret assassin.

'What, or you'll beat me with your big stick?'

I glared up at him. 'You did it, didn't you?'

He was all innocence. 'Did what?'

With a cry, Trouble squirmed from beneath Scranway's weight. He flung off his dressing gown. Again he held up his fists to parry, bounced on his feet. 'Come on, Scranway! Fight me cleanly.'

'I'll kill you!' Scranway's fist swung out.

Trouble danced back, dazzling in his silk pyjamas. 'Coward!

Filthy coward!' He tossed back his head, flicking hair from his eyes.

Scranway plummeted forward. Trouble darted away, but Scranway grabbed his collar. Silk ripped. Trouble was against the wall, with Scranway's fist poised to strike, when a voice roared:

'Boys! What do you think you're doing?'

Mr Gregg stood in the doorway.

Scranway, trembling, pointed to Hunter. 'That little bastard killed him.' His voice, at first a whisper, became a shout: '*He killed him!*' And Scranway would have hurled himself at Trouble again, Mr Gregg or no Mr Gregg.

The pause was fatal. Trouble plunged, punching with the force of a hammer blow.

Scranway crashed to the floor.

Seconds ticked by, and he did not rise.

Wearily, Mr Gregg advanced upon the hefty, supine boy. Trouble doubled over, nursing his knuckles. It was as if he did not yet know what he had done; none of us did. In the end it was Ralph Rex, Jr who skittered forward, spun Trouble around, and grabbed his hand, raising it above his head in a winner's stance.

First came one hesitant cry, then another; then cheers, rising up in a joyous surge, ringing against the ceiling, raining down like a benediction upon the benighted McManus II.

Telemachus, Stay

Fame is not always bestowed fairly. Take my Aunt Toolie: she has never enjoyed the legendary status that should, I think, have been hers. Several times during my career as a biographer I have tried to write about her, but always it seems she evades my grasp. Years ago, following the success of *Auntie Mame*, I proposed to my publisher a life of Tallulah Sharpless, the angle being that here was a real-life Auntie Mame, one quite as formidable as Mr Patrick Dennis's creation. Aunt Toolie, the one-time Queen of Bohemia, should tell her story in her own words; my role would be to arrange them. The book, I hoped, might become a classic of sorts: the story of a shy, gawky Southern girl who parlayed the small legacy that enabled her to live independently into a position as grande dame of Greenwich Village, something between landlady, hostess, procuress, and matchmaker for all manner of Village types: writers, artists, actors; drunks, derelicts, dope-fiends. Sometimes brilliant, sometimes absurd, Aunt Toolie fostered, even created, the career of more than one celebrity. She deserved to be more than a behind-the-scenes figure, a bit player in the biographies of others. My editor was enthusiastic; alas, Aunt Toolie was not. By then, her Village days were far behind her. Why dwell on the past? There is only the future.

Such perpetual anticipation is, of course, typical of Aunt Toolie. So it is left to me to recall who she was in those ramshackle days when I struggled to make my way as a writer in New York. Then (as now) my aunt is at all times onstage: a clattering assemblage of earrings, brooches, and bangles, in myriad shapes of brass, glass, and celluloid, and long swinging ropes of faux pearls. Stabbing the air with a cigarette holder that juts up at forty-five degrees, she flaunts flowing gowns of purple, orange, emerald, or gold, wrapped in stoles (often moth-eaten) of sable, mink, or ermine. Her lipstick is bright red, her powder corpse-pale; somewhat above where her eyebrows used to be she has pencilled surprised semicircles, and a spangly band holds back her hennaed, bobbed hair.

Her age? Thirty? Forty? Fifty? Impossible to guess.

Her talk is all of young friends. She calls them her protégés and each, she insists, is bound for fame: Misses Maisie and Daisy Mountjoy, the Songbird Sisters – golden-haired Maisie, copper-haired Daisy – who one day will fill Carnegie Hall (in fact, to my aunt's delight, they fill many a burlesque theatre); Miss Inez La Rue, the choreographer, Doyenne (so she calls herself) of Modern Dance; Mr Danvers Hill, her principal dancer (who decamps, disappointingly, to Tripoli, in pursuit of an Arab sailor); Mr Copley Wedger, a rich boy going through a Bohemian phase, whose talents remain unknown but undoubtedly will be prodigious, or so Aunt Toolie assures us; rumour has it that he is prodigious in other ways.

Of Aunt Toolie's circle, some were failures, some successes, but she loved them equally: Miranda Cast, the sculptor; Jackson Daunt, the songwriter; Benson Roth, acid-tongued critic (in later years, a *New Yorker* legend); Zola May Hudson, leading light in the Harlem Renaissance.

In those days, I regarded myself as a poet. More truly, I was a jobbing hack, a filler writer and book reviewer, though I might (with more accuracy still) have been called Aunt Toolie's secretary. Day after day I lit her cigarettes, mixed her cocktails, answered her letters, received her guests, and tramped the streets with piles of her invitations, which she inscribed on little silver-edged cards embossed with what she insisted was the Sharpless crest. The century was in its twenties, and so was I. Naturally, on leaving Yale, I had headed back to the place I called home since my days in France: Aunt Toolie's huge shabby apartment above a speakeasy in an alley off Christopher Street. When my father died on the Pont Saint Michel, Aunt Toolie became all the family I had.

Wobblewood, as her apartment was known, took its nickname from its treacherous floorboards. Half of them had buckled with damp or in places rotted through, and supplementary planks, sheets of cardboard, old doors, a legless table, several prone bookcases, and an antique Russian chessboard did their best to supply the lack, with ratty carpets flung on top. At Wobblewood, the energies of Greenwich Village gathered to a point. There, I wrote the poems that I imagined would make me famous. There, I first grew drunk on bathtub gin, and woke up for the first time with a stranger in my bed. And there, one blustery November evening in 1926, I met again the boy – the man – whom I would always call Trouble.

Aunt Toolie had thrown one of her many parties. Each party had a purpose, or began with one. The goal this time was to premiere that now-celebrated atonal composition (the beginning, critics said later, of modern American music), Arnold Blitzstein's *Sonata in No Key*. Blitzstein, a wiry, wild-haired Austrian who, at that time, spoke barely a word of English, was my aunt's latest discovery. She had found him sleeping rough one night in Washington Square Park and, upon learning he was a composer, became at once convinced of his genius. 'It's frightfully *moderne*,' she told her guests, enthusing about the work they were shortly to hear. 'Oh, the bit where he beats on saucepan lids… a commentary,

71

Arnold says, on the alienation of the worker from the means of production.'

That night, as on many a night before, while guests mingled against walls hung with avant-garde posters and paintings, I guzzled gin, knowing I would regret it later, and was not sorry to be drunk by the time Blitzstein bashed out *Sonata in No Key* on the tuneless upright – and the saucepans on top of the piano, ranged in order of size.

I was wondering when it would be safe to slip away when Aunt Toolie appeared beside me and whispered beneath the cacophony, 'Darling, I need your help. One word: Agnes.'

'Not again!' For months my aunt had been in one crisis or another over this runaway Catholic schoolgirl, a would-be actress of no discernible talent who gloried in the stage name of Agnes Day. Few of our circle had time for Miss Day; Aunt Toolie had all the time in the world.

'Let me guess,' I said. 'Another career debacle? So soon too! Or perhaps it's love. Is Matterhorn still the one?'

'If only! Matterhorn' – Aunt Toolie's name for a mountain-climber beau of Miss Day's – 'has gone, I fear, the way of all flesh.' (Whether this meant he had fallen to his death or merely ended his tenure in the lady's affections, I did not manage to ask.) 'So many lovers, and all bagatelles – shallow diversions of restless girlhood! It's time she was settled. You know what this means, darling? Copley Wedger. They're both here tonight. I'm relying on you. Lead the horse to water. And this time, make her drink.'

'Such confidence in my abilities!'

Wobblewood grew wilder as the evening wore on. By midnight, revellers from the speakeasy downstairs had joined us, presumably without being invited. Where Agnes Day had gone, I had no idea. For a time I talked to the Songbird Sisters, although this was difficult, as golden-haired Maisie leaped in to answer any remark addressed to Daisy, while copper-haired Daisy seemed always eager to leave, yet reluctant to do so without her sister. Later I succumbed to the attentions of a Spanish lady said – by Copley Wedger, an expert in such matters – to be a *notorious prick-tease*. The lady, known popularly as Conquistador, propelled me to the door of my room before turning abruptly, pecking me on the lips, and spiriting herself away. I was disappointed and relieved.

'Limehouse Blues' blared from the phonograph, and couples, trios, and blissful solitaries were stomping recklessly on the hazardous floor by the time Aunt Toolie, sober as always, demanded of me whether Miss Day had agreed yet to marry Copley Wedger.

'What I can't understand,' I said, 'is why you're so keen for her to marry at all. What could be more bourgeois?'

Aunt Toolie pulled my nose and I howled.

Dutifully, I sidled off to look for Miss Day. I ended up in the annexe at the back of the apartment, a sort of boxroom on a grand scale, with paper peeling from the walls in strips and clutter heaped precariously in cobwebbed piles. My quarry, outlined by the moon through an open window, squatted on the fire escape. Awkwardly, ashplant slipping, I clambered out to join her. No rain fell any more, but the tiles and chimneys and well-like yard below were black mirrors, sleek with wetness.

I should have liked to sit with Miss Day, but my leg made it impossible. Sadly, I looked down at her. She was beautiful. That night she wore chunky costume jewellery and a yellow beret, beneath which she had swept up her long black hair. Her face was silvery in the pale light. And what did she see? A prim bookworm with a bad leg. I wore a spotted bow tie, a tweed jacket with leather-patched elbows, cord trousers, and argyle socks.

There were cuts on my neck where my razor had slipped while negotiating the territory around my Adam's apple.

My position with Miss Day was a peculiar one. We seldom spoke – I was shy around her – but Aunt Toolie had told me so much that I felt I knew her intimately. Her employment disasters formed a never-ending saga. Miss Day had adopted many careers while awaiting her Broadway break: stenographer, waitress, swimming-pool attendant, factory girl, bakery assistant. Each career ended ignominiously. The library at Columbia fired her for reading the novels she should have been putting on shelves. St Vincent's Hospital let her go for talking to patients instead of mopping out the wards. Her days as an usherette at the Shubert Theatre ended when she was discovered in a compromising position with an audience member in the back row. Defensively, she had pointed out that the fellow was an old flame. Only yesterday a theatrical booking agency had fired her; it seemed she had got two of the acts mixed up. 'A children's pantomime,' Aunt Toolie told me, 'and a burlesque show. Dear Agnes! Was there ever such a girl?'

I was about to venture a remark on Arnold Blitzstein, and whether Miss Day thought he was the saviour of Western music, when a voice startled me: 'Sharpless! It *is* you, isn't it?'

At the end of the balcony, hunched over the balustrade, was a small man in evening dress with long, pale hair. A cigarette glowed in his hand. He had turned to me, and his eyes glittered.

Of course, I knew him at once.

Not since the night he knocked out Eddie Scranway had I seen Trouble. That victory had seemed at the time a new start, a marvellous beginning. In truth, it was an end. Next term, Trouble was gone from Blaze. Scranway's father, the head of the Board of Trustees, had taken up the matter, demanding expulsion. Trouble was sent to a day school on Long Island. *It's ever so progressive*, he wrote to me. *Boys and girls are mixed, and we have swimming lessons in the nude.* For a few months we exchanged letters, but, as is the way with prep school boys, neither of us kept it up. But I thought of Trouble often and wondered what had become of him.

Eagerly, I moved forward to shake his hand. How diminutive he was! He had barely grown since Blaze. Next to him I felt lumbering, absurd. When he asked me why I was at this party, I explained that the hostess was my aunt. 'Don't tell me you know Aunt Toolie too.'

'Oh, I came up with some fellows from the place downstairs. Not sure where they've gone. That apparition's your aunt? Quite a legend, it seems.'

'I didn't know you were in New York,' I said.

'I've been abroad. I've been all over. I'm just back from Europe.'

Only after some moments did I realize that Agnes Day had gone. She must have slipped back inside while Trouble and I were talking.

Our old intimacy might never have been broken. He suggested we needed a drink. That night, in an apartment swirling with smoke and chatter and squawking jazz, huddled on one of my aunt's shabby sofas, we learned about our lives since we had last seen each other. Swiftly, I passed over my days at Yale – my scholarly career had been less than glorious – and announced, with a firmness that surprised me, my ambitions as a poet. Did I reveal, that night, that it had been Trouble, and the strange magic he created around him at Blaze, that first had stirred me to write? I suppose not. I was more interested in him: in the many schools and several colleges from which he had been ejected; in the weeks with a singing teacher in Vienna, which ended his ambitions for an operatic career; in the months on a ranch in Montana, where the senator had hoped that his son would learn at last to be a man; in the career as a travelling salesman, Trouble's bid for independence, which had ended with his return home after only two weeks on the road. His latest travels – he grimaced – had been with an elderly professor from Columbia, an old friend of his mother's. The professor sought to introduce his pupil to the art treasures of Europe; the pupil (so he claimed) took it upon himself to explore more worldly matters.

Trouble narrated all this with delightful drollery, and I was longing to hear more when he glanced at his watch, sprang up, and said, 'Christ! I'm taking Mama to church in the morning.'

I thought he was joking, but he pushed his way through the crowd, calling back to me above the clamour: 'Come to tea one afternoon! At Mama's. She likes to meet my friends.'

Trouble had sent me an address in Gramercy Park. The sky gleamed softly there, a yellowish haze above barren trees, as I stood fearfully before great double doors. Brass glowed against black. Gas, like a captive star, flared in a cage above my head. I stepped into the hall, and, as the butler helped me out of my coat, my eyes darted, almost suspiciously, over the chequerboard floor, the gesturing palm fronds, the broad red-carpeted staircase cascading around mahogany bends of banister. Teacups tinkled in a chamber close by.

When we meet those who are to be important in our lives, first impressions often carry no clue of what will come. With each of the Pinkertons, on the contrary, I recognized at once that something fundamental, an epoch in my life, had begun. Kate Pinkerton was not a large woman, but as she presided over the tea things, stiff-backed beneath metallic heapings of hair, she had about her something as immemorial as the grand house that enclosed her like a shell. She was the daughter of a great political family. A Manville had been Attorney General under James K. Polk; Secretary of War under Ulysses S. Grant; Secretary of State under Grover Cleveland.

Graciously, barely moving, Kate Pinkerton inclined her head towards me. Her gown, of a green so dark it was almost black, was a fussy, Edwardian affair of trailing skirts, lacy ruffs and a bodice upholstered in ridged, scalloped patterns. Fixed at her neck was a dark brooch that flashed a reddish gleam.

To my embarrassment, I had been the last to arrive. Trouble, immaculate as ever, sat close to his mother's sofa in a spindly Georgian chair. Catching my eye, he winked at me and smirked. Four others took tea with us that afternoon: an ancient lady with a wattled neck, who represented a charity for unwed mothers; a little balding gentleman from the Audubon Society, who pecked his teacake like one of the less compelling common or garden birds and straightened, too often, the creases of his trousers; an artistic lady, whose views on a new production of *Manon Lescaut* would be sought with assiduity by her hostess; and a shabby, sack-like old fellow who was, I learned, the professor who had endeavoured to show Trouble the art treasures of Europe. As I took my place the professor was speaking in a low, rumbling baritone about some dreary academic controversy at Columbia. I could not envy Trouble such a companion.

I was sitting uncertainly, resenting the frail tea things, when Kate Pinkerton asked me, 'You're a college man, Mr... *Sharpless*?' She pronounced my name with a curious precision, as if she thought it odd.

Trouble leaped in: 'Woodley's frightfully clever, Mama. He's a writer. He'll win the Pulitzer one day, mark my words.'

The great lady eyed me appraisingly. 'I trust you shall be a good influence on Trouble. You know we call him Trouble? Our little jest.' She went on, 'I'm afraid the poor boy's not forgiven us for summoning him back from the Old World.'

'Might he not resent such barbarism?' The professor, it seemed, was fond of being contrary. 'Why, we should have chirruped our way across the world like cicadas, restlessly in quest of new aesthetic pleasures. But lo! Shades of the prison-house close upon the growing boy.'

Kate Pinkerton said, 'You refer, I take it, to my husband's office?'

Trouble twisted his mouth as I learned of his new engagement: a position on the senator's staff. This, I supposed, like the ranch in Montana, represented an attempt to tame the feckless son; yet each time Kate Pinkerton looked at him, her breast swelled and something softened in her eyes.

Talk turned to the Administration of President Coolidge. Kate Pinkerton held forth without interruption, and though I understood little, I did not repine; I wanted not so much to listen to her as to bathe, indeed luxuriate, in her patrician waters. A remarkable woman!

I had not expected the senator to appear that afternoon, but just as the tea party was breaking up, there was a commotion in the hall and a round of cursing: 'Gad! Gad!'

Alarmed, I glanced at Kate Pinkerton, but – as if with equilibrium born of much experience – she rose smoothly in her long, rustling gown and made her way to the hall. Her calm tones could be heard assuring her husband that no inducement to rage, no, not the worst that smug little shopkeeper (she meant Calvin Coolidge) could do, was worth this fuss.

The elderly lady pursed her lips; the Audubon Society gentleman trilled that, alas, he really had to go; the artistic lady tittered; and the professor smiled for the first time that afternoon.

The emergency was brief. Kate Pinkerton, bearing her husband like a trophy won in war, floated back towards us over seas of Turkey carpet. The great man, pince-nez glinting, acknowledged his guests. His head, I observed, seemed too large for his body. From his centre parting, thinning hair splayed in grey grooves, plastered to a pinkish skull; his waistcoat, hung with a fob, strained across his belly like a sausage skin with buttons.

'And this,' declaimed Kate Pinkerton, propelling him towards me, 'is Mr… *Sharpless*.'

Something passed across the senator's face: a look that for an instant I thought was fear. He exchanged glances with his wife. I could not imagine what blunder I had committed. I was about to stammer out some apology when the cloud, all at once, was gone, and he gripped my hand, twinkled behind his pince-nez, and boomed, with the politician's practised bonhomie: 'Mr Sharpless! Pleased to meet you, young fellow!'

Gratefully, I fell back into Trouble's orbit. That year, as fall turned to winter, I lived for his invitations. How I relished the jangle of the telephone; the postcards with their cryptic clues; his grinning face appearing above the desk where, escaping Wobblewood, I read in the New York Public Library.

Often our expeditions were disreputable. With Trouble I found myself in Negro haunts in Harlem, thrilling to the shriek of brassy horns; in speakeasies with mobsters; in brothels, where even the most hardened ladies exclaimed over his charms. Many a time we reeled down dark roads with a couple of girls in his rattling jalopy. Many were the mornings when I woke, head pounding, uncertain where I might be. At a stranger's house? Wobblewood? Sharing

Trouble's bed at Gramercy Park? Sometimes our pleasures were calmer: at movie houses, where Trouble gazed worshipfully at Louise Brooks (he liked to say she was the girl for him); in the bleachers at the Polo Grounds; in the YMCA gym on Seventh Avenue where again I was his second, loyally on hand as he pounded at a punching bag, stripped to the waist in shimmery flapping shorts.

Kate Pinkerton invited me to tea again. On the appointed day, I groomed myself with especial care. My hair sparkled with brilliantine and my suit, fresh from the cleaner's, creaked like cardboard as I ascended the tall steps in Gramercy Park one dark afternoon in December.

Through the drawing-room curtains shone a burnished glow.

I was surprised to find no other guests: I had expected Trouble, at least, and I quailed as Kate Pinkerton, like the figurehead of a stately ship, crested up to greet me from her stiff-backed sofa.

In a voice I had to strain to hear, she said, 'So kind of you to come, Mr Sharpless, so kind. I do like to keep up with Trouble's friends' – then added, as if sensing my unease, 'I'm afraid it's just you and me this afternoon. You don't mind putting up with an old woman?'

My teacup, when I took it, trembled in my hands. I glanced at the fire, the books, the paintings, lighting seldom on Kate Pinkerton's face, imperturbable beneath her metallic hair. At her neck, like a fastener holding her head to her body, glowed the dark brooch.

'Forgive me, Mr Sharpless, but you don't sound American.'

I explained that I had grown up in France, and other places besides, with a father who had been in the consular service. When Kate Pinkerton raised an eyebrow questioningly at the past tense, I told her that my father was dead, and she said that she was sorry, so sorry, and sounded as if she were. She adjusted the brooch, insisted I have some seedcake, and asked me brightly where else my father had been stationed. Her interest, I assumed, was feigned, mere politeness, but the performance was smooth as any politician's.

'Turkey?' She nodded. 'Well, well... Ceylon? So *useful* an island.' She gestured to the teapot. 'Indochine? Mmm... And Japan? Fascinating. Tell me, what *do* you recall of Japan?'

'Nothing. I was a baby.' But an image came to me: a hillside, studded with boxy houses; a harbour, with water blue and glittering; boats, rocking hypnotically; and a sense of sadness as a large hand led me from my vantage point, drawing me back into a shadowy house. Strange, these deepest recesses of childhood: days we have lived through that leave so little residue – only shards of feeling and image, such as remain from a dream mostly forgotten.

'Nothing?' Kate Pinkerton, smiling, might have been relieved, and I could not think why. 'I should have liked to travel,' she mused. 'Can't you picture me as some heroine of Mr James, urbanely conducting romantic negotiations in a stately Parisian ballroom?'

Jamesian heroine? Never! I could see her only as the distinguished political wife, a personification of the ship of state. Clumsily I applied my cake fork to my cake, which was delicious.

'But we Manvilles were never ones for Europe,' she went on. 'Nor anywhere foreign. Daddy' – the word surprised me, coming from Kate Pinkerton – 'liked to say that America was a world unto itself. A continent stretches before us! Its riches, ours to reap! God has given bounty enough in these United States to build heaven on earth! Why look beyond our shores? Perhaps he was right. Poor Daddy! The outbreak of the Spanish–American War was a blow to him. I think our victory shocked him even more.

What, he cried, do we want with Puerto Rico, with Guam? What do we want with the Philippines? What have we done but acquire an empire, just like the British we rebelled against? My brother died in the Cuban campaign. Daddy never got over that. James was to have succeeded to Daddy's senatorial seat – and, we hoped, to become president one day.'

I was about to say I was sorry, when Kate Pinkerton added in a brisk voice that all that was long ago. 'Time goes,' she said, 'time goes on' – but there in Gramercy Park, with the curtains closed against the twilight, with the fire, with the soft rustle of her gown as she shifted on her stiff sofa, time seemed arrested, held in a suspension that could never break.

She poured more tea. Silence extended around us like a spreading pool and, feeling myself obliged to speak, I asked whether Senator Pinkerton would again seek his party's nomination for presidential candidate. Though he had lost, as I recalled, in 1920 to James M. Cox, many felt he should have put himself forward in 1924, when John W. Davis proved an unworthy challenger for that unctuous Republican, Calvin Coolidge. Lately, voices had been raised in the senator's favour: *The Party Needs Pinkerton! Pinkerton for President!* What the senator stood for I could not have explained, though his views on foreign entanglements, I gathered, would have disappointed his long-dead father-in-law.

Kate Pinkerton asked if I considered myself a good friend of Trouble's. I said I hoped I was, and she nodded. My last question, I decided, must have been too forward; she had skimmed over it as if I had never said it at all.

'But, Mr Sharpless, what can I tell you that you don't already know? You've divined my son's history. Plumbed it to its depths. Witnessed some of it. Which of his schools was it you attended

– Blaze? I had high hopes for him at Blaze. Visions of glory. The headmaster was discreet. Still – oh, the disgrace!'

'Disgrace!' I said, too hotly. 'Trouble was a hero. He fought the school bully, a fellow twice his size, and won. It wasn't his fault the bully's father headed up the Board of Trustees.'

'So an injustice was done? The world is full of those. Alas, we cannot right the wrongs of the past. But is it not incumbent upon us to prevent the wrongs of the future? Tell me, Mr Sharpless' – and here her voice became a purr – 'do you think you might dedicate yourself to my cause?

'This country of ours,' she swept on, 'lies in a parlous state. I know, I know – you look at the prosperity all around us, the automobiles thronging the streets, the glittering towers that jut the sky, and think we're on top of the world. The years since the war have been a remarkable time for America – and for the world, since America is in the world. But has our ship a secure hand at the tiller? Coolidge rides triumphant on a following wind that seems likely never to end. But – swiftly enough – winds turn or slacken and fair days turn to foul.

'Meanwhile, from other lands come ominous tidings. They called the Great War the war to end war. I fear it is only the beginning of a new and more terrible chain of wars. We shan't escape them. Daddy's world is dead. Foreign entanglements are our destiny. You see what I'm saying, don't you? What is to become of this country? What is to become of the world? The next election is crucial. The right man must win. But all too easily the right man may be swept aside. People will talk, Mr Sharpless – talk, I mean, unkindly. What they say, in the scheme of things, may be trivia, the merest tittle-tattle. But tittle-tattle can do grave damage. We can't stop them talking. Therefore, we must give them nothing to talk about.'

Kate Pinkerton's rhetorical skills impressed me, but as she warmed to her theme my attention slipped; her words became only sound, divorced from meaning, breaking on far shores of my awareness. Abashed, I wondered what she could want from me.

Her next words were disquieting. This ship of state could turn in an instant. 'But I'm told you're a poet.'

She urged me to recite one of my efforts. For a moment, I almost believed she wanted to hear it.

'Indulge an old woman, Mr Sharpless.' That year, Kate Pinkerton would have been forty-five years old; her face was barely lined; yet, sitting before me in the soft light, she might have been the embodiment of an ancient femininity, goddess of a vanished, immemorial race.

An urge to use the bathroom came upon me. I would have liked to fling myself from the room, rush from the house, and not come back. Instead, I lowered my teacup and recited, almost in a whisper:

> With sighings soft the summer comes
> > To me again, bereft,
> Bowed down by mutability
> > And all the love I've left;
>
> By fortune spurned, and desolate,
> > What comfort can there be
> In hedgerows rich with marigolds
> > For such a wretch as me?

Kindly laughter tinkled over the teacups. My soul sank, but I had known it would. 'Aren't you a little young, Mr Sharpless, to be bowed down by mutability? And how much love *have* you left?'

'I know it's not good,' I said, my face burning.

What had I done? I had given myself away, delivered myself wholly into her power.

'Not good? On the contrary,' she said, 'most amusing. But not, I dare say, in the contemporary idiom. You realize, Mr Sharpless' – and again she smiled – 'that my son's nickname has more than one meaning? Trouble is trouble. And troubled too. Never forget that.'

She leaned towards me, and my knee jumped as she touched it – briefly, lightly – with long, cool fingers. And at once I knew where she had been leading me and all that it entailed. She was taking me into her service, reposing in me a fearful trust.

'I'm glad Trouble has a friend,' she said in a soft voice. 'You'll take good care of him, won't you?'

Wildly I gazed at her and struggled not to cry.

Of course Trouble was troubled. I tried to see his fecklessness as charm, and such a view was possible – but only to restless eyes: to the boon companions of bathtub gin, to the whores with hearts of gold, to the flapper girls who shrieked as he accelerated, long after midnight, down a dark upstate road. What risks he took! He drove like a man escaping demons. He drank until he was comatose. He mingled with crooks and low life and revelled in their company. He neglected his work at his father's office. Often the senator was absent in Washington, and Trouble placated his father's deputies with excuse after excuse: a sudden cold that confined him to bed; papers he must look up in the public library (his father, he said, had telephoned him); electoral business that took him away for days.

'I want to go back to Europe,' he said one afternoon when he should have been at the office. 'Or somewhere. Anywhere.'

We stood on the boardwalk at Coney Island. Muffled in scarves and overcoats, we faced the heaving Atlantic like explorers at the prow of a ship. Cotton candy, on long sticks, jutted up in our hands. We had been on the Wonder Wheel and the carousel, and Trouble had had his fortune told. Behind us, a calliope played 'After the Ball', and the melody dipped and soared, buffeted by the wind. Trouble wore no hat. Bright hair flicked about his forehead.

'But what will you do?' I said. 'Don't you have an ambition?'

'I'm looking for my way. Someday I'll find it. You're a poet, Sharpless. You don't know how easy you have it, seeing your way clear like that.'

'Clear?' Nothing was clear. Kate Pinkerton, laughing over her teacup, had shown me the truth: my poetry was a sham. I was a journalist, and that was all. Not even a good one.

Trouble said he had to get away, to escape.

'From what – from your family?'

'I hate my father. I wish I had no father.'

Sugary pink clouds dissolved on my tongue. 'You don't know what you're saying. My father fell down in the street and died. Don't you think I've wished he were alive again every day since then?'

'What do you want me to do, feel grateful? Bless my good luck?' In the chill wind my own face, I knew, was reddened; Trouble's remained smoothly pale, like a mask. 'Look at the senator, and look at me. I'm nothing *like* him, am I? Mama must have had an affair. The senator married her to cover the evidence. Why else would a Manville throw herself away on a naval lieutenant? That's all he was, you know. Lieutenant Pinkerton, a nobody. His father ran some fleabag hotel in Atlantic City.'

I gripped the boardwalk rail. My cotton candy reeled away on the wind and I dropped the stick through a gap between the planks. 'I'm sorry, I can't see your mother having an affair.'

'You can't see her at all. I've always known that something was wrong, as if somewhere there were a hidden key, and all I had to do was turn it and everything would make sense. Sometimes I remember another life, a different life, and imagine I was stolen from it when I was young. A smell, a texture, a rustle of fabric, something sets me off and I'm back there just for a moment. It happened in Paris, in the Louvre. It happened in a tailor's on the Upper East Side. It happened' – he paused – 'back there, in the fortune-teller's booth.'

The Atlantic swelled towards us, consequential as time. Gulls screamed in the sky. Trouble, I knew, was possessed by strange, deep-set moods that came upon him like an overspreading cloud. One evening, on a jape, we had found ourselves at a college production of *The Mikado*. It was bad, but bad enough to be funny; only Trouble, sitting beside me, seemed unamused. He twisted his hands. During 'Three Little Maids from School' he bolted from his seat. I found him in an alley outside, pale and shaking, but when I asked him if he were sick he shook his head almost angrily and demanded that we find a drink, another drink.

Ships – two of them, far apart – laboured blackly against the grey horizon. To my relief, Trouble brightened. 'Guess what the fortune-teller said? I'll become a gentleman of great importance and marry an exotic beauty. That would have to be Louise Brooks, wouldn't it?'

That evening I was meeting 'Gustus Le Vol at Benedict's, a Village diner much favoured among Aunt Toolie's crowd. I had been surprised to hear from Le Vol; since leaving Blaze he had been out west and had written to me seldom. I wondered if we still had anything in common.

It was a Friday, and Benedict's – 'Eggs', as we called it – was crowded: the usual mixture of college students, writers, artists, and general riffraff, eager for their steak or eggs or goulash washed down with bitter coffee, before they jangled out into the night, ready for pleasures of a less innocent kind.

A hand waved to me from a rickety table. Le Vol was hemmed in on all sides. The editorial committee from a magazine called *Explosion!* was meeting close by, arguing over its latest manifesto; at the next table, a bushy-bearded mesmerist leaned forward lasciviously, caressing the hand of a fey-looking girl; behind them, a party of tarts caroused so loudly that one suspected their coffee had been supplemented with the contents of an illicit flask.

Le Vol stood and shook my hand. He had barely changed. Le Vol as a man was Le Vol as a boy, only more so: coily red hair coilier and redder, long limbs longer, frayed cuffs more frayed.

He asked me if we couldn't go somewhere else. 'I was hoping for a quiet talk.'

'We will. First, eat! I'm starving, aren't you?'

'New York City's a bit much for me, I suppose. Too big. Too crowded.'

'Where is it you've been – Wisconsin, Wyoming?'

A waiter plunked down dog-eared menus. Le Vol, packing his pipe, barely glanced at his; I knew what I wanted already and he said impatiently that he would have the same. 'The thing is' – he rushed on – 'I met Morrison Reeves in Cody. Can you believe it?'

I had no idea who he meant.

'What Reeves taught me, it's amazing! He's been working on a big project for years, documenting conditions of life and labour throughout the western states. Men laying railroads. Men working land. Men building dams. And I was his assistant – me!' cried Le Vol.

'What Reeves doesn't know about pictures, it's not worth knowing.'

Reeves? Now I remembered: the socialist photographer. A magazine I wrote for had reviewed one of his exhibitions a few months before. Excitedly Le Vol reached into a satchel, drew out a manila folder, and fanned gleaming black-and-white eight-by-tens across the table. I glimpsed stubbled, ugly faces, pickaxes swinging, dirt roads fading into long perspectives.

He lit his pipe. 'How you can live in this rabbit warren, I don't know. Life out west's hard, but it's real.' He riffled through the pictures, showing me a forest, a lake, a mountain range. 'And the space! Wind in your hair. Pastures rolling for ever. The smell of pines, thick and resinous. There's a world out there, Sharpless. It's big. It's frightening. But beautiful too.'

I praised the pictures, and meant it. 'Reeves is really something.'

'Reeves?' said Le Vol. 'These are mine.'

His eyes grew bigger and he leaned across the table. 'Reeves gave me an introduction to his publishers. That's where I've just been. They want me to do my own book, can you believe it? *The Wild West Today* – oh, it'll be wonderful, the things to see, the places to go! I've an old Model T back in Buffalo. That'll be my covered wagon. I'll set off…'

There was more, much more. The waiter brought our meals: scrambled eggs and sausages with hash browns on the side, but I had lost my appetite. Le Vol had always made me uneasy and I thought I knew why: I felt as if he were judging me, and I feared his judgement was right. Shovelling back hash browns, he launched again into the wonders of the West.

My attention drifted until a hand gripped on my shoulder and I twisted back to see Trouble. With barely a glance at Le Vol, he slumped into a seat beside me. Stricken-eyed, he seemed on the verge of tears.

'I'm done for,' Trouble declared. 'I'm done for. It's the senator. He's found out I've been skipping work.'

'How? Did somebody rat on you?'

'He says he's taking me to Washington. Can you imagine? I'll never be out of his sight. Mama's mad, furious. Going on and on about how I've let them down –'

'Trouble, you're not a child. You're twenty-five.'

'Yes, and it's too late! Do you know how many things I've failed at now? Do you know how many second chances I've had? I've been chucked out of every school I've ever set foot in. I tried to be a singer – that was for Mama. I tried to be a rancher – that was for the senator. I couldn't even make it as a brush salesman – and that was for me! I'm not like other people. I can't *do* things like other people. Nobody wants me except the senator, and all I can do is let him down because I hate him, and I'll keep on hating him until the day I die!'

He was shouting. I was mortified. 'Calm down.'

'Don't tell me to calm down! Why do people tell you to calm down when you've every reason to be upset?'

Le Vol, stiff-faced, had bundled his photographs back into his satchel. Whether Trouble remembered Le Vol I could not be certain, but Le Vol remembered Trouble, of course, and didn't like what he saw.

'Still thick as thieves, the pair of you,' he muttered, in what I took to be a disgusted tone. Sinkingly, I wondered how to tell Trouble that this big shabby fellow across the table required my attention too, when salvation came in the form of a colourful apparition, flapping towards us across the crowded diner.

Seldom had I been so glad to see Aunt Toolie.

She looked exhausted. She had not removed her none-too-clean mink, and her cheeks were as bright as the hair piled beneath her cloche. Quickly, she gave us each a pecking kiss ('School reunion? How charming!'), fingered Trouble's lapels ('A man of taste, I see'), and landed in the seat alongside me ('No, no, couldn't eat a *thing*. But you boys carry on'), before nudging me, glancing sidelong at my plate ('Darling, if you're just going to *leave* that…') and snapping imperious fingers for a waiter ('Ketchup! Where's the ketchup?').

I said, 'I thought you were meeting Miss Day.'

'She left a message,' Aunt Toolie replied, shoving a knife into the ketchup bottle. 'Expects me to find her at the Captain's Log – that dive! Oh, but such a day! This morning I had Maisie and Daisy threatening to break up their act – why, why can't those girls see they belong together? I put my foot through the kitchen floor. Then all afternoon there was Copley Wedger – you know Wedger's, the department store? Rich as Croesus, that fellow, absolutely *top drawer*,' she added, for the benefit of our table companions, 'and he was stomping about in a rage – though not in the kitchen, thank God. I said, "*Darling, Agnes loves you.*" Now there's hope over expectation, for a start. "*A girl likes to play hard to get, that's all.*" Did he listen? He was incoherent, though admittedly a bottle and a half of bourbon had something to do with that.'

'Agnes Day's a Catholic schoolgirl,' I explained to Le Vol. 'Well, lapsed. Quite a lot, actually.'

'You'll help me find her?' Pleadingly, Aunt Toolie gripped my hand. 'If ever a girl was running after the wrong crowd, it's Agnes. It's time I brought my moral influence to bear.'

'Le Vol and I—' I began, but Le Vol, to my surprise, waved aside my objections, polished off the last of his eggs, wiped his mouth, and declared that of course we must find this remarkable young woman.

Rising, I held out a hand to Trouble. 'See you tomorrow?'

'Sharpless! Don't you think I'm coming too?' He sprang up, and something in his manner alarmed me. He was too excited, too eager.

I tried to apologize to Le Vol as we picked our way through the crowd.

Aunt Toolie grabbed me in the doorway.

'Darling,' she muttered, 'I expect you to be on form tonight. Agnes has a new flame, I'm convinced of it. We've got to put a stop to it. Copley mustn't know. There he is, all six floors of luxury departments and a doddering paterfamilias possibly drawing his last breath *even as we speak*, and that wretched girl gallivants after any piece of lowlife that gives her the time of day!'

'And this from the Queen of Bohemia?' I said, incredulous.

'What do I care about Bohemia? I care about love.'

Aunt Toolie had no time to say more. Gathered in the street, our little party linked arms at Trouble's insistence and scuffed off through the snow. Others on the sidewalk had to move out of our way as we snaked merrily around a fire hydrant, then out into the street between automobiles.

That was the beginning of an odyssey that lasted until after midnight. Trouble took charge. At the Captain's Log he bounded up to the door, rapping confidently; inside, he greeted the barman with a hail-fellow-well-met air and turned to us, beaming, to ask what we wanted.

The place was packed. I craned my neck through the gloom. In one corner, jammed on a narrow podium, a college-boy band – slickers in white ducks – blared out 'Riverboat Shuffle'. Couples stomped in time; others huddled in booths; many embraced; the air was dark and smoky. Uneasily, I inspected the nautical decor: the nets that hung from the ceiling, the snaking hawsers, the ships' helms, the foxed engravings of Cunard liners. Aunt Toolie, shouting in my ear, said that Agnes could not be here yet; Trouble balanced four elaborate cocktails on his way back from the bar, whipped them past obstructing shoulders, and deposited them into our hands. Dutifully I tried to talk to my aunt about Agnes, but before I could get far she was hugging a party of flapper girls she knew from God-knows-where: uptown tourists in spangly gowns. For a time Trouble expatiated to me on the subject of my aunt ('Why can't she be *my* aunt? She's wasted on you'), before skittering off, leaving Le Vol to launch into fresh rhapsodies about Wyoming until Trouble returned, dragged Aunt Toolie back into our clench, and declared that the lady (he had it on the best authority) had left earlier, bound for the Plaza.

Through gathering snow we hauled ourselves towards Sixth, where a cab, flagged by Trouble, swept us uptown.

'The Plaza?' I said to Aunt Toolie. 'The new fellow can't be quite the lowlife you thought.'

At the Plaza I feared the doormen would turn us back, but all that came were acknowledging nods for Trouble, who made his way around the Palm Court with the efficiency of a minesweeper before informing us, in a bemused voice, that the young lady and the gentleman had finished their meal and taken themselves off to a certain coloured establishment.

Of the club in Harlem I remember little, only jostling elbows and shiny dark faces whirling in a raucous subterranean haze; then we were in the night again, piling into a flivver driven by one of Trouble's pals, our destination a roadhouse on the city limits, where the young lady and the gentleman had, apparently, said they were headed. Blearily, I thought we should let Miss Day be. What were we doing, chasing this silly girl? We were on a fairground ride, whirling faster and faster. Speed was all that mattered; the speed was too much, but we couldn't stop. All we could do was go round and round.

The roadhouse was a dive more disreputable than the last, but Trouble, after abandoning us with a party of pinstriped gangsters, informed us after an hour or so that we'd made a little mistake. The lady and the gentleman were in Manhattan after all, at a party on the Upper East Side.

'What? You're crazy! You're as bad as you were at Blaze!' Le Vol, enraged, flung himself at Trouble, but I calmed him, saying that we were all overwrought. Trouble brushed aside the incident ('Hot-tempered, aren't they, the redheads?') and the next thing I knew we were standing on the highway, hitching our way back into Manhattan.

Trouble picked up a ride for us soon enough.

When it ended, we stood before a vast, imposing apartment building that soared above Park Avenue. We crossed a marble lobby; we rode in an elevator – a universe of its own, bright as summer, all mirrors and gold and engraved floral curlicues – ascending dreamily as if towards the heavens. Gates opened, disgorging us into a glittering panorama. An orchestra sounded; there was the plash of a fountain; laughter rippled, civilized, urbane.

Bedazzled, we wandered through this palace of mahogany and gold, one magnificent chamber opening into another, miles above the darkened city. Oil paintings, sumptuous portrayals of Christian and classical themes (a Titian? – a Rubens? – a Raphael?), flared gorgeously from each panelled wall; ceilings, pendulous with chandeliers, seethed with gilt and mouldings thirty feet above; drawn-back curtains of red velvet framed in what looked like proscenium arches the spangled geometry of the city at night.

Dominating a central chamber was a broad imperial staircase of marble and gold, sweeping up towards mysterious higher reaches of the penthouse. The place might have been a Renaissance palazzo, spirited to the heights of a Manhattan skyscraper. When Le Vol asked me what prince this palazzo might belong to, I could only shake my head. Trouble exclaimed delightedly. I asked Aunt Toolie if we could still be in the same city of Wobblewood and 'Eggs' and the Captain's Log, but her attention remained fixed on the object of our odyssey.

That object came upon us like a vision, as if, in the culmination of a quest, we had penetrated to the heart of the world. In the middle of Manhattan was a penthouse; in the middle of the penthouse was a dance floor; and in the middle of the dance floor, on slick parquet, a creature of jewels and silver, too radiant to be real, circled in the arms of a darkly handsome man.

Aunt Toolie gasped: 'Agnes… Copley!'

Trouble turned and laughed at us. He sounded crazy.

'I knew! I knew all along! They told me at the Captain's Log! I've led you all on a wild goose chase!'

Champagne floated by, borne on sparkling salvers; Trouble – ready, it seemed, for fresh pleasures – slipped into the party; Le Vol, a shabby scarecrow, moved as if to pursue him, perhaps to strike him down, but guests in tuxedoes, furs, and spangly gowns milled too thickly to let him pass. Aunt Toolie, beside me, choked back a sob, thinking, no doubt, of those six floors of luxury shopping; I put an arm around her, said, 'All's well that ends well!' and she rested her head against my shoulder, watching in wonderment as her protégée circled in the arms of Copley Wedger. We could forgive Trouble's joke. 'Sometimes, darling,' Aunt Toolie said, 'the world is a well-ordered place.'

I agreed. The evening was over: the curtain, at that point, should have fallen on the comedy.

But more was to come.

Le Vol fought his way back to the elevators. Alarmed, I called his name and struggled after him. Oh, but I was drunk, drunk! Pain throbbed in my damaged leg, but I flung myself into his way, cutting off his path, just before he could slip through the elevator door.

'Come back to Wobblewood. I'm sorry about tonight.'

'Me too. I told you about Wyoming and you weren't even listening.'

'I was.' I had heard some of it.

'And I thought you could come with me! We could be a team: Le Vol, the man who does the pictures; Sharpless, the man who does the words. Why not? You want to be a writer.'

'I *am* a writer,' I said, too loudly.

Le Vol laughed. 'You have to write *about* something, Sharpless. What have you written, since we left school?'

'I'm working on a sonnet sequence.'

'Sonnets? Didn't anybody tell you this is 1927?'

'What's that supposed to mean?' I said. I would have added that several editors were eager to print my work, but at that moment my attention was diverted by passers-by: a band of Orientals, three in a row, dressed identically in funereal suits. Something about them intrigued me, and I realized I had seen them, or others like them, before: already, through the shimmery haze of this party, I had seen them many times, arms upraised with trays, backs bent to bow, heads nodding solemnly to others of their kind. They were servants: a private army of sleek, slender young men with gleaming oiled hair and sallow, mask-like faces. The prince of this palazzo, it appeared, was a man of distinctive tastes.

When I turned back to Le Vol, he was gone.

And where might I find Trouble? It was useless. Bodies pressed hotly against me from all directions. An Oriental appeared at my side, proffering a champagne glass. I glugged from it gratefully.

Hours later, or perhaps only minutes, I found myself in a plush armchair, gazing at the dance floor. The lights had dimmed; the orchestra, behind music stands like monogrammed shields, played one of the hits of those years in a languorously slow arrangement. *Who… stole my heart away? Who… makes me dream all day?* Stars blurred in my eyes: from the champagne, from the chandeliers, from the lovely gowns. Brilliantine, diamonds, and blue driftings of smoke flared and died away in the elegant gloom. Gentlemanly hands, banded at the wrists in cuffs crisp as paper, smoothed the naked backs of girls with shingled hair. Dreamy solemn faces turned in my direction, then turned away. Like a spectre, my spirit moved between the dancers.

Far off I thought I saw Aunt Toolie towering over a portly, bald gentleman as she circled in his arms. Hardly handsome, but undoubtedly top drawer. Good old Aunt Toolie! I would always love her.

The band slipped seamlessly into another slow number.

I thought about Le Vol. Naturally, I rejected his view of my life. But Greenwich Village was closing on me like a trap. Many a college crony had made his way to Paris and sent back ecstatic reports about life on the Left Bank. Why languish in America, this puritanical backwater where money was all that mattered, where progress was measured in automobiles rolling off assembly lines, and alcohol was illegal? 'The business of America is business,' said President Coolidge, but it was no business of mine. I asked myself if I had ever really been American: I was an observer of Americans, that was all, tethered to their gravity but not of their world. Life beckoned – and where was life but Paris? In Paris, my talents would mature. I would master the contemporary idiom. I would strike out on radical paths. I would sail away, gripping the railings of a

Cunard liner, as the Statue of Liberty, and all its false promises, filled less and less of the sky.

Even then, I knew I would never go.

From close by came a flurry of voices. Behind a potted palm a young man-about-town with copious coppery hair thrust aloft a glass and clashed it against those of his companions. Their conversation, or rather his, was all gossip, and gossip about only the best people. Had they heard, cried the young man, that a certain heiress had whitewashed the wainscoting in her Connecticut country house and replaced the priceless colonial furniture with pieces *très moderne*, made from glass and steel? And what of a certain young gentleman? Oh, it was too much! A subway bathroom! His disgrace was complete. But Miss Something-or-Other! Could she really be holed up at the Waldorf-Astoria, after that dreadful business with…? They must investigate! They must stake out the place!

The coppery hair, curled tortuously, shimmered and flashed.

'And then,' he declared, 'there's Yamadori.'

'Yama-what?' said a girl, and giggled.

'My dear, I'm speaking of our host. What, you didn't know we had one? Surely you didn't assume this prestigious event, this lavish offering of hospitality of which we are all partaking so fulsomely, simply sprang into being by magic? Did you suspect that no presiding intelligence had conjured it into life? Why, Yamadori's a legend, a mystery – an *enigma*, that's the word! A prince of Japan. See his servants with their yellow, blank faces, gliding here and there! Decorative, aren't they? But where's their master? They say he hasn't lived in Japan for years. Tangier, Cairo, Monte Carlo… he's an international playboy. Everywhere he plants himself, his soirées are endless. Now this palazzo! Shipped from Venice, every brick and tile, and rebuilt in the sky! How long he'll be in New York nobody knows, but one thing's for certain: he'll have this town at his feet.'

'A Jap?' said a hulking fellow. 'Not sure I'd like a Jap.'

'You will! Parties every week, and every season a masked ball – the Blood Red Ball, that's the next one. Yamadori's winter bash. We'll all dress in red. We'll drink red sparkling wine. We'll smoke red cocktail cigarettes. There'll be red fireworks at midnight. Even the invitations will be written in red. They say the ink will be his own blood.'

'Goodness!' said an old woman. 'So what's he like, this fellow?'

'Yamadori? Let's see. Some say he's a prince among men, and among princes too. They're the ones they scoop off the floor at six in the morning, with many an empty Vecchia Romagna bottle rolling beside them. Some say he's the vilest of snobs. They're the ones who never get invited. To some, he's worse still: curse of whatever town he lands in, foreign interloper, villain of the blackest dye. Who's to say? Is he even here tonight? Maybe he's watching us, concealed behind the walls. See that painting? Maybe he's cut out holes in the eyes.'

'The guy sounds like a nut.'

'A *nut* who could eat John D. Rockefeller for breakfast.'

Applause rippled across the dance floor; at the podium, Paul Whiteman whisked his baton like a magic wand, grinned plumply, and propelled his famous orchestra into a jazzy cacophony.

'The chugalug! The chugalug!' came excited cries. It was the dance craze of the moment. A trombonist flared out his slide; cymbals simmered, a snare drum snapped; as if by magic, fashionable persons in dishevelled evening dress turned themselves into a twisting train, doubling over, one hand hooked to the hand in front, one to the hand behind. I expected only to watch, but no one was exempt; with a laugh, a girl darted towards me, wrenched me up from my chair, and I found myself enfolded in the heaving dance. A chugalug choo-choo running around the track, we curled our way about the mighty palazzo, in and out of the Renaissance rooms, watched by holy men, nymphs, cherubs – and, perhaps, Prince Yamadori.

Heels in the hundreds stamped on parquet. Voices whooped *woo-woo!* and everyone bobbed up, miming the vigorous tugging of a cord. I became one with the rhythm. On and on went the sinuous dance; whose hands I held, I had no idea, only that one was the girl's, one a boy's; together they pulled and pushed me along.

The line broke up, giving way to wild, free dancing.

Where was my ashplant? Trouble, far from me, pirouetted from one lovely girl to another; at last, solitary, he flung out his arms and whirled in a circle like a spinning top. Onlookers cheered.

Beyond the bandstand, a half-open doorway beckoned to me. Groping, almost slithering to my knees, I found my way to a bathroom, where I pissed, swaying dangerously, half into a urinal, half on the floor. The bathroom, startling in its modernity, dazzled with whiteness.

I leaned against a sink, feeling sick.

A voice came: 'I brought you this.'

Le Vol stood behind me. He held my ashplant.

'Didn't you leave? You left hours ago,' I said.

'What, and miss the free champagne?'

'Why did you come tonight?' My voice was bitter. 'You didn't have to come.'

'Shouldn't I see how the other half lives? Well, now I've seen it.'

'What are you talking about?'

'I wanted to see what you preferred. Or whom.' Le Vol stepped towards me. Smiling, almost fatherly, he pressed my ashplant into my hand. 'I meant it about Wyoming,' he said. 'Come with me.'

'Me, out west? I'd better find Aunt Toolie.'

'Or Trouble?' said Le Vol. Then he was gone.

'Mr Sharpless! Good of you to come.'

The senator struggled up from a capacious armchair. In one hand he held a burning cigar; the other he stretched towards me, and my own hand, as it sank into his, felt like a sculpture made of chicken bones and wire. His eyes, huge behind his pince-nez, fixed mine intently.

'Drink!' he boomed (a command, not a question), winked at a waiter, and indicated to me the chair beside his own.

Carefully, I descended into slithery ancient leather. Light, weak with winter, fell through mullioned windows, glinting on the axes, maces, and shields that lined the walls. Flames roared in an immense stony fireplace. I might have been on the stage set of a play, a murder mystery set in a Scottish castle. Faintly, sounds of traffic drifted up from West 44th Street. The doorman, I had feared, would never let me in. That I, Woodley Sharpless, should be lunching with the man almost certain to be our next president seemed scarcely credible.

The waiter supplied me with a Scotch and soda, and I noted without surprise that alcohol, Prohibition or no Prohibition, should be served freely in this bastion of the American elite.

'Your health, my boy,' said the senator, and told me, as his wife had done, how much he liked to meet his son's friends. 'You've become important to him, Mr Sharpless. That means you're important to me.'

From the first, he assumed a conspiratorial air, determined, no doubt, to get me on his side. He was likely to succeed. Had I considered refusing this invitation? Never. Not for a moment.

'Quite a place, eh?' He gestured around the lounge. 'You realize, of course, that I've no right to be here?'

'I was thinking that.' I flushed. 'About myself, I mean.'

'No, no! You're a college man! I'm no alumnus. From the age of fourteen I sailed the seven seas. My father-in-law got me my membership. Pulled strings. He was good at that.' Luxuriantly, the senator drew back on his cigar – unconcerned, it seemed, by the ash that fell on his paunch.

'Oh, some might object,' he mused. 'They objected to a lot about Senator Manville. Pork-barrelling. Logrolling. One rule for the rich. You scratch my back, I'll scratch yours. Mud was flung, but none of it stuck. Or not for long. He was a pragmatist, my wife's father. Everything I know about the art of politics, that man taught me. He hated my guts, of course.'

'Oh?' I had read many a Pinkerton profile. His father-in-law, it was said, treated the young B. F. Pinkerton as a son.

Nervously, I sipped my Scotch. I had come to talk about Trouble and wondered when we would start. Weeks had passed since the party in the penthouse, weeks in which Trouble had holed up at Wobblewood, never going home to Gramercy Park. He said he never would.

'Hated me, yes,' the senator continued. 'Who was I to pay court to a Manville girl? Don't get me wrong, I wasn't as lowly as they say. Perhaps you've heard of my father's little empire: the Excelsior, finest hotel in Atlantic City. But I was hardly cut out for the family firm. Restless boy, I was. That's why I went to sea. But I was looking for my true calling. Isn't that the problem a lot of young fellows have? Thrashing about. Trying to find your way. Before you do, it's hard. I know: it was hard for me.'

I braced myself. Trouble, I assumed, was just around the corner.

But not yet. The senator sighed. His eyes grew fond. 'Good place for a convention, Atlantic City. My favourite. One summer when I was on leave from the Navy, they had every Democrat in the country there. Quarter century back, I suppose. The Excelsior was full to the rafters. Bunting, rosettes, Old Glory: you couldn't move for the red, white and blue! I met my wife at that convention. A brilliant afternoon. There I was in my lieutenant's uniform. She wore a white dress. Trailed after her down the boardwalk. Carried a parasol, she did. White parasol. Turned to me and said nothing. Just looked. Smiled. So I smiled back and said to myself, "That girl will do. Yes, decidedly, that girl will *do*."

'After that, we used to go for long walks together, all the way down the beach, until the town was far behind us. I'd tell her about places I'd been – Lisbon, Tripoli, Montevideo… She loved to hear about my journeys. Only later did I find out that her father was Senator Manville. The old bastard offered me money to take myself off, but I told him I wasn't to be bought. Told him I loved his daughter. Old Cassius respected that. Eventually.'

'So he didn't hate you, really? Not once he knew you.'

'He made the best of things. A pragmatist, as I said! Whatever I am today, I owe to that man. I said so at his funeral and I meant it. He was a great man. One of the great American statesmen.'

I wondered what Le Vol would say to that.

Trouble seemed no closer as the senator urged on me another Scotch and began a disquisition on Calvin Coolidge. To my surprise, his speech was temperate. The senator might almost have been sorry for that fatuous Republican; but never mind, he seemed to say – soon, under President Pinkerton, all America's wrongs would be put triumphantly right.

By the time we moved into the dining room, I was drunk, and

glad that I seemed called upon to say so little. The senator ordered a bottle of burgundy to accompany our ox-tail soup (he said he always had the ox-tail soup) and saddle of lamb. When a group of men in expensive suits stopped briefly at our table, he engaged them in lively banter. One was a celebrated industrialist: I had seen his picture in the *New York Times*.

'You won't know Mr Sharpless,' said the senator. 'But you will. One of the coming men.' And he winked at me.

The meal had progressed to brandy and cigars when he remarked casually, 'Your father, he was in the consular service.'

I nodded, as if to confirm this, but could tell he already knew.

'That walking stick of yours, it belonged to him. He was a fine man, Mr Sharpless.'

'You knew him.' It seemed inevitable.

'In Nagasaki. Good old Addison Sharpless – there was a man a fellow could rely on. And you, my boy, were just an infant in your cradle.' An edge came into the senator's voice: a curiosity that seemed more than idle. 'You remember nothing, I suppose? About Nagasaki.'

I shook my head.

'Me, I was a young lieutenant in those days, on the USS *Abraham Lincoln*. I remember the boats in that long harbour. I remember the hills that rose behind it. I remember the houses with paper walls.' Big eyes fixed me squarely. 'I dare say he talked about that time. Your father.'

'I asked him about it – Japan, I mean. But he said nothing. I don't think he was interested in the past.'

'No? Hmm. Maybe he was *too* interested in it.'

A dulled oil painting of George Washington loomed behind the senator's head. He gestured to it. 'You know I'm seeking nomination again,' he said, and I felt bereft: I wanted to go on talking about my father. 'What's your view, Mr Sharpless? Do I stand a chance this time?'

Naturally, I said he did. President Pinkerton!

'Soon I'll be assembling my team around me. The faces won't be the same. Young men, that's what I want. Young men with a future. Fund-raisers. Campaign organizers. Writers. Press officers.'

Yes, I nodded. Yes, yes.

Then came the part I had not expected: 'You've a growing reputation, Mr Sharpless.'

'Me?' I had no reputation at all.

'Don't think I haven't had my eye on you, my boy! I can spot talent from a mile off. I can see what it is. And what it could become. You're too good for those rags you write for, and you can tell them Senator B. F. Pinkerton said so! Tell them when you quit, and come to work for me.'

I looked down, confused. Were we going to talk about Trouble? Blunderingly, I said I planned to go to Paris.

The senator smiled. 'No hurry. Think about it, my boy.'

'Trouble.' I lowered my book.

Snow flurried at the window. The afternoon was dark and I had switched on the lamp beside my bed. Often that winter I spent whole days in bed, huddled thickly like a caterpillar in its cocoon. Trouble, smiling faintly, leaned against the doorjamb. He had crossed his arms over his chest.

'Shall I join you?' He flung out splayed hands, Nijinsky-like, or that was the intention, and leaped, and landed on my covers. I cried out. 'Aunt Toolie's had the most marvellous idea,' he said, rolling over and crushing me. 'The ponds in the park are frozen. A skating party – what do you think?'

'I think you're heavier than you look, little boy.' I struggled out from under him. If his intimacy with Aunt Toolie filled me with envy, I did not want him to know it. Hour after hour she hooted at his jokes, urged him to sing, told him he should go on the stage, and shimmied with him to 'Tiger Rag' on the phonograph. That morning I had come across her sobbing in his arms; quickly I withdrew, but found later, crumpled on the bumpy living-room floor, the letter that had caused her distress: a love letter from her girlhood in which a fellow called Colby Something, Jr declared he adored her passionately. Would she be his bride? The date was twenty years ago. She had never shown the letter to me.

Trouble plucked the book from my hands. 'What's this rubbish?'

'Tolstoy.' I plucked it back. It was one of the Graustark books by George Barr McCutcheon. I had loved them as a boy. 'Trouble, we've got to talk. What are you going to *do*?'

'Do? What do you mean?'

'You came here just after the holidays. It's February now.'

'So you've got a calendar.' He bounded up and ranged my room, inspecting books, pictures, knickknacks. The room, mean as it was, was my haven, my retreat. I wanted to tell him to get out.

Instead, I said, 'You're not going back to Gramercy Park, are you?'

'Aunt Toolie says I can stay here while I work things out.'

'She's my aunt, not yours.' My words sounded harsher than I had intended.

'You want to come skating, don't you?'

'Yes, and cross-country running. Who's got skates anyway?'

'You rent them, idiot. But Aunt Toolie remembered there are some old ones in the annexe. I said I'd look. Help me.'

I pushed back the covers. How I longed for warm days!

Even in my cocoon I had been wearing my overcoat. With ill grace, I followed Trouble to the back of the apartment. His only concession to the cold was a scarf, shoplifted (I had seen him do it) from Wedger's department store. That day he wore a Fair Isle pullover, Oxford bags, and two-tone shoes.

'You look like the Prince of Wales,' I said.

In those days, the young David Windsor was an idol in America, the world's most eligible bachelor. Trouble laughed and I flushed, remembering a drunken Englishman at one of Aunt Toolie's parties, who bellowed uproariously the refrain: *I've tossed off a chap, who's tossed off a chap, who's tossed off the Prince of Wales!* Trouble thought it frightfully droll.

In the annexe the light was a seeping pallor and the cold so bitter that my teeth chattered. Quietly, as if clutter were reason for reverence, we prodded here and there, moving willow-pattern plates, a family of marionettes, and waterlogged heaps of sheet music: Stephen Foster, Chas. K. Harris. Something dreamy filled the scene, something strange. Trouble tilted a rocking horse, pressing down its head, but halted it when the rockers squeaked too loudly. A banjo clanged as I knocked it. Why had Aunt Toolie kept all this junk? She must have brought it from the old Sharpless house in Savannah.

I wondered why she had never married Colby Something, Jr. Perhaps Trouble could tell me, but I was never at ease with him now. Since my lunch with the senator, I felt I had betrayed him. Yet what had I done? I had no intention of taking up the offer. For a man determined to be president, a son like Trouble was a liability. Working for the senator, I would be on his side. My job, nominally, might be speech-writer or researcher; in truth, I would be Trouble's minder. The idea was monstrous. It also filled me with a certain base excitement.

A cheval glass shuddered in its frame as we passed.

'Where *are* these skates?' I said, as if I cared.

'Aunt Toolie said they'd be in a chest.' Trouble, moving a rack of gowns, exposed a cabin trunk in a corner. Across the lid were stickers, plastered askew: SHANGHAI, HONOLULU, NAGASAKI. A name was visible on the side, the letters flaking: B. A. SHARPLESS. Beasley Addison. The trunk had been my father's. It must have been shipped back from France, along with me.

Perturbed, I told Trouble that this was not the place. He paid me no heed. Perhaps I should have asked him to leave the trunk alone, but I saw his fascination with it and could not intervene. He broke the rusted locks. He lifted the lid. Rushing up at us came the scent of incense. Marvelling, Trouble reeled out a length of fabric, embroidered brightly: flowers, peacocks, dragons. A kimono. He slipped his arms through the sleeves and tied the sash. In the grey light, the silk glowed with inner fire. Excitedly, he plunged into the trunk again. He drew out a fan and flicked it open, revealing a painted butterfly.

'Mirror, mirror!' He swivelled towards the cheval glass and posed, head back, fluttering his eyelashes, half-concealing his face with the fan. I should have laughed, but in this strange garb Trouble might have been alien, a creature of a reality quite different from my own.

'Did I ever tell you,' he said, as if it followed, 'about the face I imagine? It's a woman's face, and she's looking at me with eyes as black as night – Oriental eyes. She stares and stares and I think she's going to cry. But there's something too brave in her, something too strong. Sometimes I see her face before I sleep, hanging like a mask before my eyes.'

'I'm sorry, Trouble – I'm sorry.' I was barely aware that I spoke, or why. I moved towards him. I touched him. He moaned and stumbled against me. I cradled his head against my heart. I told myself this could not happen: this could never happen. Time distended, stopped, and I thought of other lives I had not known, other people I might have been. If, in the universe, there were infinite worlds, why should I live in this world? Boundaries rose high around all my desires. I wanted to pass through them easily, freely. I ran my hand through Trouble's hair. I touched his bent neck: just touched it, held fingertips to the delicate, pale skin.

We might have remained like this for hours, days, but now the voice came: 'Benjy, where *are* you?'

We sprang apart. Rounding a corner of the clutter, Aunt Toolie laughed. Smoke curled from her cigarette holder and she huddled in a much-burned dressing gown. 'Oh, it's vile in here. Let's just *rent* skates.'

Trouble removed the kimono and flung it back in to the trunk.

I have always hated the New York subway. I hate the concrete, the metal, the glaring electric light, the tracks beneath their treacherous drop. I hate it when it is crowded and I fear I shall be crushed in the press of bodies; I hate it when it is quiet and every echoing footstep makes my heart jump. I hate it when it is hot. I hate it when it is cold. I hate the shriek of the incoming trains.

Trouble loved the subway. On our way uptown I watched him, as if he were a stranger, shuddering in the streaky black mirrors of the windows. Often his smile flashed. His hands gestured expansively. Wearing a red deerstalker that Aunt Toolie had presented to him, he chattered too loudly about Louise Brooks, King Oliver, cocktail cigarettes, and how much he wanted to go back to France. Several times he ridiculed the senator, agreeing with a recent Republican smear, even adding an anecdote of his own. Aunt Toolie, in moth-eaten mink, watched me with an expression I could not make out.

By the time we reached Central Park, the light was failing already. Only the hardiest skaters remained on the ice; I, of course, could never have joined them, but my companions were determined. Like a fool I kept up a commentary of sorts – 'Brrr! Isn't it cold?' and 'I don't know how you can do it,' and 'To think, I could be in bed now' – as they donned their skates.

Trouble took charge of Aunt Toolie, hustling her out on the ice before she was ready. Their voices drifted back to me. Aunt Toolie fell several times, squealing in delight; Trouble, who skated with superior grace, laughed at her immoderately, but kept close watch on her. When, far out on the ice, she was about to fall and teetered, flinging out her arms, he swooped towards her, grabbed her hand, and swept her back on course. For a time she accepted his guidance, looping this way and that with him, cutting a figure of eight; then, growing confident, she broke free. He skated around her in circles, then Aunt Toolie circled him.

The sun, diffuse and orange, burned low through a wintry mist. I sat on a bench. Gripping my ashplant between my knees, I rested my chin on its knobbly top and stared across the frozen lake. Score marks gleamed on the grey-white surface like the cat's-cradle trace of a dance of knives; black trees, gaunt as pylons, rose around the shore. I heard the laughter. I heard the cries. The skaters grew unreal to me, phantoms circling in the declining day.

Passing my bench came a curious group. All were Orientals. At their head, striding forward, was a slender youth, aged perhaps fourteen or fifteen; behind him, struggling to keep up, were three little men, none of them more than five feet high. Each had dressed with elaborate neatness, as if from a Wedger's winter-wear display; but while the boy's coat, hat, and gloves were of bright

110

yellow, the three men wore black. Only the boy had rented skates. Perching on a bench some way around the lake, he donned them with quick, capable hands.

A little comedy played itself out. Exuberantly, the boy gestured to the ice, while the attendants, standing about the bench, remained solemn, as if to dissuade him from a course so risky. One shook his head. One flung up his hands. One might have been about to restrain the boy, but seemed abashed and drew back. The boy, it seemed, was an object of peculiar respect. He had none for his attendants. Laughing at them, he launched himself on to the ice.

When he fell, almost at once, the attendants gasped; one covered his eyes and I thought of the Three Wise Monkeys: see no evil, hear no evil, speak no evil. The boy scrambled up; within moments, he cut a remarkably graceful figure. The attendants, like palace guards, remained by the bench. Curious, I watched the boy vanish into the distance.

Aunt Toolie hobbled over to join me. I lit her a cigarette.

'Our friend Benjy' – she blew out a long stream of smoke – 'is too *small*. I never feel he's quite anchored to the earth. Now take Copley Wedger: a girl could feel safe with a man like that.'

'I thought you and *Benjy* were getting on rather well.'

'Darling, you're not going to resent me, are you?'

'Who's resenting?' But I did. At a party at Wobblewood two nights before, Aunt Toolie had been unusually silly. Dressed, at 'Benjy's' insistence, in flapper-girl garb, she paraded haughtily amongst the guests, cigarette holder jutting just so, and I felt an impulse to slap her. Worse still was her skittishness with 'Benjy'. He had slicked his hair and wore white tie and tails; both of them mocked the guests, and their mockery grew worse as the evening wore on. Interrupting Arnold Blitzstein at the piano, Aunt Toolie demanded that they put 'Fidgety Feet' on the phonograph; she shimmied to it flamboyantly, all by herself. Later, 'Benjy' played at being a dog, crouching on hind legs with hands curled like paws, while Aunt Toolie held crackers above his head and snatched them away as he lunged up for them, yowling. In the end, she pelted the crackers at him in handfuls until he chased her down the stairs, caught her, and kissed her.

'I know you've been miserable since Agnes,' I said.

'Agnes! Ancient history.' I supposed she was: not once, despite promises, had the new Mrs Copley Wedger descended to her old haunts. But what did Aunt Toolie expect? Secretly, I had always hated her protégés. What was I to feel though, when her protégé was 'Benjy'? Eagerly, she began saying what a tonic he was, what a broth of a boy: Benjy this, Benjy that.

I snapped: 'Do you have to call him *Benjy*?'

'It's his name: Benjamin. No need to be lugubrious.'

'I'm not lugubrious,' I said.

'You are. You're Mr Lugubrious.' Aunt Toolie pouted and patted my head. 'Don't you know you're first on my list? My special charge. My sacred trust. My dear, dear boy.'

'You packed me off to Blaze as soon as I arrived.'

'It wasn't all up to me. Provisions had been made.'

'Oh, provisions!'

She stiffened. 'Darling, you must admit you were difficult. Christ, you were impossible! You'd just tried to kill yourself.'

'I didn't!' But what had I done? I thought of the automobile that had shattered my right leg. How many times had I played that scene over? Each time it felt real, as if the accident were happening again: the green boxy sedan ramming into me, sending me sprawling, while the driver, too late, blared his horn, as if to silence the crunch of bone. The moment, I thought sometimes, had been the greatest of my life: the time I stopped traffic in the Champs-Elysées.

Wildly, I had run from the honey-coloured house that meant only a coffin in the front parlour, and silent servants, and the concerned lady from the consulate, and the weeping Latin Quarter mistress, who had to be asked to leave. As I ran, tears blinded my eyes, but I needed no eyes; if I ran fast enough I could fly: fly faster than time. And I flew, only to be snatched back suddenly to earth. In my shock I felt no pain, not at first, only bewilderment that I didn't, that I couldn't, rise up and keep flying, outstripping the leaden chronology that said only, in its remorseless drumming march, that my father was dead… that he was dead… that he was dead.

Aunt Toolie touched my hand. 'Take care of Benjy, won't you? Friends like him are rare. In Savannah, as a girl, I paced beside the railroad tracks and wished the train would take me away – away, like your father. Have you ever thought why he travelled so far? Couldn't stand his ruined Southern family, that's why. Couldn't live on a desolate plantation with empty slave shacks rotting out the back. What boy of spirit could? What death-in-life, to know your world is ruined before you've had your chance! Oh, if I'd been a boy! But wherever I was going, I'd find a friend. That was it, you see. Not fame, not wealth, but a friend. There's nothing more important.'

I agreed there was not, and almost asked her about the man who would have married her, but she tossed aside her cigarette and rose, ready to return to the fray. On the lake's brink, she turned to me. 'I say, look at that Japanese boy, all in yellow. Rather fetching, isn't he?'

'How do you know he's Japanese?' I said.

But of course he was. Again I looked at the boy's attendants. I had seen them before: Yamadori's servants. And what connection, I wondered, had this boy with Yamadori?

Aunt Toolie said, 'Your father adored the Japs, of course.'

'Did he? He didn't stay long in Japan.'

'Something happened there. Some scandal, I think. Upsetting, whatever it was,' she cawed back, and slid away from me. Trouble, in a stately arc, cruised towards her; behind him, threading with insolent aplomb between plaid-jacketed burly youths and red-cheeked laughing girls, I saw the Japanese boy. How graceful they looked, these phantoms of the ice! I loved and envied them. I imagined slipping outside myself, joining my spirit with the circling figures: I was Trouble; I was Aunt Toolie; I was the Japanese boy; I was all of them and none of them, captured in the pattern.

My eyes flickered shut.

In my dream I skated, revelling in my prowess. Trees thrust upwards, barren-branched; snow piled in drifts; but between the obstructions ran a web of icy paths where Trouble and Aunt Toolie and the Japanese boy and I careered in enthralling, unending chases. As I whizzed down entangling roads of ice, I felt I might take to the air, vanish into realms above the clouds.

I skidded into a clearing. Paths branched in all directions. For a moment I thought I had lost the others, but a red deerstalker flashed: Trouble, circling on a frozen lake.

I called his name. I called again.

The lake was growing larger. Round and round went Trouble in his revolution of nothing, but I had no power to reach him. Mist hung low over the lake, and the sun glowed red as the ice began to crack, radiating from the centre in a star. I called – 'Trouble, please! Trouble, no!' – but he plummeted into the depths. A hand waved up, then was gone, as if the lake had swallowed him, leaving only the deerstalker trembling on the waters.

I opened my eyes. I felt feverish, shivery. For a moment I failed to recognize what was wrong. Cries came: I thought they

114

were cries of joy, the usual exultations of wheeling skaters. What alarmed me was Aunt Toolie, suddenly beside me, staring wide-eyed over the lake.

'Christ,' she whimpered. It might have been a prayer.

As if my dream had been prophecy, a crack had opened in the middle of the ice, shattering the frozen surface. Screaming skaters struggled for the shores. From the depths of the chasm, an arm waved and waved. My palm covered my mouth, as if to hold back sick.

My dream was real. No: this was not my dream.

Three little men in black slithered on the ice, desperate to reach their young charge. One skater, a blundering would-be hero, wriggled on his belly towards the crack, calling to his friends for rope, rope. Then came the saviour, in the red deerstalker, swooping forward, plunging fearlessly into oblivion. Aunt Toolie screamed. The splash, on the icy air, sounded like an explosion.

I thought I would collapse, but I stood, swaying, watching in horrified rapture as Trouble, drenched, his deerstalker lost, flailed back to the ice, tugging the Japanese boy behind him. Aunt Toolie buried her face in my chest, sobbing as if tragedy had destroyed us. But there was no tragedy here. In triumph, Trouble carried the boy in his arms.

Trouble didn't seem small. He was a giant.

Like moons orbiting a planet, the three attendants surrounded him. The boy was spluttering, jerking his limbs. I hung back, holding Aunt Toolie. The boy slid from Trouble's arms. Only for a moment had he been in the water. He had been in no danger, no danger at all. Grinning, he slapped his saviour's shoulder before the three attendants hustled him away.

The red deerstalker bobbed on the water.

***

Nothing was the same after Trouble's valiant act. The *New York Times* – on the front page, no less – took up the story: HERO OF THE ICE: SENATOR'S SON RESCUES PRINCE'S NEPHEW. Senator Pinkerton, quoted copiously, said that his son's bravery was only what he expected. Benjamin (a Pinkerton through and through) was that kind of boy! A Pinkerton presidency, he seemed to imply, would bring about a world in which such boys were commonplace.

A prominent picture of Trouble accompanied the story. The *Times* photographer captured him at the height of his youthful beauty: that hair! those eyes! that dazzling smile! To my knowledge, that photograph is the best ever taken of him. 'Oh, Benjy! They'll want you for the movies,' Aunt Toolie cried admiringly, as the three of us huddled over the paper in her cold kitchen the next morning.

Trouble was glum. What he was wanted for, he knew already, was not the movies; it was Senator Pinkerton's presidential campaign.

Rapping came at the door, and Aunt Toolie laughed. 'The movies?'

Trouble went to answer it. Only after some moments did I sense that something was wrong. The voices drifting back from the drawing room were strange. And strangely quiet.

I hauled myself out of the kitchen and went to see.

Inside the door stood three of Yamadori's servants – the same three, I assumed, from Central Park. Trouble, hearing the thud of my ashplant, turned back to me, a curious wonderment playing in his face. When I asked him if anything were wrong, he shook his head.

He said no more. He packed a bag and left with his visitors.

That was the last we saw of him at Wobblewood.

Perhaps a week passed. One chill afternoon, the telephone bell jangled, and, answering it, I heard Kate Pinkerton's voice. She came to her point directly. Would I accompany her to the Blood Red Ball?

'Prince Yamadori's ball?' I was bewildered. 'But surely—'

'You realize *everyone* in New York will be there? Quite an opportunity for a young man on the make.'

'I suppose so.' *On the make?* Was I on the make?

That Kate Pinkerton should telephone me was startling enough. Here I was, in a filthy dive in the Village, with spongy crumbling floorboards and spreading cracks down the walls; there she was in Gramercy Park, dark ancestral portraits arrayed behind her displaying secretaries of this or that, of war or treasury, of commerce or state, under president after president since the founding of our nation.

Her voice dropped, assuming that persuasive timbre I had come to dread. 'The ball, you realize, is two nights away. You know what this means? Trouble needs you. *I* need you, Woodley.'

Woodley? She had never called me that before.

'On hand, as it were.'

'For what?' I said, though I feared I knew.

'Perhaps we might… well, we might bring him home.'

How weary the world has grown of Yamadori's parties! Turn to any memoir of the *haut monde*, recalling those riotous years before the Crash, and Yamadori is there: in Hollywood, in Rome, in Rio, in decadent Berlin, or on the Côte d'Azur, presiding like a puppet master over the revels. Through many a season, the world's elite descended upon his latest lair. Imagine New York that night of the Blood Red Ball: the limousines rolling down

Park Avenue towards that great tower topped with his palazzo! What cargoes they disgorge: gentlemen in top hats and vampiric capes; girls with spindly arms and swinging beads; Rubenesque women in boas and feathery hats, all of them in red, all of them masked. Behind those masks hide many famous faces, the titled, the rich, the merely notorious, mingling promiscuously: Mr Cole Porter, the Aga Khan, Miss Elsa Maxwell, Miss Greta Garbo, the Duke of Verdura, Mr Duke Ellington, Mayor Jimmy Walker, Miss Nancy Cunard, Mr Al Capone, Mr Al Jolson, Mr Newton Orchid, the Chester Beckers and the Ripley Snells, Mr Theodore Dreiser, Prince Frederick Leopold.

Gliding in a limousine with Kate Pinkerton, as if towards my destiny, I shivered once, though the car was warm.

'I trust,' she said airily, 'you've been developing your craft.'

'I've given up poetry,' I replied. 'I'm writing a novel.'

'Oh?' She sounded curious, but asked no more. I was glad and disappointed. My novel was called *Telemachus, Stay*. It would be nothing if not contemporary. The action, set in Manhattan over one Fourth of July, was to begin with a lengthy prologue ('Overture', I liked to say), which I imagined weaving like a sinuous jazz tune through streets of squalor and splendour, from Park Avenue penthouses to Harlem dives, Garment District sweatshops to Woolworth Building offices, alternating between hard, 'objective' presentation of the city and sudden vertiginous descents into the consciousness of this or that character, most of them the merest passers-by. What followed, in so far as I had worked it out, was to be an account of a dissolute young man called Eugene Telemachus and the various pointless things he did to fill up his day. I saw the book as a commentary on the post-war world. It would be nine hundred pages long, with each chapter written in a different experimental style.

I studied Kate Pinkerton. She had explained no more about the purpose of the evening, but there was no more to explain. Trouble would be here. And we were here to save him.

Floodlights lit the vast apartment block. Under the canopied entranceway braziers burned on either side of a broad vermilion carpet. A servant, materializing from behind the flames, assisted us from the car; Yamadori's men wore black, but had hidden their faces behind maroon lacquered masks. Snow had fallen earlier, and the slushy sidewalk gleamed with reflected fire. Kate Pinkerton took my arm, and with a surge of pride I led her into the marble lobby. Her costume was an eighteenth-century gown with enormous hoopskirts; mine, which she had sent to me, the chequered garb of a harlequin. Our masks: a jewelled shield for the lady's eyes; for me, a shell of skull-like porcelain that fitted with eerie precision over the top half of my face. Skywards we swept in an art nouveau elevator. Kate Pinkerton's breasts, powdered whitely, swelled out from her beaded bodice. I loved her.

As we entered the palazzo, the swooning tones of a full orchestra, reeling its way through a Strauss waltz, encircled us in silky skeins. Like a dazzled page by his lady's side, I entered the first of many salons where robed and furred nobility once bowed in stately conference. Within gilded walls emblazoned with frescoes, against mighty canvases by Titian and Veronese, guests garbed in every variety of red clustered in elegant groups or revolved, with many a whirl of tailcoat and gown, in the roseate twilight of red-globed chandeliers. Through an archway I glimpsed the broad imperial staircase I had seen before, stately in its thrust of marble and gold: a stairway to the stars.

'Tell Prince Yamadori' – Kate Pinkerton clutched a servant's sleeve – 'that the senator's wife has arrived.'

Masked revellers surrounded us. To my left stood a group of

long-legged girls, each in burgundy high heels, damask stockings and a skirt the colour of cherries, stretched across her thighs; one sported a ruby cigarette-holder, into which she had fixed a strawberry-coloured cocktail cigarette. To my right a squat elderly gentleman, cheeks alarmingly rouged, squired a carrot-haired young man in obscenely tight shorts, cerise in shade; there were carmine leotards, carnelian capes, a fuchsia bridal gown complete with veil; I saw lapdogs, doves, and leaping, chattering monkeys magicked into myriad flaming shades as I guided Kate Pinkerton to a beet-red leather sofa. Glasses floated towards us, borne on trays by the masked servants; I plucked one free and proffered it to her, but she waved it away. I wished she would speak to me. What was she feeling? What was she thinking? Did she really expect that Yamadori would come to her? Quaffing pink champagne, I wondered how, in any case, the prince would find us in this bedizened sea.

The waltz ended; there was applause; then, just as I was becoming annoyed with a party of young bucks who stood in front of us, flicking ash with a cosmopolitan air, a fellow dressed as Charles II (a Charles II dipped, wig and all, in cranberry juice) bowed extravagantly to Kate Pinkerton and asked if the lady would care to dance. I thought she would rebuff him; instead, she rose and took his hand. Could this be Yamadori? And where was Trouble? I tried to keep Kate Pinkerton in sight, but soon she was lost to me in closing ranks of red.

Slipping away from the young bucks, I searched for another of the floating trays. Somebody, not a servant, handed me a raspberry-coloured cocktail cigarette, but made no offer to light it.

Voices came from close by.

'Weird!' said a woman. 'So this guy, the Jap, could be anywhere?'

'Mingling,' said a man. 'Must be. Like a spy.'

'Japs, ugh!' said another. 'There's something evil about a Jap.'

'They say he ran away from something in Jap-land. Something big. I heard he killed a man.'

'I heard he killed a woman.'

'I heard he betrayed the emperor.'

'I heard he was sentenced to hara-kiri. But wouldn't do it.'

A hand gripped my arm.

'Darling, there you are! It *is* you, isn't it, Woodley?'

I held up my ashplant. 'The deductive powers of a Holmes! Enjoying yourself, Aunt Toolie?'

'Ecstatically. Thank goodness Benjy sent me an invitation.'

'So he's getting on well with this Japanese prince. That's where he is, isn't he? With Prince Yamadori.'

Aunt Toolie might have been hurt, insulted by Trouble's behaviour. But if she were, she would not let on. 'Have you heard about the fireworks? Come midnight, the sky bursts into flame. They say it'll be the most spectacular display Manhattan's ever seen. Do you like my costume?'

'Milkmaid, caught in Mafia bloodbath?'

'Marie Antoinette – *after* the guillotine. See this ribbon around my neck? But darling, hide me. There's a *man* over there.'

'What man?' I was in no mood for games.

Aunt Toolie slipped behind my back, but extended one garnet-coloured fingernail over my shoulder, pointing towards a portly fellow in a madeira toga who stood some distance away, looking lost. His bald head, crowned in russet laurels, glistened under the twilight chandeliers as he turned this way and that, blinking with a worried air through goggle-like spectacles.

'Didn't you see me dance with him last time we were here?' said Aunt Toolie. 'He's a tiger. A hound on the scent. Won't take no for an answer. I declare, he positively ravished me with his eyes.'

'The cad! Shall I challenge him to a duel?'

'Certainly not. That's Grover Grayson the Third, the radio millionaire.' And with a flourish, like Isadora Duncan making an entrance, Aunt Toolie stepped out from behind me. 'Yoo-hoo!'

At once, Grover Grayson III spotted her. Approaching, beaming broadly, he looked like a chipmunk.

'Excuse me,' I said. 'I need a drink.'

What I really needed was air. Whether that was possible in this magic kingdom I could not be sure. I pushed my way through the crowd. Between fluted columns a doorway stood open. I slipped through it and found myself in a stairwell. Ascending, I came to a garden in the sky.

How glad I was to escape a world of red! Here the noise from the ball was muffled. Here was solitude. Here was peace. Here also was a garden deep in winter. Snow lay in pale patches over bleak parterres and lawns. Weeds had pushed through the paving. Like the chambers below, the garden appeared to have been imported, in one piece, from some ancient estate. Manhattan stretched beyond the garden's high walls, glittering like stars. I could have been floating far out in space, perched on a fragment of an exploded earth.

I sat on a bench in a dark glade. Branches clotted above my head. Cold pressed through my costume and I shivered. In front of the bench was a pond. Ice crusted half its surface; the exposed water looked black and viscous as oil. The cigarette, unlit, still drooped between my fingers.

Something splashed me. I swivelled around. The branches, I thought, were trembling. Was there fruit on that tree? Or was this garden enchanted?

A second splash: a stone. And this time, laughter.

'Who's there?' I demanded.

The laughter came again, a branch creaked above, and a young man slipped down beside me.

He bowed, bending from the waist.

'My greetings.' The accent was foreign, precise, and the figure boyishly slight, dressed in the dark uniform and mask of Yamadori's servants. The fellow's impudence startled me. He sat beside me, lit my cigarette, then produced one of his own and lit that too.

His lighter was a rich man's, golden and weighty.

'Given up on the ball, then?' I said.

'Is dull now. I come here. I like come here.'

'And sit in your tree? And splash the prince's guests?'

'You funny, sir. You look and look, wondering who there. You a clown, clown in circus?'

'Almost. Harlequin.' I held out my hand.

A smile appeared beneath the mask: generous, brilliantly white. We sat in silence, smoking. Cold as I was, I had no wish to return inside yet. Something sickened me, even horrified me, in the Blood Red Ball, as if Yamadori's guests were victims of a plague, carousing and cavorting in a vain attempt to escape the fate that would destroy them.

I asked the boy, 'So what's he like, this prince of yours?'

'But don't you know – you, the American?'

'I'm *an* American. The place is crawling with us.'

'I watch you come with lady – great American lady.'

'You've heard of Mrs Pinkerton?'

'In Japan long ago. Only young lady then. She take what she want.'

I had eaten nothing all day, and the cigarette – strong, Turkish – made me feel dizzy. Behind the boy's mask, his eyes were deep and dark. 'You seem to know something about Mrs Pinkerton.'

'Lady, I think, no friend of Uncle.'

I had guessed, of course, the identity of the boy. With a plunge half of envy, half of fear, I thought of Trouble bearing him back across the ice. 'You're Prince Yamadori's nephew.'

'Funny, hah?' He flicked away his cigarette. It fell into the pool, sizzling into lifelessness. 'I, Isamu, never meet American lady, but I, Isamu, know things about her you not.'

'What do you know? Tell me.'

I expected him to draw back, as if I had gone too far, but he said, matter-of-factly: 'Uncle sad man. Long ago in Nagasaki, he in love – ah, so in love. But his love, she die. Poor Uncle! He travel far, far across seas. There he find crowds, music, laughter, but none of it make up for lady he lost.'

'What's this to do with Mrs Pinkerton?' I said.

'Hah! Is everything!' Isamu leaped up on the edge of the pool. Pacing, he slipped a little, almost fell, then steadied himself with airplane arms. 'Lady, Japanese lady, love man from America. American go away. Lady have baby, baby with hair yellow as sun. American say he come back to Nagasaki. For him, she drive dagger into belly and die.'

'Because this man left her – this American?'

'Uncle, he angry, so angry! Never forgive American who sail away.'

These were my first inklings of a story I felt, paradoxically, I had always known: Nagasaki, the American lover, the promise that he would come back one day. Something stirred in me, something great and terrible. I rubbed my hands against my icy upper arms.

Isamu said, 'American and new wife take boy away.'

'To America? This can't be true. It can't.'

Laughingly, he swept towards me. 'But is, is! And Uncle is sad man.'

I gripped Isamu's arm. 'You're saying Mrs Pinkerton took this boy? Her husband's bastard son?'

'Uncle would have raise boy as own. Love him.'

'Because he loved the lady?'

'Come, I show you.'

'Show me?' I was confused, but Isamu tugged me to my feet.

Across the garden wall, the lights of New York were a sinister bright sea, a violation of nature like an enchanter's spell. Snow shuddered from the air, and I felt as if the world would never be warm again, as if day would never come.

The boy led me below. I could barely keep up with him, dragging myself down a different staircase from the one I had ascended. We passed along a corridor. The party noises were louder, but they still came from beneath us; we were somewhere on the upper floor, the highest level reached by the grand imperial staircase that led up from the ballroom.

Through a servants' entrance, a low door in a corner, we entered what appeared to be a Renaissance library. The room was long and narrow. At one end, through mullions of wide windows, snowy pallor illumined a desk, a Persian carpet that curled up at the edges, and a zigzagging screen pushed back against the wall; what lay beyond was dark, but I was aware of serried books rising to the ceiling and smells of leather, mould, and dust.

Isamu crossed to the desk. He flicked on a green-shaded lamp, reached into his pocket, and took out a key. Lamplight disclosed more clearly the lineaments of the room: a carved stone fireplace; a portrait of some bearded worthy in a ruff; clustered leather library chairs; little low tables. The screen (Japanese, painted with reeds and pools and flying cranes) seemed at first the only Oriental touch, but I saw a teacup on the edge of a shelf, a vase on a mantelpiece, and a little golden figure of the Buddha in a windowsill. At the far end of the room, massive doors stood between pillared columns.

Below, frenetic jazz had replaced the stately waltzes.

Isamu unlocked a drawer of the desk and produced two items. The first was a heavy, leather-bound album. With reverence that surprised me, he spread it beneath the lamp.

The second item was a dagger.

'The dagger,' I said, 'that she killed herself with?'

The handle and scabbard were made of gold and silver, inlaid with precious stones. Isamu pulled forth the blade; it flashed in the light. 'Dagger, it belong to lady's father. Words on blade in Japanese,' he said.

I peered at the etched characters, a web of meaning with no meaning for me. Isamu translated: '*When cannot live with honour, die with honour*. Sad words, very sad.'

I agreed they were. I imagined the dagger, dark with blood, as it slipped from the lady's hand. Isamu sheathed the blade again.

He turned a page of the album. 'And here is lady's picture.'

Our shoulders touched as we gazed at the photograph. Fixed in sepia was a Japanese girl, young, almost a child, in traditional dress, posed against tatami mats and papery walls. With her dark hair heaped high and dressed elaborately, and with her expressionless pale face, she seemed at first a creature wholly alien to me, and yet when I looked in her eyes they were eyes I knew too well.

'Her name,' said Isamu, 'is Cho-Cho-San. They call her Madame Butterfly.'

A key clunked in the doors.

'Quick!' In a flash, Isamu slapped off the lamp and drew me, with a suppressed laugh, behind the screen.

We had just concealed ourselves when the brighter lights of a chandelier filled the library. Then came voices: one low, one high and pealing. My heart hammered and, peering through a crack in the screen, I saw one of Yamadori's servants urging Kate Pinkerton to take a seat, to make herself at home, while Kate Pinkerton, fingers interlaced, demanded to know how much longer she must endure these games. She had removed her mask and flung it down contemptuously as the doors parted again, opening the way to a squat, bulky personage in magnificent scarlet robes patterned with curlicues of interlacing gold. Oil-black hair, swept into a topknot, surmounted a toad-like face with bulging eyes lined heavily in kohl, and thick purplish lips like chunks of liver. I was startled: I had pictured Yamadori as a fey creature, a man made of gossamer.

The servant withdrew at a flick of his master's fingers to a station by the wall. In all that followed, I was aware of this masked boy, a second Isamu, watching what happened from another angle.

'My lady.' The prince bowed deeply.

Kate Pinkerton inclined her head. I wished I could see her face.

'Prince,' she began, 'I've come to plead with you.'

'My lady, so hasty? This is not our way.'

'What time have we for *ways*? I'm only asking you not to destroy all that I've built over these many years.' Carefully, she toured the room, tracing a finger over shelves, the back of a chair, a big varnished globe of the world, like a lady of the house checking for dust. Then, quietly, she turned and said, in a voice soaked in sorrow:

'Oh, Yamadori! How can you be so cruel?'

'Was I the one who promised a tender girl my life, then left her?' His voice was soft too. 'You think of that girl as some meaningless dalliance of your husband's youth. Madam, I would not like to judge a woman harshly, but you know nothing of love.'

'Am I incapable of the feelings of a mother?'

'You are barren, I believe – barren all through! I saw it in you from the first. Did you not see yourself as the spirit of compassion, forgiving your husband the sins of his past, taking in his bastard to bring up as your own? Yes, you would be the embodiment of all your Christian virtues! Some would praise you, but I saw a woman determined to control all around her. Can you deny it? Your husband you work like a puppet master, tethered to you by strings of guilt; his son you keep captive in a web of lies. Is he to know nothing of the girl who bore him into the world, the girl from whom you stole him?'

'You don't understand! The girl was a prostitute.'

'And who made her one? Madam, you speak of the lady I would have married had your husband not intervened.'

'Oh, Yamadori! I know all about your ridiculous wooing.' Kate Pinkerton's voice was pitying. 'We all did. Even the girl's servant used to laugh about you. You were a joke, a buffoon.'

'You think I don't know it? I was barely more than a boy. But never can I flee from the sorrow that gripped me then. Listen, hear the music welling up the stairs! Gay, is it not? But what light can it bring to the blackness I carry within me no matter where I go?'

I might have been watching a scene onstage. Kate Pinkerton had met her match, a performer every bit as grandiloquent as she. Neither, I suspected, was really listening to the other. Their words were arias they knew too well, honed by the resentments of decades. While Yamadori's words spooled out, Kate Pinkerton shook her head as if to say *no* and *no* and *no*; I thought she would stop her ears, but she swung back to him. She went to him like a lover. She clutched his robes.

'Then you understand! Then we're alike! For hasn't the blackness been in me too, since those days in Nagasaki? Call me a foolish woman, call me weak, for what did I see when that girl proved her love in death, but a passion that would always be denied me? You say I thought her an inferior, a thing of no consequence. Never! From the moment I saw her stricken and bloodied, I knew that any love I had ever felt had been a rattling empty shell. The girl triumphed in death. Call *her* cruel. With the cruelty of a passion that would not be appeased, she left the rest of us ruined: you, me, my husband.'

'Your husband?' Yamadori flung her off. 'You dare speak of that viper in my presence?'

'Viper? No viper! What was he but a foolish young man, as you were?'

'You go too far. Had he any goodness in his heart, could he ever have left that girl? Very well, dispute the word *viper*. I offer you another: *murderer*.'

'Yes, a murderer, and I married him!' cried Kate Pinkerton. 'You say he made your beloved girl into a whore, but whores were what he wanted. And since then, all the time pretending to love me, he has flitted from whore to whore. This, the man who would be President of the United States! Prince, I am sorry you have suffered, but can't you see that I have suffered too, and not for a matter of months, not for a few youthful years, but for a lifetime? He has abused me as deeply as a woman can be abused! I've withered inside! Pluck out this heart, fling it to the floor, and what would you find but dust and ash? Yet you would take from me my son, the one glimmering of love that redeems my emptiness.'

She broke off, sobbing. Yamadori's next words were resolute.

'Madam, I claim no virtue. In these empty years I have consoled myself with many a lady – seeking, always fruitlessly, the shadow of that perfection I could not value fully until it was lost. Do you think I don't understand the wiles of common women? If you have felt all you claim to feel, you could not dispute that you – in comparison to the girl I loved – are of a piece with the most worthless of your sex. You plead with me for compassion. Your tears flow. But your heart is ruled by selfishness. It is you who are cruel. You have built a kingdom based on lies, and now, when your kingdom must crumble, you beg me to let you keep on lying.'

'What a fool I was to come here.' Kate Pinkerton spun the globe of the world. 'I thought I was speaking to a man of feeling, but I wasted my words on a whited sepulchre. Don't talk to me about truth! This is vengeance, the vengeance of a heart incapable of love.'

'It is you who cannot love.' The words came from the masked servant, who strode away from the wall, stretched a finger towards Kate Pinkerton, pointed, and intoned like a mantra, 'Liar. Liar.'

Then this servant, who was no servant at all, discarded his mask and his dark wig. Kate Pinkerton shook, almost convulsed, and I longed to comfort her as everything slipped from her, the edifice of years crumbling like a sandcastle at the inundations of the tide.

Yamadori's lips curled. 'Now, madam, you understand. Already, the crisis has come to pass.'

'Why did you do it?' Trouble said coldly. 'Why, Mama?'

Her voice cracked. 'Would you be an Oriental, and a bastard? Can't you see, I've saved you from shame!'

'You've saved the senator. You've saved yourself.'

I staggered, and the screen crashed to the floor.

'Mr Sharpless!' Kate Pinkerton shook her head. 'You disappoint me gravely.'

Her words stabbed me, killed me.

'Sharpless! So now you know,' Trouble was saying. Yamadori

was upbraiding his grinning nephew. But all was not yet over. Violent hands flung back the doors and there, in a crimson opera cloak, stood Senator Pinkerton. He was drunk. No mask concealed his flushed face, and his hair, dislodged from its customary grooves, hung dishevelled over his heavy forehead.

'Pinkerton! What is the meaning of this?' Yamadori said.

The senator made no answer. He strode towards his son. 'Bastard. Ungrateful bastard. What do you think you're going to do, swan around the world with this filthy Jap?'

Trouble's words were icy. 'Why not? It'll get me away from you.'

'Ben, no.' The senator reached for him. Trouble flinched. Loathing flashed in his face, but fear too, as if his father, at a drunken touch, could drag him back to his old life. 'You're my son.'

'Then why do you hate me?'

'I love you. Don't you know that? From the moment I first held you in my arms, I loved you.'

'Enough.' Yamadori's great sleeve rose, glittering, as if to sweep the senator from the room.

'Filthy Jap!' Reeling, the senator pushed him in the chest. They grappled; Yamadori called for his servants, but his opponent's attention was distracted: Trouble had rushed for the great doors.

'Ben, wait!' The senator lumbered after him.

It was time for the fireworks. A fanfare surged from below; lights plunged to blackness, and, through the great windows of the high palazzo, explosions in every shade of red flared around the building. The phosphorescence, flowering and fading, plunged the scene into visionary strangeness, as the senator and Trouble faced each other at the top of the imperial stairs.

Crowds held me back and I could not reach them; nor, over the explosions, could I hear their words. I could only watch the anguished tableau – flung arms, flung-back heads – that seemed

131

to be enacted not just in the silence but with the deliberation of mime, and all its inevitability: inevitable, that clutching hand, slapped away, then returning; inevitable, those words from bared teeth, from corded neck, that denunciation that might sever everything, or, instead, in the fury that it raised, tighten every bond it sought to break; inevitable, that hand that struck out, sending the smaller figure tumbling down the stairs.

And there at the bottom of the stairs, crashing through the crowd, was Aunt Toolie. Her words were lost to me also, but I knew them: 'Darling!' – yes, first 'Darling!', as she fought her way towards the sprawled, inert form; then, as her gaze travelled upwards to the caped figure at the top of the stairs: 'You've killed him – you've killed him!'

Sparks, the colour of blood, cascaded across the sky.

Between the Acts

Stories are strange. Nothing is stranger than stories.

Years passed before this one was clear to me – I pieced it together from fragments, like a shattered ancient relic, and not until after Senator Pinkerton's death did I believe I had it complete – but in memory it seems that everything was revealed to me on that night of the Blood Red Ball. Later I saw the story as a succession of scenes unfolding, vivid with the passions, but not quite real, like Japanese woodblocks come weirdly to life.

The place is Nagasaki: a house on Higashi Hill, overlooking the harbour. White screens slide back and a dark polished terrace juts into lush gardens. Goro, the nakodo – the marriage broker – shows his latest client the house. Exotic, is it not? So very Japanese! The perfect love nest for Pinkerton-san!

Lieutenant Pinkerton is a dashing fellow, big and handsome, filled with bonhomie and bent on pleasure. A local geisha girl has bewitched him with her charms. The *Abraham Lincoln* is becalmed in port. Why should he not contract a marriage with the girl? Sailors in these waters know all about such marriages. What Goro offers is prostitution, though the word, or any word like it, does not pass his lips. Unctuously, he offers a contract for the bridal bower: a lease of nine hundred and ninety-nine years, no less, with the option to cancel at the end of every month.

Wedding festivities begin. The first guest is Sharpless, the American consul. But does he display a wedding day demeanour? No: Pinkerton is his friend; he admires his friend, but cannot approve this marriage. The girl, says Sharpless, is young, too young; loving her American with a credulous passion, she cannot see how lightly he will treat her devotion. Must Pinkerton, to gratify a passing fancy, bruise the wings of this little Butterfly? But Pinkerton has no time for his grave friend. Guests are milling in earnest, and here, radiant among them, comes the Butterfly herself! Has there ever been so charming a girl? No photograph does her justice. This is no waxwork fixed in sepia but a fluttering gay creature, at once child and woman.

She tells the Americans her story. *I fifteen years old. Noble family fall in world. Father, dishonoured, commit ritual suicide. Mother, left in poverty, not provide for me. Had no choice but to become geisha. But now, what change of fortune! How happy am I to enter upon honourable marriage!*

Watching her, Goro the nakodo smacks his lips. He thinks her the most accomplished of all his charges: a harlot of genius! But Goro's heart is too corrupted to know the truth. For everything the girl has said is sincere, and, as if to show this, she reveals that she has renounced her religion. At the Christian mission house in Nagasaki, the girl has been received into her husband's faith. If her family knew, they would disown her. But she cares only for the new life that awaits her.

The commissioner reads out the marriage contract. Bride and bridegroom sign their names. The joy is general. Wily Goro has been nothing but thorough. Food and drink flow. The house spills over with guests. Look at the girl's relatives, feasting with abandon! Look at that old rogue Uncle Yakuside, carousing drunkenly at the American's expense!

The girl's face is filled with joy. Does Pinkerton not believe he really loves her? What thought has he for the attritions of time? There is only this moment, with its promise of bliss. And

Sharpless, what feelings stir in Sharpless? Envy, undoubtedly – for must he not love the girl himself? But sorrow too, a soul-harrowing sorrow, for the destiny that awaits her.

An intruder bursts upon the scene. Look at his rage! Look at his fury! Is it a madman? It is the Bonze, Butterfly's most eminent uncle, a holy man of high degree. Word of his niece's apostasy has reached him. Wicked girl, to betray the faith of her ancestors! He curses her. Pinkerton laughs at the madman. But Pinkerton does not understand. The girl's other relatives join the denunciation. Even the drunkard Yakuside is filled with righteous indignation.

Wicked girl! Cursed be the girl! To betray her ancestors!

Pinkerton, growing angry, clears the house. Butterfly sobs. What has she done, to marry an American? What has she done, to forget her race and kindred? But she loves Pinkerton too well to be downcast for long. His caresses restore her. All will be well, won't it? Weep no more.

Three years pass.

How rapidly Butterfly's happiness has flown! For, of course, a few months after the marriage, the *Abraham Lincoln* sailed away. Pinkerton said he would return when the robins nested in spring. Lightly enough he flung out the words, and Butterfly believed him; though robins, she fears, may nest less often in America than in Japan.

Seasons come and go. The funds left by Pinkerton dwindle. Penury awaits. Butterfly tells her maid, Suzuki, that Pinkerton will come back. One fine day, she declares, we'll see a thread of smoke above the sea, coiling up from the far horizon; closer and closer the ship will come, until cannon thunders in the harbour, signalling its arrival; one fine day I'll wait for the man who climbs

Higashi Hill from the crowded city below; at first a speck, he will grow and grow in my sight, and at the summit of the hill he'll call my name. One fine day.

Suzuki does not believe a word of it.

Enter Sharpless, the consul. He has received a letter from Pinkerton, who is returning after all. Still, Sharpless is grave: Pinkerton has married an American lady and has asked his old friend to break the news (gently, of course) to Butterfly. Sharpless, for now, has no chance to proceed. Goro the nakodo is here again; Butterfly, the marriage broker insists, must take another husband. Look at the fine suitor he offers her this time! It is Prince Yamadori, a Japanese nobleman who has lived much abroad. Yamadori is a posturing fool. Absurdly, he pleads his cause. Yes, he has made other marriages, it is true, but all his other wives he will cast aside for the love of Madame Butterfly.

Outraged, she refuses to listen. She has a husband! And her husband will return! Sharpless despairs. What, he asks Butterfly, if Pinkerton is not to be trusted? Perhaps, he ventures, she should accept Yamadori. She turns from him, affronted. She will never give up Pinkerton. And, as if to prove that Pinkerton must be hers again, she runs to fetch the little boy of whose existence neither Pinkerton nor Sharpless has been apprised before.

The boy's name, declares his mother, is Trouble. But on the day of his father's return, his name shall change to Joy.

Now comes the sound of cannon from the harbour. A ship! A ship! Butterfly rushes to the terrace. The vessel flies an American flag, and, looking through the telescope she keeps for this purpose, she sees that its name is the *Abraham Lincoln*.

Pinkerton has returned! Deliriously, Butterfly calls to Suzuki. They must celebrate his homecoming! They must strew flowers throughout the house! For hours they work in the garden, cutting every flower; soon, flowers fill every space; petals carpet the floor; the fragrance is overwhelming as Butterfly arrays herself in her wedding garments and decks out Trouble in his finest clothes.

Night falls. Oh, when will Pinkerton come? In the shoji screen that is drawn against the darkness, Butterfly, Suzuki, and Trouble make three holes, and through the holes they watch expectantly. Hours go by. Trouble sleeps. Suzuki sleeps. Butterfly thinks none should sleep. Her vigil can end only when Pinkerton returns. Slowly, a new dawn bleeds into the darkness.

Waking, Suzuki persuades her mistress to rest at last: is she not to look her best when her husband comes? (Poor Suzuki! She has had the measure of Pinkerton from the first.) Suzuki sends Trouble out to play in the garden. But look, here comes Sharpless – and Pinkerton is with him! Suzuki is startled: were Pinkerton's promises true after all? Receiving him warmly, she tells him how her mistress has prepared for this homecoming: the costumes, the flowers, the vigil. What joy will fill her now!

Every word is a dagger in Pinkerton's heart. He had only wanted Suzuki's advice on how to break the news to Butterfly of his marriage. Suzuki sees that something is wrong and, turning towards the garden, she becomes aware of a lady standing there: a foreign lady, in a sweeping gown. It is Kate Pinkerton – and perhaps, even now, her gaze lights upon the boy called Trouble; and Trouble, leaving off his play, looks up at her wonderingly.

Kate Pinkerton sails into the house as Butterfly, alerted by voices, emerges from her chamber, filled with excitement to greet her husband again. Instead, she stops and stares.

She sees Kate Pinkerton. And, in a trice, Butterfly knows.

Despair fills Sharpless. The tragedy, he thinks, is upon them now, but he is precipitate. Butterfly is calm, surprisingly so; it is Pinkerton, bidding farewell to the life he knew in this house on

Higashi Hill, who is overcome with emotion. What a carefree fellow he has been! All that has gone now. Never, he realizes, shall he be free from remorse. Never, he realizes, shall he forget Butterfly's eyes, gazing at him in sorrowful reproach. He is ready to curse himself. He is ready to break down. But the women display exemplary calm. Is Kate Pinkerton shocked by her husband's past? Not a bit of it! The little Japanese girl is a charming plaything, delightful; as for the child, they must take him back to America and bring him up as their own.

Butterfly takes this in. Of course: Pinkerton shall have the child, if he only comes back in... oh, half an hour. The Americans go. The calm, they know, is only on the surface: Butterfly's heart is broken. Pinkerton knows it, and knows he will always feel shame for what he has done. Kate Pinkerton knows it, but steels herself. Sharpless knows it, and for the rest of his life will feel a sense of failure, exile, and loss. Perhaps he guesses what will happen next.

Butterfly is alone. What has she done that she must pay this price? The Bonze has cursed her, and his curse has come to pass. She has abandoned her religion. She has betrayed her country. She has trusted in love, and love has let her down. She takes up the dagger that her father used to commit ritual suicide. She unsheathes the blade and kisses it. She recites the words engraved on it: *Die with honour when you can no longer live with honour*.

The time has come. But now Suzuki pushes back a screen to admit the boy called Trouble. He rushes to his mother. She sweeps him into a last embrace. She loves him: loves him. Oh, let him look into her face – deeply, searchingly, never to forget her! It is for you, she tells him, that I do what I do. It is for you, little boy, that you may go across the sea. She breaks from him, ties a blindfold around his eyes, then, with her gaze still fixed upon him, retreats behind a screen, where again she takes up the dagger. She plunges it into her bosom and emerges, tottering; she falls, but just has strength enough to drag herself across to the boy and embrace him again, before she sinks down.

Returning, Pinkerton and Sharpless find her lying dead.

ACT THREE

After Tokugawa

The world is webbed by imaginary lines: latitude, longitude, the lines are not there, but seem as real to us as mountains, rivers, coasts. Spin a globe to the Pacific, and all the way down the watery hemisphere runs the International Date Line. As a boy I thought of it as a seam, as if planet earth had two halves, tacked jaggedly together. Travel westwards, and at one moment it is the date in America, at the next (jump!), the date in Japan, a day later. We have passed through a barrier. We have entered another world.

'Tell me again – temples and pagodas?' I said, as our ship drew into a long, thin harbour.

'Great Temples of Kyushu, that's what the *Geographic*'s paying for.' There was an edge in Le Vol's voice. This was the first of our commercial projects that he, not I, had arranged. I had thought it odd when he suggested it, and wondered why it appealed to him. 'Mysteries of the Orient. Buddhist chanting. Incense. Gongs. Think you can work up something on that?'

Gentle hills, blue in spring, rose over a clutter of port and town. As we lugged our suitcases down to the quay, I wondered if anything in Nagasaki would stir my memory. I supposed not: I had been an infant, barely more than a baby, when my father was the consul.

Le Vol had changed his shirt and shaved for our arrival. This surprised me, but I was not surprised at all when he discoursed knowingly about the Mitsubishi shipyards, which loomed, grey and forbidding, on the other side of the harbour. Did I know, he demanded of me, how much Japan spent on ships, tanks, and airplanes? Without them, the war in China could barely have begun.

I sighed; I was tired of the war in China. It had become Le Vol's subject, his *idée fixe*. For six years, Japan had fought a war of conquest on the mainland; by now, much of China lay under Japanese occupation. Western powers, imperial to the core, were outraged at Japan's imperial expansion. But Japan would not listen, withdrawing indignantly from the League of Nations.

'Shouldn't you be researching temples and pagodas?' I said.

'That's your job. I just take the snaps.'

'I suppose so.' In my suitcase was a Baedeker and an illustrated book called *Mysterious Japan*.

Evening gathered pinkly in the sky. Our ship, a merchant steamer, had deposited us at an inauspicious dock, all slithery timbers, tangled hawsers, and brown wiry wharfmen hurrying in every direction. High above, cranes held crates suspended by spidery threads; shadows, black and boxy, slithered over pungent clutter, and I wondered if I should have entrusted the arrangements to Le Vol. He was not the most reliable of business partners.

We had just completed customs formalities in a shabby timber office when a fellow in a chauffeur's uniform slipped towards us, grinned and bowed, took our luggage, and ushered us in the direction of a stately Lincoln sedan. Deep wrinkles seamed his face and his teeth were yellow, waggling pegs.

I said to Le Vol, 'A step up from our usual welcome. Good hotel?'

'Let's just say I've exceeded myself.'

The Lincoln – brown and gleaming like shoe leather, inside and out – swept up hilly, winding roads above the harbour. Cherry blossoms burgeoned in a fleshy, pink riot as we turned smoothly this way and that.

It had been some years after the Blood Red Ball when I ran into Le Vol again at a diner in New York. Then, as now, he was the shabby fellow he had always been, red-haired and gangly, only a little more weather-beaten and wrinkled about the eyes, as if he spent too much time squinting into the sun.

'Still taking snaps?' I had asked him, and he had looked at me almost pityingly and informed me that he was in town for the opening of his new exhibition. He was ebullient. The Crash (to most, a calamitous end) seemed to him an exciting beginning, the final crisis of capitalism that preceded a new order. Bemused, I listened to his analysis for a good half-hour before he realized he had asked me nothing about myself and demanded to know what I had been doing.

I hesitated to tell my story. What had I become but an ageing journalist, hustling for freelance work, living in a single shabby room in Greenwich Village? Wobblewood was no more. The Queen of Bohemia, surprising all her circle, had found her ideal friend at last in the form of Grover Grayson III, the radio millionaire. Following a lavish wedding at the Plaza, the couple decamped to California, where Mr Grayson was building up his interests in the movies. I could have gone with them; Aunt Toolie insisted, but I demurred. It was time I made my own life. Yet what was my life to be? I had left Paris too late. The Crash seemed only to confirm that an era had ended. Boatloads of Bohemians made reverse Atlantic crossings. The Lost Generation was finding itself again. I knew I would never write *Telemachus, Stay*.

Le Vol, a little hesitantly, asked me what had become of Trouble. I tried to explain what had happened at the Blood Red Ball.

'How his father must hate him!' Le Vol drew on his pipe.

'He said he loves him.'

'But the cat landed on his feet. He's all right?'

'Depends what you mean by *all right*.'

Trouble's fall had left him with a concussion, fractures of his right hip and thigh, and extensive bruising. For six weeks he lay in a hospital bed; Kate Pinkerton visited him every day, and so did I. The senator's contrition was piteous, but his son refused to see him: not clamorously, but coolly, calmly.

One day I came upon Kate Pinkerton sobbing. Trouble's bed was empty. Seeing me, she sprang up and left, not speaking, and I burned with shame, as if I had assisted his escape.

Le Vol said, 'So he walked out into the night?'

'And hasn't been seen since. Do you ever imagine just walking out on everything and starting a new life?'

'I've got one, in case you haven't noticed.'

'Maybe I need one too.'

'Oh? I'm heading west again,' Le Vol began, and, lighting his pipe, he informed me that a writer he had worked with for the last three years had just defected to Hollywood. 'The fool! He'll be sorry. It's a new world. There'll be no burying our heads in the sand any more.'

'I suppose you think I've been doing that,' I ventured.

'We're heading into a key period of history. Someone needs to document it. We'd make a good team: Le Vol, the man who does the pictures; Sharpless, the man who does the words.'

Destiny, it seemed, was calling me again, and this time I answered. In those years of Depression and New Deal, Le Vol and I crisscrossed America. We sought out breadlines and soup kitchens. We stood in fields where the soil had blown away. We travelled with hoboes in boxcars. For the Public Works Administration, the Works Progress Administration, the American Federation of Labor and the Tennessee Valley Authority, we chronicled the construction of dams, roads, and railroads. Several of Le Vol's pictures became iconic images: young men in the Civilian Conservation Corps digging mud in a field in North Dakota, like Russian peasants, anonymous and enduring; oil raining from a gusher in Texas, drenching jubilant workers black; a dust storm approaching an Oklahoma farmhouse, while a Model T in the foreground struggles to escape along an arrow-straight highway.

We staged exhibitions, published books, and contributed copiously to federal archives; critics – and more than a few political activists – valued our work highly, but neither of us earned much money. Inevitably, we were forced to supplement our income with commercial work. Le Vol was dubious, even disgusted, when I urged these projects upon him. Often, I knew, he was tempted towards sabotage, and I did my best to make sure he did not turn the tourist guides, industry promotions, and magazine features that paid for more than gasoline and steaks in cheap diners into parodies of what they were meant to be. Resignedly, he followed me to Alabama for a piece on beauty pageants ('Miss Southern States'), to California for a guidebook to Beverly Hills (*Mansions of the Stars*), to Lake Superior for a brochure on a shipping line. For *Life* we went to London; for *National Geographic* to Anchorage, Havana, and Guatemala City.

Then came Nagasaki. It was April 1937.

'What is this place?'

The Lincoln had come to rest on a gravelled drive. The chauffeur held open a door for us. With an air of triumph, he gestured towards a veranda wreathed in vines. The house was modest but prosperous.

'Didn't I tell you?' said Le Vol. 'I wrote to the American consul. He insisted we stay.'

The chauffeur, waddling ahead with our luggage, led us into the long, low bungalow. On the threshold of the hall, following his lead, we removed our shoes. Lining the walls were framed photographs of past consuls, stiff-collared gentlemen with moustaches. My father's eyes watched us, and I wondered that Le Vol should not exclaim, startled by a picture that looked so much like me; but then, I had no moustache and wore no stiff collar.

My room was comfortable, if furnished sparsely: whitewashed walls, white-quilted bed with mosquito netting, cherrywood dresser with spindly legs. Beside the bed was a bookcase. Briefly, I inspected sun-faded spines: Alain-Fournier, *Le Grand Meaulnes*; E. M. Forster, *The Longest Journey*; Henry James, *The Ambassadors*; Pierre Loti, *Madame Chrysanthème*.

The blinds were drawn and I raised them, revealing a broad lawn that stretched to a line of conifers: my father's lawn. Breathing deeply, I imagined rain that had slithered down the glass in the days when Teddy Roosevelt and Emperor Meiji were alive, and so was my father.

Far out on the lawn, a lean gentleman stood against the sunset. He had set up an easel and stood painting; what he painted I was too far away to see, but I imagined the subject as suitably Oriental: sprays of pink blossom surrounded him on the trees. Dressed in a cream suit with a panama hat, he had about him the air of an imperial official, retired to indifferent leisure. He stepped back, surveying his handiwork, before, as if he sensed me watching, he turned towards the house.

* * *

That night we dined on mats at a low table, where a bent-backed old woman supplied us abundantly with noodles, rice, seaweed, and fish in delicate strips. The consul, whose name was Clifford T. Arnhem, had assumed a silken robe and sat comfortably in a half-lotus; beside him, with downcast eyes, a Japanese girl of the geisha type knelt, unmoving. Scented breezes blew in from the gardens; lights flickered in paper lanterns.

'Your health, good sirs, and welcome.' Mr Arnhem raised a tumbler of sake. A twinkly-eyed old roué who had, I gathered, taken this posting a decade earlier after long years in the State Department, he sported a curling white moustache and a red cravat, arranged, I suspected, with meticulous care. Dark spots stood out on the backs of his hands.

'Kiku and I,' he added – the girl would not eat with us – 'have few guests in these troubled times. But Mr Sharpless, you look uncomfortable – and you an old hand in the Orient, I hear.'

'Hardly.' I feared Mr Arnhem was mocking me. My legs, unsuited for crossing, jutted out at an awkward angle, and I displayed no talent for chopsticks. Eyeing the steaming bowls, I wondered if many consuls had adopted so thoroughly the customs of the natives. I had been right about his painting: pictures signed *C. T. A.* hung all over the consulate; most were watercolours and all were executed, with little finesse, in the style known as *Japonisme* – cherry blossoms, lotus leaves, girls in kimonos wielding fans.

Mr Arnhem expatiated upon the delights of Nagasaki-ken ('Great Temples of Kyushu? The greatest are close by') and assured us that his driver, whose name was Goro, would be at our disposal throughout the length of our stay. Every so often I glanced at Kiku. Twin dabs of scarlet shone from her lips. The girl might have been a china doll, and every bit as brittle.

I did my best to make conversation. 'Tell me, Mr Arnhem, do you fear there will be a war?'

'There is one,' Le Vol interposed, 'in China.'

'I meant with us,' I said. 'Senator Pinkerton seems most concerned.'

The senator had become a key figure in the Roosevelt Administration. That he should ever be president seemed unlikely now, but some said he was vice president in all but name.

Mr Arnhem stroked his moustache. 'Look at it this way. Japan has shown herself to be the imperial power of the East. The world is a pie. For years, Europeans have carved out their slices: Spanish, British, French, Dutch, all have had their share. Lately, Americans have tucked in too. And now Japan comes to the table. She has proven her power. On what grounds is she to be turned away?'

'That seems a little cold-blooded, sir – if I may.' Le Vol's face had flushed. 'Empires are brutal. And empires clash. We'll be dragged into an Asian bloodbath that will last for years.'

He might have said more, but Kiku, at this, leaped up with a cry. As she hurried from the room, the patter of her little stockinged feet resounded down the corridor like a bird's rapid heartbeat.

'Poor child!' Mr Arnhem laughed. 'I've been teaching her English. Not a good idea, perhaps.'

'She's frightened of war?' Le Vol said.

'Frightened – so I flatter myself – that I shall leave her.' Mr Arnhem laughed again, leaned across the table, and slapped Le Vol on the back. 'Women, eh? I've had them white, black, brown, red, and yellow, and haven't they always been flighty, emotional things?'

After dinner he suggested we take a turn in the garden. When he offered us cigars, I shook my head. The garden had grown chilly, but scents of blossom hovered on the air. From an open window I heard sounds of sobbing. Disturbed, I imagined I would go to Kiku, comfort her. But what could I say?

Le Vol, striding ahead with Mr Arnhem, praised our host's generosity before returning to the Chinese war.

'Perhaps we pushed them into it. Japan had shut out the world for hundreds of years. Would she ever have opened up without Commodore Perry? No Perry, no black ships in Edo Bay, no army raging across China now. Funny, isn't it? We thought modern war was something just for us. But all they had to do was watch and learn. And don't they learn quickly?'

Cigar smoke, like echoes lingering, traced the gestures of Le Vol's hands. I hung back, studying the gardens. Insects flickered by, ghostly in moonlight. The consulate was built on an angle on the hill. Through a gap in the trees, I saw a low wooden gate and a path, descending steeply, leading to a clutter of tiled roofs, telegraph poles, and overhead wires like a web. Music, some martial air, drifted up faintly. I looked back at Le Vol and Mr Arnhem. They were far away. They had forgotten me. I sidled to the gate.

In the alleys below there were few wanderers. Jaundiced street lamps, scattered above, made splashes of light. Here, the music I had heard before was louder, coiling out from an open doorway. I bowed my head and entered a barroom, a place of flickering lanterns and blackened low beams, like the cabin of an ancient ship. Faces loomed above shadowy benches. On the bar stood a frilly-horned phonograph, crackling out the martial-sounding song.

'Sake.' The barman, a pigtailed elderly Chinaman, pushed a glass towards me. I shook my head: *No, no sake*, I tried to say, but already he had hobbled away from me, slipping into semi-blackness, where he squatted, eyes shut, swaying his head to the music. I leaned, half turned, against the bar and drank. I took in my companions. Every face was old: seamed, parchment-brittle. Only one fellow appeared to be Western, a Slav perhaps, but his features, like beaten bronze, stretched Orientally over cuttlefish cheekbones.

The phonograph crackled into silence, and the Chinaman wound the handle. The same song played again; heads nodded for the opening measures. Two old fellows mumbled under the music; I wondered if they were talking about me, but I thought not. I was invisible. There was something timeless in this place, something weightless, as if nothing here could have consequence. A second sake appeared beside me. Between soundings of the martial song I heard the wash of the sea. It was closer than I had thought.

A man leaned beside me. At first he was only a mouth, a gust of spicy breath through big, jutting, peg-like yellow teeth. Why he spoke to me I could not imagine; then I realized he was speaking English. He was Mr Arnhem's driver.

'Hah! But Sharpless-san, you see my suffering, no? To think, my old friend to be wrapped in funeral robes! How fat he look in them, like a fugu fish! Ah, many time we drink, drink' – he gestured about him – 'and I say, *Good Yakuside-san, our days they grow short, but mine, I fear, shall be short by more, and yours*' – he laughed, a little hysterically – '*yours, the sorrow when we part…* and treacherous Yakuside-san, he nod, he smile, he say, *Hah! old friend, you die half already, your eyes are like weasels, your knees are like raisins…*' – did he really say *weasels*? Did he really say *raisins*? – '*you, you join your ancestors any day now*. And Yakuside-san, he lie, he lie!'

Only slowly did I realize that the fellow was telling me about a dead friend. I wondered how long ago the funeral had been. That day? Yesterday? Months ago? Years?

'Yakuside-san and I, we have understanding,' he said. 'Business we do, business here and there. But stories that went around after that – that *business* with his little niece, they lies, Sharpless-san, all lies, lies. Me, I blame the Bonze...' He slugged back his sake. His driver's uniform had frayed at the collar.

'Goro, isn't it?' I said. 'That's your name?'

His breath was overpowering. 'All of us, we look same to you, no? But, Sharpless-san, I know you at once! When I see you last, you tiny baby. Now look like father – like father come back. Who in Nagasaki not know that honourable man? I pleased to say he my friend. Perhaps he speak of me, in those years after he go away – Sharpless-san, I nakodo!'

I began to feel drunk. 'I thought your name was Goro.'

'Goro the nakodo – man who make marriage.'

'You married them?' I said. 'The lieutenant and the girl?'

'No marry! Me man of business, not holy man.' He said it as if a man of business were the better thing to be, then grinned, and the grin made me feel slightly sick. 'I, Goro, help them meet.'

'A pimp?' I had not meant to say it aloud.

'He is drunkard.' It was the Chinaman. Filling our glasses again, he splashed the counter. 'Every night, with Yakuside-san...' He flung back his head and mimed a glugging motion. 'Every night, till head it fall to bar.'

'Shut up!' Goro waved the barman away. I downed another sake, and at once wished I had not. Goro's mouth opened and closed; his yellow teeth waggled. Now he was saying something about the days, years before, when he had been with Sharpless-san and Pinkerton-san on Higashi Hill, and I asked him if he would take me there, but just then the barroom fell silent.

In the doorway, half in shadow, stood three Japanese soldiers. A young officer stepped forward. Blearily, I took in his rounded cap, his tight collar, the leather strap that crossed his chest. Pacing forward, he held in one hand a thin stick like a schoolmaster's cane and slapped it in a slow rhythm into the palm of the other. Stopping before one bench, he inspected the elderly drinkers before moving on. No one spoke. I thought myself barely visible in the gloom, but before the officer stalked out again, his eyes fixed on mine and I felt singled out, threatened, as if he had marked me down as an adversary to be crushed.

Sighs and nervous laughter rippled around the barroom after the patrol had gone. Goro slapped me on the back, beckoned the barman for sake, and demanded that I drink, drink.

Moths flurried around glimmering lanterns.

'Where did you go?'

I had woken more than once in the night, startled each time to find myself beneath gauzy netting. Restless dreams disturbed me. Again I was in the bar with Goro; again his toothy face thrust into mine, but he spoke Japanese or just nonsense-words, gobbling away like a turkey cock. I sank under the tide of talk; I saw his face twist; then he drew away and there behind him, fixing a liquid gaze on me, was the young Japanese officer.

'I said, "Where did you go?"'

Sunlight, for some time, had pressed behind the blinds; now it filled the room, and Le Vol turned back from the window.

'Please.' I pressed my face into the pillow.

'Goro brought you home. You were stumbling and swearing. And in the consul's house! What are you playing at?' He pulled back my mosquito netting. 'Come on. Koshi-byo awaits.'

'The temple? Baedeker's by my bed.'

'Baedeker? I want Sharpless.'

'You go.' I pulled my face from the pillow – temporarily, I hoped.

Le Vol had shaved, dressed, slicked his hair.

'What's with the grooming?' I said. 'This isn't like you.'

'And this isn't like *you*. You're still drunk, aren't you?'

'I'm sick!'

'Well, you can't be. Do you want the Pulitzer or not? This story's going to be big.'

'Great Temples of Kyushu!' Le Vol could not be serious. 'Calvin Coolidge said the man who builds a factory builds a temple. Do you think it works the other way around? Does the man who builds a temple build a factory?'

'Up! Mr Arnhem is at our disposal – and Goro and his automobile.'

I told Le Vol to go ahead. 'I'll catch up with you.'

'I'll bet!' He flung up his hands. 'Damn you, Sharpless.'

'Close the blinds, will you?' I called, but he had gone.

I rolled on to my back. I flung a forearm over my eyes. From outside came the chugging of the Lincoln sedan, then tyres crunched over the drive.

When I rose at last it was afternoon. The house was quiet; even the bent-backed maidservant did not come when I called. I searched the kitchen for coffee, but found none. I glugged down several glasses of water.

My plan was no plan at all: I would walk into town and wander without direction. If my odyssey brought me to Koshi-byo, well and good; but as I reached the end of the consulate's drive, I found, when I rounded a vine-covered wall, a rickshaw-puller standing idle. The fellow, after the manner of his tribe, was wiry, naked to the waist, and strangely ageless, a wizened boy, his teeth brown with chewing-tobacco as he grinned and said, 'Koshi-byo?'

'Higashi Hill.' I settled into the rickshaw like an invalid, drawing a rug across my knees. The sun struck brightly at my eyes. We rattled into streets thick with people and stalls and cluttered storefronts. We crossed a canal; automobiles honked like geese and streetcars trundled by, tugging at overhead wires. I glimpsed a temple, scaly with ornament like a dragon's back. Might this be where Le Vol had gone?

The rickshaw disconcerted me; its swayings and bumpings, its openness to the streets, made me feel vulnerable and strangely ashamed. Grimly, I concentrated on the puller's knobbly back, until the pressing streets gave way and we climbed between houses spaced wider apart and spring trees shedding sticky buds.

Now the air was sweet and I forgot my queasiness. Buildings scattered down the hills like pale boxes. The harbour, far below, flashed in the sun. We passed through a screen of cypresses and before us was a house, a low, ethereal affair of papery walls and black beams beneath an overhanging terracotta roof. The garden was broad and long, with ornamental boulders, curving paths, and raked pebble borders. Slipping down from the rickshaw, I felt as if I had reached a centre that I had skirted all my life.

Like a thief, I moved through the garden. An ornamental pond smelled noxious; no fish flickered in the reedy water. Making for the lawn's edge, where the hill sloped downwards, I surveyed the harbour. Yes, I thought. From here, one could follow all the ships that came and went.

I made for the house. The veranda, unbalustraded, jutted out from creamy walls. The steps that led up to it were an arrangement of stones. The quiet was hypnotic. One of the walls had been slid back, opening the way to an interior deep in shadow. Old timbers creaked beneath my feet; I might have been on the deck of a sailing ship. I removed my hat, my shoes; I stepped through the screen. Inside, the sparse room was not as dark as I had expected. Inner screens, some partially opened, led to other rooms. The place was a magic box; the configuration of the walls could be changed at a whim.

'Hello?' I said, though I thought the house was empty.

Tatami matting muffled my steps as I passed from room to room. Incense drifted on the air, and something, perhaps a gossamer insect, brushed my face. Beside a cabinet of lacquered teak leaned a samisen, that strange slender banjo-like instrument played in Japanese prints by delicate young women with downcast eyes. I had never seen a real one before.

'Hello?' I said again, and heard a sound of humming. Shadowy against a screen stood a ghostly, kimonoed figure with hair heaped high, turning a fan in an upraised hand.

'Ah, but he come – American come.' She snapped the fan from her face and stepped towards me. This was no ghost, but a woman all too real – her hair unravelling, her face seamed and sagging beneath its mask of make-up. Her teeth were poor and there was sourness on her breath as she looked up at me, slapped my arm with the fan, and said, 'Come, American.'

We stepped into a chamber that stood open to the garden. I was back on the veranda where I had begun; a tea table had appeared, arranged neatly with a peculiar large metal vessel, porcelain bowls, and cups without handles. Cherry blossoms splayed from vases nearby, and on a plinth stood a telescope, a dark, tapering cylinder banded in brass. On each side of the table was a flat, pale cushion. The old woman descended with surprising grace to one, and gestured to me to take the other.

Clumsily, I lowered myself. The woman's face was grotesque, the paint thick as a clown's, the eyes yolky and rimmed in red. She dipped the ladle into the teakettle; I sipped the bitter, steaming tea. The ceremony would have proceeded in silence, but from time to time the old woman hummed or let slip a muttered phrase, sometimes in Japanese, sometimes English: 'American here?' or 'Ship in harbour?' or 'Sharpless-san, he fix Mr B. F. Pikkerton, no?'

'You're the girl's maid,' I said. 'Suzuki.'

And all at once the old woman, as if in response to her name, leaped up and rushed to the plinth. Jamming an eye to the telescope, she called out words I could not understand and beckoned to me excitedly.

Her fit was over almost as soon as it had begun. Leaving the telescope spinning, she resumed her place and carried on sipping tea. She only muttered, as if it were expected, 'Mr B. F. Pikkerton, he no come today.'

The longer I sat with Suzuki, the stranger the scene became. Gently, she picked out a song on the samisen. Her voice, to my surprise, was beautiful, and I listened as in a trance, wishing I could understand, but before the song was over she flung down the instrument and covered her face. Her shoulders heaved. I went to her, but when I stole an arm around her she flared, screaming and clawing at me, shrieking out curses until I escaped ignominiously. As I slithered down the stony steps from the veranda I barked my shin, and braved further blows as I scrambled back for my ashplant.

The rickshaw-puller waited for me outside.

'Koshi-byo?' he said, and I nodded, but only because I did not know how to tell him to take me back to the consulate. Something wet coursed down my cheek, and I dabbed at it with my handkerchief: Suzuki's nails had drawn blood. I had left behind my hat and shoes. Blankly, I watched the rickshaw-puller's brown, bent back, its jutting vertebrae suggestive of some ancient,

160

stubbornly persisting form of life – something repellent, reptilian – as we jolted down from Higashi Hill.

In town, spidery entanglings of wires meshed the sky like a net, as if to keep the citizens trapped; the streets were dirty, crowded, reeking. Everything was as it had been before – but no, it was not.

Cries filled the air. There was a thunder of feet.

The chaos, even as it descended, seemed unreal: unreal, the loud report, like a shot; unreal, the crowds pushing, flooding out from the alleys, filling every space between rickshaws, bicycles, automobiles; unreal, the shouting, the blasting of horns.

Young men pressed from all directions, jostling and angry. Fists punched the air; words screamed from flung-back throats. Where had the riot come from? How had it erupted? All at once it was there, and I was in the middle of it.

I cried out to the rickshaw-puller, but he paid me no heed, struggling as best he could to liberate us from the fray. Something slammed the side of the rickshaw, sending it rocking. I gripped the arc of the canopy, wondering if I dared jump into the street. Could I make it to the sidewalk? But on the sidewalk, there was only the same swarming, angry crowd.

Horns bellowed, loud as the shouts and screams. Then, blasting through the throng, came a long, dark sedan, like a president's car, sweeping one hapless fellow on to its hood.

The Lincoln! I had no way to reach it.

Soldiers had appeared, mounted on horses. One struck at rioters with a club. One fired shots. My rickshaw-puller lost his grip on his vehicle and was carried away from me, sinking under the human tide. I was flung against one side of the chair, then the other, then out into the street. The rickshaw overturned and covered me like a shell.

I scrambled out. I struggled to my feet. I was pushed down again;

I forced myself forward. Where was my ashplant? A camera flared, burning my eyes. I lost my footing. Shots rang out again. Rearing over me, whinnying, was a horse. The rider, a Japanese officer.

I would be crushed. Horse and rider blocked the sun, then veered away, and I whispered (for, after all, I knew that rider, that officer from the bar): 'Isamu… Isamu.'

Another figure fought its way towards me. Le Vol! He wrenched me upright. We plunged through a door. The chaos was muffled; leather protected us, brown and slithery as polished brogues.

'Pleasant afternoon, Mr Sharpless?' said Clifford T. Arnhem.

I lay, breathing heavily, in Le Vol's arms. His camera, big and boxy, jutted at my spine, and through a glass partition I studied the back of Goro's neck: like the upholstery, it was leathery, brown.

'Communists.' Mr Arnhem bit the end from a cigar. 'Communist agitators. What do the fools want? Don't they understand this country is on the brink of greatness?'

To my surprise, Le Vol made no protest at this, only extricating his limbs from mine, winding down the window, and taking more shots. The riot had subsided, leaving a street strewn with debris. Goro drove on slowly. We passed corpses and overturned vehicles, one on fire.

Glumly, I thought of my missing ashplant.

'This is just the beginning,' Le Vol was saying. 'Mr Arnhem's arranged an important interview for us tomorrow, Sharpless. Big wheel in the government, this fellow. No drunken philandering tonight, eh? This is where you come into your own.' He tapped the window. 'Who better to explain all this? And China too! The inside story, from their point of view.'

'Great Temples of Kyushu, indeed!' I said.

'I love temples,' said Le Vol. 'Without them, would the *Geographic* have stumped up for our tickets? Don't worry, I'm shooting temples too. Anyway,' he went on, 'this fellow you're interviewing, he's a Jap nobleman. Years ago he was a rootless playboy, living in the West. Back home, he's the fiercest patriot. What did you say his name was again, sir?'

'Yamadori,' replied Mr Arnhem. 'Prince Yamadori.'

'This isn't like Yamadori,' I said.

'Yamadori isn't like Yamadori – politics, Sharpless!'

'Since when does a playboy get up at five?'

We trudged through early-morning streets. Gravely, I placed my ashplant ahead of me. Last night before dinner, Goro had appeared in my room, bowed, and presented me with the gnarled black stick, held horizontally across his upturned palms; he was a servant, I realized, of exceptional powers.

Deserted in the dawn, the broad thoroughfare with its trolley-car tracks might have been anywhere. Only the hand-painted signs above the stores suggested Japan. We were a few streets back from Dejima Wharf, somewhere between Chinatown and Nagasaki Station.

I asked Le Vol the name of Yamadori's hotel.

'City's finest. Built over thermal springs.'

We crossed the road. Between stores selling fish or rice or radios, an imposing façade stretched the length of a block. Festooned with statues and Doric columns, it looked like an Austro-Hungarian palace, but for the sense that it was all lathe and paste: Vienna via Hollywood. As Le Vol led me through a pair of mighty doors, young men in bow ties bent low, and a desk clerk, proud in pince-nez, gestured to an ugly ottoman.

'We're expected,' Le Vol said, impressed.

The young men resumed their tasks: one, polishing a brass

plate by the elevators; one, wiping with a damp cloth each leaf of an aspidistra; one, fluffing cushions on sofas and chairs. The desk clerk, pince-nez glinting, scratched solemnly in a ledger, as if recording deeds of conquest in imperial annals.

Le Vol was nervous, his hands twisting as he asked me, in a murmur, whether I had my questions ready. I was irritated but not worried. Le Vol would do the talking; my task was to take notes, and afterwards put them in order. 'You don't think he'll tell us much, do you?'

'This is where you come in, Sharpless. The human touch. Old pals, aren't you?'

'Hardly. What's he doing in Nagasaki, anyway?'

'Inspecting the shipyards, says Mr Arnhem.'

I expected we would be called up to Yamadori's suite, and was confused when the young men fell into formation by the elevators. A counter clicked from top floor to ground. The desk clerk, straightening his jacket, joined the line of young men; Le Vol rose and prodded me to my feet, just as the doors slid back to reveal a stately figure illumined in the mirrored box.

Yamadori had changed since the Manhattan days. The Playboy of the Western World had vanished beneath a military bearing. There was something of the samurai about him. The huge, toad-like head, with its livery lips and staring eyes, had stiffened, like a carving; a tight collar circled the jowly chins, and his squat, broad torso had been shoehorned into a blue uniform, heavy with epaulettes, medals, and braid.

The boys, the desk clerk, and Le Vol and I bowed as the prince strutted forward. A sword in an elaborate, curving scabbard jutted from his left hip, and his boots were high and gleaming. Emerging behind him were three impassive servants, each in grey-green military uniform.

Yamadori, with a faint smile, inclined his head to Le Vol and me, then turned to the desk clerk and barked harsh-sounding words in Japanese. The exchange ended with Yamadori dealing the fellow a blow and the fellow, cringing and cowering, accepting his fate as if it were deserved.

'My secretary,' the great man explained, 'has been delayed in Tokyo – government business, you understand. He was to have joined us this morning. But, it seems, is late. Come.' He snapped his fingers and pointed not to the elevator, but to a far wall of the lobby. Dutifully, with hotel staff bowing all the while, we trailed after the prince and his retinue. Carved doors, sleekly lacquered, loomed from dark-papered walls; young men, like compliant machines, opened them at our approach, revealing an antechamber of glowing marble. Confused, I stole a glance at Le Vol as we made our way down a curving staircase into a windowless, subterranean realm.

Everything below was as fine as in the lobby, but stark and simple: Japanese, not Austro-Hungarian. Broad corridors, lit dimly by lanterns, stretched in several directions. The air was humid, oppressively so, and I heard, from somewhere out of sight, a soft lapping of water.

'A bathe!' cried Yamadori. 'Always the best way to begin the day, don't you find? Especially when one has spent the night not in sleeping but in talking on the telephone to this minister and that.' He sighed. 'But such are the times. Soon, none shall sleep.'

A servant opened a slatted door.

'We'll change in here,' declared Yamadori.

'Prince' – Le Vol, I could see, was losing patience – 'we arranged an interview.'

'Mr... *Levi*, is it not?' – Yamadori smirked – 'you will appreciate that I am a busy man. Here we are, imperial affairs at a critical pass, and I choose to speak to two Americans.'

165

'What better time,' Le Vol swept on, 'to explain yourself? China's changed everything, for Japan and for the world. You know that, don't you? Once you were exotics, charmingly so. The world wished you well. Now we see you as beasts, ravening beasts.'

Yamadori's nostrils flared and he spoke rapidly to a servant, who skittered forward and took Le Vol's arm.

'The interview will be dull for the photographer,' said Yamadori. 'Besides, am I to be depicted in the act of bathing? Your American audience would find it indelicate. This hotel has a tea chamber, Mr Levi, with *most* diverting woodblocks on the walls.'

Le Vol protested, but the servant's grip was firm.

'Your friend is a man of political passions,' Yamadori observed when we were alone. He seemed amused.

'But fair,' I said, 'and just. He's not here to judge.'

'And nor are you?'

In the room with the slatted door, a bench, varnished darkly, ran around the walls; there were hooks for hanging clothes. Through a wide opening at the far end of the room was a steaming pool.

I had thought servants would be on hand to undress Yamadori, but he tugged efficiently at his collar and the many buttons of his tunic. Embarrassed, I half-turned from him as I removed my own clothes. Cursing Le Vol, I tried to think what questions I should ask. Manchuria: check. Korea: check. War with America: likely or no?

Covering myself with a small, thin towel, I prodded my ashplant over the slithery tiles, then lowered it, discarded the towel, and was about to ease myself into the steaming water when the great man appeared beside me, gripped my arm, and said, 'No. First you wash.'

'I've washed,' I said, 'earlier.'

'You wash,' he declared, and I limped after him, naked, to a bank of showerheads that protruded from one wall. Ice-cold

166

water struck me like a blow, and I gasped and whimpered while Yamadori, unperturbed, threw out remarks about the weather and the stock market; once, in a rich baritone, he boomed out a melody from *La Bohème*: '*O Mimì, tu più non torni...*'

He reminded me, I decided, not so much of a samurai as of a sumo wrestler. Lathering myself, I tried not to look at his ponderous swaying belly and the surprisingly large genitals that impended beneath it, like obscene fruit, from a frizz of wiry black; but he, I could tell, was looking at me. Acutely, I was aware of my spindly arms, my sunken chest, the disfiguring scars on my injured leg, and was relieved when he gestured at last towards the pool. No steps led down from the sides, but he slipped his bulk into the water with unexpected grace. I followed, squelching my buttocks to the tiles and pitching forward, floundering, crying out at the sudden, startling heat.

The water was opaque, a greyish green. Steam coiled around us, infused with sulphurous scent; Yamadori lay back, luxuriating, and closed his eyes. The time had come for my questions, and I struggled to recall phrases Le Vol had used, babbling out at last, 'Many of us in the West have been alarmed by the rise in Japanese militarism. Should we be – in your view?'

Yamadori sniffed, hummed.

I tried again: 'Japan, to the world's astonishment, became the only non-Western nation to defeat a Western nation in war, in the Russo–Japanese war of 19...' (1904? 1905? I decided not to risk it.) 'Is the world more inclined to censure Japanese military adventurism than that of other nations – in your view?'

He sighed; his belly rose and fell. 'Young man, why ask me this? My secretary has the answers, prepared in press releases. Am I to weary myself by repeating what has passed my lips already countless times?'

The bathing chamber was vast, greenish like the water, with a high, vaulted ceiling. Through crisscrossed panes of skylights, a dawn pallor glowed. Still we were alone, and I was both relieved and alarmed; other bathers might be banned from the great man's ablutions, but I had expected attendants, slim boys in loincloths or naked, aquatic geishas, ready with scrapers and back-scrubbers, like slaves in ancient Rome.

Yamadori sang Puccini again; his voice was remarkably pleasant. In his old life he must have spent many a night at the opera. Cautiously, I asked him whether he missed his playboy days.

For a moment I thought he would not reply; the great whale body stirred not a jot, and I felt content: I had done my duty by Le Vol. No Pulitzer Prize would come from this scene. It was over.

The pallor from the skylights grew golden; buttery shafts of radiance sank into the steam. Yamadori's baritone came again – speaking not singing – bearing pictures of an ancient culture: pagodas like dragons' scales, stacked tier on tier; the flick of fans in strange ceremonies; suits of armour flashing like jewelled crustaceans; giant torii jutting from the sea; robed figures ascending sacred stairs. This, said Yamadori, was the time of Tokugawa, the feudal regime that had ruled in splendid isolation from the world before the coming of Meiji and the birth of modern Japan.

'After Tokugawa… ah, but all of us come after Tokugawa now!'

He shifted, and the slosh of water startled me.

He went on: 'There are those who see me as a superficial man' (I had never, I wanted to assure him, entertained such a thought), 'idler, skimmer of the surface, seeker after vain pleasures. Call me butterfly if you will – a fluttering thing of no weight, no consequence!' (I never would, I almost said – no, never; but held my breath, as if some revelation were about to come.)

'I was born, Mr Sharpless, some sixty years ago: 1877 on your American calendar. A year that perhaps means little to you, but in Japan it is the year of the Satsuma Rebellion, when Takamori, last of the samurai, led his army of forty thousand against the forces of the new Meiji government. My father died in that rebellion – yes, on the losing side. Naturally, I never knew him; I was an ugly fat baby, clamped to my nurse's breast, far away in our palace at Omaru. But often I have wished I could speak to him. I should tell him he was a fool. Why cast in his lot with Takamori? Already the Meiji had entrapped us, an age of iron and lead; Tokugawa and all its gold lay as deep in the past as Lady Murasaki and *The Tale of Genji*. The golden world was over, crushed by time, from the moment the Americans in their black ships appeared in Edo Bay.

'*Manifest destiny*, that was your name for it, your progress of pillage and plunder, first across one continent, then around the world. Were you to be denied the rich ports of Asia?' He snorted. 'Ports! In the beginning, that was all. But the doors were flung open then. Our hemisphere fell into the clutches of your race. Was it our destiny to be your colony? Were we Chinamen? Were we Indians? No! We would never surrender. We would adopt your ways. Modernize. Compete.

'That was the dark bargain of Meiji: iron horses, clanking factories, telegraph wires that webbed the sky. We turned on our land as if we hated it – we had to, in order to save it. Did you know, Mr Sharpless, that your Commodore Perry was a hopeless drunkard? He died raving, eaten by the ravages of his weakness. And this, this foul-breathed swaggering American, was the man who plunged a great and ancient people into shame!'

As Yamadori's words crept over me I suspected this was a monologue he had delivered often. But should I – American,

169

though I barely felt it – hold myself responsible for Commodore Perry?

Yamadori continued: 'I grew up in ignorance, Mr Sharpless. Cosseted product of a tendril of royalty that had withered on the vine, what chance had I? Yes, there were our family lands, our old retainers; I wanted for nothing, but nothingness gnawed at my heart. My tutors encouraged me in the callow paths of pleasure. At an early age I was sent to America. Travels in Europe followed. By the time I came into man's estate, I was thoroughly cosmopolitan. Some would call me deracinated, though how deracinated can a man be whose very appearance – his skin, his eyes – proclaims his origins at every turn?

'Oh, I was not given over wholly to my foreigner's life; there was business to attend to here and I came back often in young manhood, if always with an eagerness to be off again to Vienna or Paris or Rome, and the mistresses and boon companions who beguiled my hours there. I admit I partook of the pleasures of this port – how many marriages did I contract, flickering affairs of a few weeks or months, with the sweet little protégées of a fellow called Goro?

'Then came the one girl I could not forget. I dare say I appeared a bumptious fool the day I stood before her, offering my hand. I blush to think of it. Here was my heart, enraptured, and all I could display were the gestures of the libertine, taking his pick among playthings in a house of ill-repute – for such, Mr Sharpless, is the power of vice to pollute our attempts at purity, to coarsen our overtures to our own salvation.

'Hear me, speaking like a Christian! But when that girl stood before me in a kimono embroidered with a dragon's coils, I knew I had lost myself long ago and only through her could I find my way home again. What beauty that girl possessed: a girl whose ruin, like mine, stemmed from the days of the Satsuma Rebellion and the alliances contracted by her father then – a girl fallen low, but one whom I could raise up, restoring her to her rightful place! For yes, this I would have done, had the American Pinkerton not stolen her heart.

'I was abandoned by history, Mr Sharpless. Love, when at last I found it, might have compensated for my losses. But love, too, was snatched from me by history. Could I, like my country a half-century before, have been more abjectly cast down? I vowed to leave Japan and not come back.

'And I almost kept my vow. Never once, through what remained of Meiji and the effete years of Taishō, did I return. My exile was lonely, a stage, perhaps, through which I had to pass, for while I frittered my time away in city after city, slowly something stirred in me. Yes, I had been weak. Yes, I had been a fool. But I am a prince of samurai blood. Only for so long could I be oppressed by a foreigner. In Manhattan, at the Blood Red Ball, I confronted the treachery that had worked against me for so long. Afterwards, I returned to my homeland and found, as if in echo of my own turning spirit, that the passing of Taishō had brought a new age. Under Emperor Hirohito, Japan would become a nation fit to command the world. And I would be a part of it, shape it, direct it. My time had come.'

Would Yamadori never shut up? I longed to rise from the pool and go. My flesh felt boiled, and in my irritation I blurted out, 'This can't be your time, it can't! You spoke of torii and sacred stairs. In China, Hirohito's soldiers skewer children on bayonets. They rape. They murder. They fling gasoline over houses and set them blazing. Can't you see what you're doing? You're killing the Indians. You're enslaving the Negroes. This is the logic of Meiji – the iron ships, the airplanes, the mile after mile of railroad track. This is where they lead. You haven't turned your back on America. You've become America.'

Yamadori moved towards me through the steam. 'Mr Sharpless, I've told you my story and you've understood not a word. Your ships in Edo Bay had dark and terrible powers. But your empire is over and ours has begun.' His hand, a darting fish, slithered under the scalding water, alighting on my hip. 'I could kill you, American. You're Sharpless, the consul.'

'His son. I was a child.'

'You'll always be a child.' His voice was a whisper. 'Look at you, what are you? Chicken bones, fit only to be left for the dogs! A weakling. A cripple. How can you even pretend to be a man?'

'Stop it! Keep away!' I flailed from the side of the pool, but the darting hand was adroit, threading between my spindly legs and closing upon my testicles.

Pain shot through me like electric volts. I shrieked and thrashed. I sank. He pushed me down, then wrenched me up, twisting and crushing with brutal, thick fingers. I floundered for the side of the pool; I crashed through the water, down and down; I surged up, yowling; I lay on my back, kicking and writhing; and all the time Yamadori twisted.

Then came the flash. Incandescence scythed the steamy air. There were scufflings, shouts. What was happening? I didn't know, but the distraction was enough for me to break from Yamadori. Outraged, he bellowed in Japanese, but not at me, and only when I had ripped myself from the water did I see Le Vol, holding his camera above the desperate servants' heads.

Flash! Flash! Le Vol took a second photograph, then a third, just as Yamadori whiplashed a hand over the pool's slimy edge. Grabbing my bad leg, he gouged into the scars. I screamed. Le Vol joined the fray and tugged me by the arms. I feared they would tear me in two.

Le Vol had the advantage. Yamadori was half out of the pool. With a mighty splash he fell back, and I slithered like an eel towards the changing room as Le Vol flung first one, then another, of the servants into the water. He wrenched me up, ready to hustle me away, but Yamadori, as if infused with occult power, reared up before us. Cries tore from his throat; his sumo bulk charged at Le Vol and flipped him to the floor. The camera smashed.

Yamadori raged. In an instant, he would be upon me. His uniform hung from the wall, and beneath it, gleaming in the steam, was the sword. I seized it, ripped it from the scabbard. Like lightning the blade flashed – just as the door behind me burst open and a new voice rang out.

I lowered the sword. At first I could not believe the saviour that appeared before us, dapper in Japanese military uniform: breathless, and a little astonished, but not too much, at the scene he had encountered. My scars burned, but worse was my sudden, absurd shame at my nudity.

'I've been entertaining our American friends,' said Yamadori, as if he had been presiding over a tea ceremony. 'You'll see they're somewhat ignorant of our etiquette.' Flagrantly he advanced over the tiles, feet slapping, genitals swaying, huge-nippled breasts wobbling against his sides like folds of cloth. He gestured to the new arrival.

'My secretary. But perhaps you've met before.'

Familiar, violet eyes looked at me, amused.

'What I don't understand,' said Clifford T. Arnhem, 'is what you thought you were playing at.'

'Why should we be *playing* at anything? The interview took a peculiar turn – a bath, for Christ's sake!'

'The prince is a busy man. He bathes at odd times.'

'He wouldn't let Le Vol in with us.'

'So your friend insisted? He's disappointed me, Mr Sharpless. I thought he had some sense.'

We were in the Lincoln; Goro drove, aimlessly it seemed, about the city. It was late afternoon. Until then I had spent all my time on the east side of the harbour. Now we had reached the west, and I wished we could stop; at every rut in the road, at every pothole, pain shot up my injured leg and throbbed between my thighs. My testicles, my *balls*, would be black for weeks.

Rain shivered down, pattering the windows. Shabby stores, a succession of holes in walls, reeled slowly by; yellowish faces loomed in at us through the glass. There was another pothole, a nasty one.

'Goro, drive carefully!' I rapped the dividing glass, and Mr Arnhem glowered; I was too ashamed to tell him what Yamadori had done to me. 'But Le Vol,' I urged. 'Surely they'll let Le Vol go?'

Mr Arnhem, summoned by Yamadori, had extricated me with some difficulty from military prison; Le Vol was another matter. 'What do you think would happen if a Jap photographer muscled his way in to take snaps of, say, Senator Pinkerton in his bath? The crime is comparable. Your friend has grievously insulted Prince Yamadori.'

'And Yamadori,' I cried, 'has insulted me!'

'*You* are not a senior member of the Japanese government.'

Another bump. Pain contorted my face. 'Mr Arnhem, are you telling me that *you*, as consul, can't make him see reason?'

'You presume to know what *reason* in this case might be.'

'So that's it? You're giving up on Le Vol?'

'Don't be silly. Yamadori's intention, I hope, is just to frighten him. But I can do no more today.'

174

Storefronts had given way to barbed-wire fences, scrubby fields, and, in the distance, low metallic sheds with half-built shells of ships towering above them. A checkpoint appeared ahead. With a tap at the glass, Mr Arnhem directed Goro to proceed no further; but as we swerved back towards town, I glimpsed a motorcade parked within the shipyards, and Yamadori greeting a line of naval officers. Standing stiffly by his side was Trouble.

In the days that followed, I ate my meals and drank too much and spoke of idle things, as if no desperate uncertainty beat beneath each moment like a drum. Mr Arnhem was preoccupied, busy with consular duties, and it fell to Goro to keep me amused, taking me for long drives around Nagasaki-ken and beyond. Green volcanic valleys unfolded before me, with volatile hills and steam that hissed up foully from the earth. Here, said Goro, the Christians were massacred; here, the samurai met their doom; Japan, I reflected, was a violent land, never the dreamy eternity the world thought it should be.

Goro treated me with a deference that I found humbling. One afternoon, in a teahouse in Takeo, he introduced me to a little girl of twelve or so who was, he said, a daughter of his nephew. Only after the girl had sat with us for some time, eyes downcast, and Goro had barked at her in Japanese, evidently telling her to improve her demeanour, did I realize he was offering her to me in temporary marriage. My face flushed and I did my best to decline the offer graciously. How sorry I felt for the frail, bird-like girl! How amazed I was that Goro could think me another Lieutenant Pinkerton! But I had no thought of castigating him. I feared I had insulted him and was ashamed.

That night, Goro accompanied me to the theatre. I understood little of the Noh drama, with its masked actors and sweeping robes and slow, stylized gestures. We sat on benches, some rows back, to the side of a jutting stage with pillars at each corner and a roof like a pagoda's. Once or twice I would have asked Goro to explain what was going on, but I suspected a man of his class knew no more than I. Only during the entr'acte, a knockabout affair of squabbling rude mechanicals, did he become animated, parting his yellow, peg-like teeth in laughter. When it was finished, he rose abruptly, bowed to me, and hurried away.

I assumed he had gone to the bathroom, but he did not return during the next act. Watching the robed figures make their exquisite gestures, I wondered if this act involved the same characters as the first.

Then somebody took Goro's place and tried to help me.

'It's a different play, you realize.' Yamadori's voice, hot against my ear, was barely loud enough for me to make out the words. Onstage, an actor in a golden cape writhed sinuously, holding aloft a sword that sparkled in the lights. A Noh performance, Yamadori explained, consists not of one play but of a set of plays, demonstrating successively the harmony that attains in the world of the gods, the dissensions of man, then man's repentance, his redemption, and the glory of defeating all that stands in the way of peace. 'This is the fall we're seeing now. But it isn't all, you see. There's more to come.'

The actors stamped and leaped, thumping out a ritual dance; the stage throbbed like a drum skin, and Yamadori continued, 'The play confuses you because you want it to tell a story, but it wants to evoke a mood. See how even in this violence of conflict there is colour, beauty, life? And infinite grace. Think of the story as something that happened long ago. Forget the story. We know what happens next: always the same transience, the beauty of moments passing.'

176

The resoundings ceased abruptly; there was applause, and Yamadori said quickly, 'Temple of Shofuku-ji. Tomorrow at two.'

Abruptly, he was gone, and Goro appeared once more. Furious, frightened, I wanted to ask him what arrangement he had come to with Yamadori, what bribe had made him leave me like this, but Goro, at once, was laughing loudly over the second entr'acte. Resentfully I studied his jutting larynx, his thousand pleated wrinkles, his yellow teeth with their many gaps.

All I cared about was what happened next.

In the morning I dismissed Goro and made my way about the town alone. Filling in time, I wandered along canals, sat on a bench by the harbour and drank too much Japanese beer over lunch in a restaurant with flyblown windows and meticulous table-settings. What awaited me at Shofuku-ji I could not imagine, but I felt as if I, and not Le Vol, faced criminal charges. I feared I was being watched. In the restaurant I looked suspiciously at the other diners; none looked back at me.

Shofuku-ji appeared deserted. Set back from the street over a wooden bridge, the temple gathered about it an air of quietness. A gold-painted gable, catching the sun, flashed like a signal as I ascended stone stairs. I found myself in a broad, dark hall. I moved carefully, but the varnished floors, sleek as violins, thrummed at the smallest movement.

'Prince Yamadori?' I said, emerging into a courtyard lined with pale gravel. A gong, bronze and immense, glimmered by the far wall. In the centre of the wide space, an old man in orange robes raked the stones with meditative calm. As I approached, he did not look up.

'I was told to come,' I said, my voice low.

The old man kept raking, face averted, head down. I touched his arm and he giggled; he was senile, or perhaps had acquired so great a tranquillity that every reaction was at tortoise-speed. The bent head rolled towards me, revealing eyes sleek with yellow film. 'Sharpless-san?' he said at last, and pointed to the shrine that lay across the courtyard.

Shadowy eaves overhung the entrance. Inside, sweetness hovered on the air. Light, pale and smoky, seeped through high lattices and, from the dark back wall, above an altar laid with flowers, loomed a Buddha, impassive and vast. Prostrate before the statue was a solitary saffron form. A peculiar composure filled me, and I thought how I had misjudged what awaited me.

'Trouble,' I said, when the saffron form rose. If his blondness appeared incongruous against the Zen robes, I did not consider it. There was a rightness to him, a naturalness, as he came towards me.

He smiled. 'I see you've met the Bonze.'

'Bonze?' Hovering outside was the old man, still holding the rake.

Trouble said, 'You knew he was my great-uncle?'

'How could I know that?'

Moments later the raking resumed, the languorous *scrape...* *scrape*. Trouble and I were meeting in a dream: it did not seem strange that we had not said hello, not shaken hands, not embraced.

He led me out of the shrine. We would walk in the gardens, he said, and explained that his great-uncle, now a servant, had once been a priest of this temple, but gave it up after Trouble's mother died. 'He'd denounced her, you see. Cast her out of the family for becoming a Christian. He never forgave himself.'

We passed beneath cypresses, Trouble keeping a slow pace

by my side. Shadows and sunlight flickered over his robes.

'So, you're a Buddhist now?' I said. 'You believe all that?'

'What's believing? You think you have to trust in something, be convinced of it absolutely.' I was not sure he was talking to me: by *you*, perhaps, he meant Westerners generally. 'Here, you learn that it's practice that's important. Forget belief. There are things you just *do*. All else follows.'

I said, 'But Yamadori, you believe in him?'

We had come to a stony platform overlooking a lawn. Trouble gestured for me to sit on a bench. Far out on the lawn, three young men in monks' robes competed at archery. As they stretched back their bows, it seemed to me there was no element of play in their actions, but care, a care as meticulous as the Bonze's in his interminable raking of the gravel. Punctuating my talk with Trouble came a muted *thop-thop* of arrows striking targets.

'I'd expected Yamadori,' I said. 'To see him, I mean.'

'We thought you might. But I'm the one who has to tell you.'

'Tell me what?'

'Sharpless, what did you expect to happen?' he said.

'That I'd hear about Le Vol.' I had barely thought about him.

'Oh, they've released him. I dare say he's waiting for you back at the consulate. Better be quick, though. Tomorrow, he must leave Japan. He's been lucky. I was able to change the prince's mind.'

'Thank you.' I gripped his hand.

His voice hardened. 'I'm not coming back. You know that, don't you? In America I was incomplete, always at a loss. And Mama could have told me so much. But all she told were lies. And the senator's no better. He's worse. Why does he hate me so much?'

'He doesn't. You can't forgive him – ever?'

'There's a saying we have in Japan, *Shikata ga nai*. It can't be helped. Too bad. I know what you're doing. You want me to go back and I can't. I won't. It's not about forgiving. Once I lived in the wrong world. Now I don't.'

A flush spread up my neck. 'No. You're half-Japanese, but half-American too. You grew up in America. Your family's American. How often do you play this game, dressing up in monk's robes?'

'It isn't a game. I'm at school.'

'I get it. Renounced your religion, like your mother.'

'You don't understand my mother. Don't think you do.' He reached into his robes and withdrew a small, glittering object: the dagger. Casually, he held it out to me. How beautiful were the handle and scabbard: the gold, the silver, the precious stones. I drew out the blade.

'See that writing in Japanese?' Trouble's voice seemed to come from afar. '*To die with honour when one can no longer live with honour.* I think all the time about those words.'

I said abruptly, 'There's a war coming.'

'Japan and America? All America cares about is keeping the profits flowing. Any war that's coming, they'll keep well out of it.'

The bowmen had left off their contest and stood talking; they could have been any three young men, relaxed after play. One of them waved a hand to Trouble, and Trouble waved in return.

'Tell Kate it's no good, all right?' he said. 'Tell her it'll always be no good.'

'You thought I came for Kate?'

'You did, didn't you? You're her ambassador.'

The bowmen were splitting up; one, the one who had waved, walked in our direction. His robes glowed in the sun and I thought how beautiful he was: a loose-limbed, carefree boy, bow and quiver hooked across one shoulder. How different Isamu appeared, dressed as a monk!

180

I began to tremble. The dagger glittered in my hand, as if I meant to stab myself and was hesitating. 'Trouble, this is all unreal. War will come. There'll be no place for you here. Come home. Save yourself.'

'But I have. I *am* home.' He took back the dagger, concealing it in his robes again as Isamu reached us. Addressing Trouble in Japanese, Isamu mimed an arrow-shot, cuffed Trouble playfully, raised a hand to me, then made his way back towards the temple buildings.

Envy and sorrow burned in me like fire. What Trouble had said was true: all the time, but unknowingly, I had been Kate Pinkerton's ambassador, and my mission, I realized now, had failed.

That evening, Le Vol, Clifford T. Arnhem and I indulged in a long, drunken dinner. Mr Arnhem, doing violence to a samisen, yammered out the one about Naga-sacky where the fellers chew tobaccy and the women wicky-wacky-woo; Goro, joining us, laughed over everything and nothing, then sobbed between gluggings of sake for his dead friend Yakuside. The girl Kiku, covering her mouth, told jokes in broken English. The night was hot, the doors open; insects plunged and darted about the lamps. Mr Arnhem, growing sombre, played the one about the Japanese sandman, an old second-hand man, trading new days for old.

In the morning I said goodbye to Le Vol.

'You're sure you won't come home?' I asked him.

'They're only throwing me out of Japan, not making me go to America. I can't pass up this chance. You should come too. Come on – China! It's the story we've been waiting for.'

Was I a coward? Was I a fool? I held up my ashplant, my excuse for everything, and said: 'Be careful, old friend.'

My own ship, for San Francisco, was to sail a week later, but before it left, a restlessness claimed me and I departed early, bound for Hong Kong. Goro, by the gangplank, bowed to me deeply and urged on me again the charms of his niece in Takeo. Tearfully, he babbled that she would wait for my return.

A suspended period in my life began. I lingered in Hong Kong, that peculiar British outpost that seemed so disconnected from the massing bulk of China; I travelled overland to the French city of Saigon and by ship to Singapore, secure in the embrace of the British Empire; further south to Batavia, in the Dutch East Indies; east, to Port Moresby in the Australian protectorate of Papua; north-west to Manila, in the American islands of the Philippines.

Everywhere I felt the press of strangers. Natives massed against me in promiscuous streets, and colonials slapped me on the back in clubs beneath laggardly, churning ceiling fans; I found myself driven along jungle tracks or taken shooting, or hauled off to brothels by planters who had heard I was a visiting writer. Dutifully, I investigated temples and palaces and travelled on trains past squalid shacks and dazzling lakes and lush terraced hills, but nothing could assuage the loneliness that gnawed at me like physical pain. I favoured hotels near the sea. At night, lying awake, hearing the moon tugging at the tide, I would feel as if my soul were driftwood, buffeted on the waves, and wish that one day I could be washed ashore.

In Bataan, shaving one morning, I saw that my face was bloated. My nose and cheeks were red, and my eyes looked boiled. Months had gone by. I was running out of money. I suppose I thought that if I kept close to Japan I was somehow tied to Trouble, revolving, if distantly, in his orbit.

At breakfast, I paid attention to the papers. The war in China had gone from bad to worse. For months, I had seen something strained in the faces of the colonials: the same fear, the same sense of an ending. Yamadori's threats were coming true. All across the Far East, palm trees swayed, rice paddies gleamed, rains pelted down and were soaked up by the sun, and rickshaws clattered through stinking streets: all was as it had always been, yet something was over, as if a curtain had fallen.

I sailed home via Guam and Honolulu.

Arriving in New York one blustery afternoon, I realized a destiny that had lain in wait ever since I had taken my leave from Trouble at the temple of Shofuku-ji. When I reached Gramercy Park, there were lights on in the houses. Slowly, I ascended the steep steps. The butler, with oppressive deference, showed me into the drawing room. I felt I was expected.

Trembling, I looked about me: at Kate Pinkerton, like the figurehead of a ship, unchanged in all the years I had known her, swelling majestically over the tea table. At the ornaments, the glazed spines of books, the ancestral portraits. At the guests: the lady-librarian type, hair up in a bun; this or that society lady in too many pearls; the society gentleman, sleek and neutered, whose cheeks and chin appeared greased with oil. And there, standing at the fireplace, elbow on the mantelpiece at a jaunty angle, the guest who was not a guest at all. He filled my mind like a vision: thick blond hair, neatly parted; pale grey lounge suit, with trousers knife-edge sharp; cigarette burning in a laconic hand.

As I entered, he was deep in some anecdote, but he left off when he saw me. Kate Pinkerton cleared her throat, ready for introductions, but all I could do was stand, swaying a little, in the middle of the carpet, and say softly, almost to myself:

'Trouble. You've come home.'

ACT FOUR

The Gravity of Americans

Trouble had said he would pick me up in Albuquerque.

Making my way across the army airfield on a cloudless day in early summer I saw no sign of him, and my spirits sank; Los Alamos was – what? – eighty, ninety miles away and I didn't like the idea of arranging my own transport from this sleepy-looking base. The sun beat down hotly.

In the airfield's only building, a long, low, galvanized-iron shed, a young sergeant with too many freckles stirred himself behind a counter that looked like a bar, saluted sloppily, and told me in a drawling voice that no, no sir, nobody had come for me. Grinning, he added, 'You part of that show at Los Alamos, sir? What do you make up there – rockets to the moon?'

The fellow annoyed me, but I let him fix me coffee in a chipped enamel mug, while I sat and waited on a pew-like bench. Mechanics and a pilot came and went. Some stopped to chat with the sergeant, leaning, elbows crooked, across the counter, as if with tankards of beer; none paid attention to Major Sharpless and I had begun to wonder if Trouble would ever come when a vehicle squealed up outside, cheers broke out, and a voice I knew well cried in triumph, 'Forward to victory!'

It had been the senator's campaign slogan in 1928.

Colonel Ben Pinkerton (as Trouble now was) bounded into the shed. Immaculate in his well-pressed uniform, he remained lithe and slender, the hair visible beneath his cap still blond; only later did I see strands of grey and cracks in the skin around his eyes.

He pumped my hand enthusiastically, shouldered my knapsack, and led me out to the jeep.

'I could have got a driver,' he said, 'but I thought it'd be better if we could talk properly. You're looking good. The uniform suits you – Major Sharpless!'

As I hauled myself into the passenger seat, the mechanics, hunkered in a row by the shed, studied us idly; one, a sunburned fellow with a wrench in his hand, made some smart-aleck comment I did not quite hear. Trouble only smiled, flung my things into the back of the jeep, and blasted the horn three times as he tore out of the base with a spray of gravel.

'Popular fellow, aren't you?' I observed.

'It's not about me. It's Los Alamos. They've guessed something's up and they're dying to know. Some of the stories you wouldn't believe – Flash Gordon, I tell you!'

We passed through a checkpoint and swung northwards. Trouble wore dark glasses and chewed gum. On an unpaved highway he put on speed, and I snatched off my cap before the wind snatched it instead. Dust churned under our wheels, and I had to shout, 'So it's some big scientific show, this place at Los Alamos? You're up there all the time these days – and the senator too?'

'Let's just say we're going to end this war – and soon.'

I had never doubted it. Already the Nazis had surrendered in Europe; Japan, after the firebombing of Tokyo, seemed hardly likely to hold out much longer.

I said, 'Do you think the Japs ever really had a chance? They didn't, did they?'

'Remember Pearl Harbor? Remember Singapore? An Eastern country, raining down ruin on the Empires of the West! I wouldn't bet it's over yet.'

Often I had imagined the firebombing of Tokyo: the B-29s crossing the dark skies like monstrous, malevolent insects, the bombs pounding unceasingly, the fires rampaging, consuming mile after mile of flimsy wooden buildings. How many thousands had died in the inferno? Roads had become rivers of boiling tarmac. There had been no escape.

Once it would have seemed monstrous that such destruction should be unleashed upon civilians. Today, air raids were commonplace: Guernica. Chungking. London. Rotterdam. Berlin. Coventry. Dresden. The list went on and on. And Tokyo had been the worst so far.

We cut along Albuquerque's broad, straight streets, then out again towards blue-green mountains. There was something fantastical in our surroundings, something unearthly, and I wondered what the senator and a scientific base could be doing in these ancient Indian lands.

'You're happy?' I asked Trouble. 'In your role now?'

'Role? Well, I like that!'

He had said we could talk properly. I wanted to ask him why he had come home. He had never explained. In Japan, I had believed him when he said he had renounced America. Perhaps the threat of war, when he realized it was real, had shocked him at last out of his foolish course. But he had not only come back to America; he had returned to his family as if all had been forgiven. I wished I could see into his mind, his heart. Perhaps, if I worked slowly, carefully, I could make him reveal himself. But I was not sure how to start.

He asked after Aunt Toolie, and I told her she was still happily married. 'They have a place up in Carmel – Wobblewood West! I'm going for a weekend – next weekend, in fact, if I still get that leave I've booked. I *do* get time off after looking over this base of yours, don't I?'

Two days had passed since I received my summons.

I had been bewildered. 'The senator wants me?' I said. 'But why?'

Trouble's voice fizzed over long-distance wires. 'Why do you think? A new job! How about that?'

For three years, nearly four, I had been deployed in propaganda. Trouble had secured me my commission, pulling strings in his new assignment as Senator Pinkerton's right-hand man. When my papers came through I was overjoyed, imagining I would spend the war in Washington, DC, with Colonel B. F. Pinkerton II perhaps only a stroll away down Constitution Avenue.

I had been disappointed. I wrote recruiting copy in an office in New York, then army information manuals in Richmond, Virginia. In Los Angeles, seconded to Paramount Pictures, I script-edited war films and for a time served as publicity officer, and minder, for a Hollywood he-man; too drunk for the forces, he stumped back and forth across the country, selling war bonds.

The road climbed between rocks and pines.

We had just turned a corner when the bright day shattered. First came the report, sharp as a whip crack but twice as loud, then the streak through the air, zinging past my ear.

'Duck!' cried Trouble, and I jerked back.

He accelerated wildly. Another whip crack sounded. Dust whirled up from beneath our wheels. I was almost tossed from the jeep. Crouched low, I clung to the edge of the door as we squealed around bend after remorseless bend, pain stabbing through my damaged leg with every lurch and jolt. The desperate ride had begun so suddenly; it was as if we had plummeted from one world into another, a world of wild caprice where nothing mattered but speed and flight. We almost hurtled over the edge of a cliff.

When we slowed at last, Trouble arched back his neck and I saw his Adam's apple straining in his throat. Whether he was frightened, I could not be sure. Flushed, I clambered back into my seat.

'What *was* that?' I asked, when I could speak again.

'Sharpless, please' – he turned to me, earnest – 'don't tell the senator. Please, just don't.'

'What?' I said. 'I don't even know what happened!'

He put on speed again. I feared he would say no more, but after I had sat in silence for some moments, numb with shock, he said flatly, 'Sniper in the rocks. Must I spell it out?'

'Well, *yes*. Why do I get the feeling this has happened before?'

'Just don't tell the senator. Please, Sharpless.'

We drove on down the dusty road.

Los Alamos lies on a verdant mesa some seven thousand feet above sea level. The first sentry post had been several miles from the base, a stripy barrier beside a hut stuck alone in the woods, where two crew-cut privates loitered on duty, rifles at the ready. Closer to the base came two further checkpoints: gates in fences topped with wire, opening the way to a collection of huts and hangars sprawled across the mesa like a boomtown on Mars.

'Main Street,' Trouble announced as we passed between stores and bars. Another jeep, driven by a corporal, nosed by us with a honk; a becalmed truck, juddering smokily, with a cargo of crates stamped US ARMY, blocked half the road; men, some uniformed, some in lab coats, and one or two secretarial-looking women crossed Main Street here and there, but the place had about it a sense of sleepiness, as if, in these weird mountain lands, human imperatives could not count for much. None of this is permanent, the mesa seemed to say; boomtowns turn into ghost towns soon enough.

The base, Trouble informed me, had been built on the site of a school for boys called the Los Alamos Ranch School. Commandeered by the military some years before, the original school, with its stately timber buildings, could be glimpsed between the mean, low clutter that had overwhelmed it.

'You can bunk with me,' he added, pulling up beside a low galvanized-iron hut. Our route had taken us some distance from Main Street, weaving between lines of similar huts, and I wondered how I would ever find this one by myself. The ground outside was dusty, deeply rutted. Duckboards did service for sidewalks; laundered clothes, unstirring in the heat, hung on lines between the huts, and electricity poles jutted untidily skywards.

'You're not telling me the senator lives in one of these places?'

'Don't be silly. The VIPs are in the old school buildings. Not for us, alas. Space is tight up here.'

We made our way into a single-room apartment. The heat under the tin roof was savage. Sunlight pressed behind a drawn blind, and two metal cots, made up precisely, stood side by side; there were lockers and simple chairs, but no strewn magazines, no empty beer bottles, no ashtrays filled with butts. On the sill beneath the window was the room's sole ornament: a twist of branch with two jutting twigs, a desiccated piece of debris retrieved, perhaps, from a desert roadside.

'This one's yours.' Trouble thumped down my knapsack on a cot. 'Tonight, it's dinner with the senator. But you'll want to wash up, I guess. I'll show you to the showers.'

'Shouldn't you tell me what all this is about?' I said.

'What, and steal the senator's thunder?'

Curiosity consumed me, but when I returned from the showers Trouble had vanished, leaving a message in neat handwriting, telling me that something was up – some sudden duty – and our

192

dinner must be postponed. I found it strange to think of Trouble as an important, responsible man.

That night I found my way to the mess hall alone, and had applied myself to a surprisingly edible rabbit stew when a fellow across the table said to me, 'I know you. You're one of us.'

The voice suggested Brooklyn, and the face that blinked into mine belonged to a journalist I had met some years back, a plump, round-faced fellow who looked perpetually eager to please, like a schoolboy stabbing up his arm to answer questions in class before any other pupil had a chance.

'Sharpless, ain't it? I'm Miller, remember? You'll be replacing McKenna, then?' he asked me.

I suppose I looked blank.

'Tell you fuck-all, don't they?' cracked a dishevelled, rangy fellow who bore some resemblance to the actor Robert Mitchum, complete with waggling, ill-made roll-up in a corner of his mouth. 'And once you're here, you can't go back. Unless you do a McKenna.'

'Can't?' I said. 'What is this place, a prison?'

'Hush-hush. Stands to reason, don't it? McKenna, he went loopy. Let's hope you don't do the same.'

'Raving, tearing his hair,' said Miller. 'This foul-mouthed bastard's Meyer, by the way – and *that* one,' he added, pointing to a young man with thinning blond hair and round gold-rimmed spectacles, 'is Maybee – Miller-Meyer-Maybee. Think of us as the Andrews Sisters. Maybee's LaVerne.'

'Yes, quite an amusing little corps we are,' said Maybee in a Boston Brahmin voice, looking me over with patrician eyes. 'I prefer to call us the End of the World Archivists – I'm an historian,' he explained, not without pride, and asked me what my own 'discipline' might be.

'Propaganda, ain't it?' said Miller, and Maybee, somewhat sourly, pursed his lips.

'Nobody's told me a thing yet,' I said. 'I'm not even sure what all this is *for*.'

Meyer, or Robert Mitchum, laughed. 'Fucking hell, you really haven't heard of the Manhattan Project?'

Maybee rolled his eyes. 'It *is* secret, isn't it?'

'What's going on in Manhattan?' I said, foolishly.

'Not Manhattan – here! It's a code name.' Meyer called down the refectory table, 'Hey, fellas, this fucker don't know about the Big One!'

'The Bomb.' Miller puffed out his plump cheeks, then expelled a spitty explosion. Droplets sprayed my face. 'It's the ultimate weapon, ain't it? Ming the Merciless! Just one and we can flatten a city. Enough of them, we can wipe out the world.'

Startled, I looked between grinning faces.

'I told you,' said Maybee, 'we're the End of the World Archivists.'

'End of the Japs, anyway,' said Miller.

'Hah! If the fucking thing works,' said Meyer.

'It will,' said Maybee. 'And take the world with it!'

Meyer spat on the floor. 'I'll believe it when I see it. The cash they've wasted on this thing, you wouldn't fucking believe,' he said to me. 'Billions! And all because of some rumour the Krauts were building one too. So we had to get there first.'

'But the Germans have surrendered,' I said.

'Noticed that, did you?' said Miller. 'He's sharp, this one!'

I wanted to know more, but a girl appeared between Meyer and Maybee and asked, with a hand on the shoulder of each, if they would be at the dance that night. Meyer offered up his Mitchum smirk – 'Sure thing, honey' – and Maybee, who seemed awkward with women, blushed bright red.

I thought I might as well go to the dance. Confused thoughts filled my brain as I tagged along after Miller-Meyer-Maybee. In a noisy hall, leaning against the bar, I drank too many beers and watched the base's too few girls whirling in the arms of excitable young men. I wished they would dance to something other than Miller's namesake. Glenn Miller was missing; his plane had vanished somewhere over the English Channel, but still he haunted every jukebox in America, a ghost pressed into wax. Again and again a girl punched in the numbers for 'Yes, My Darling Daughter', and no one seemed to mind.

Maybee turned his attentions to me. And was I, he asked, the Sharpless who had worked with that left-wing photographer fellow, Augustus Le Vol? He said he had one of Le Vol's books at home, and I was surprised: I had not thought the Boston Brahmin would take much to Le Vol's work, but it seemed he admired him aesthetically, if not politically.

'So what's Le Vol doing in the war? Still a red?'

I wished I could change the subject. There was nothing to say: Le Vol had sailed to China and never come home. I had tried and tried to find out what had become of him, but Le Vol, like Glenn Miller, might have vanished into the air. If he had stayed on in China, I only hoped he had kept out of Japanese hands. After Pearl Harbor, with the American fleet safely out of action, a lone white man in East Asia would have been in constant danger. Le Vol might have been in a prison camp or dead.

Only after I had left the dance did I realize there were no street lamps on the base. I stumbled in the dark, tripping once in a pothole and once on the edge of a duckboard.

When I got back to our hut, Trouble was not there. I resolved to wait up, but lay down on a cot – his, not mine – and fell asleep. I dreamed: reveries of Asian faces screaming out of fire, buildings falling and puffed cheeks exploding with spit, while all the time 'Yes, My Darling Daughter' played.

Not until my second evening did I meet the senator. Trouble accompanied me to one of the old school buildings. Perhaps it had been the headmaster's house; some distance from the rest of the base, it was a solid, sprawling bungalow surrounded on all sides by broad verandas.

A cocktail party was in progress when we arrived. Someone played a piano; privates acted as waiters, and faces smiled at Trouble as he guided me through the crowd, introducing me to generals, chiefs of staff, Washington insiders. Names blurred and so did features, but by the time I was ushered into the senator's presence, I had practised my banter sufficiently to respond to him with ease.

I had followed Senator Pinkerton's career with fascination. Everywhere in the war, I detected his hand. When America's battered industries were galvanized into life by military demand, I could hear his patriotic words ringing out in the Senate, demanding that it be so; when, after a shocking series of Japanese victories, our fortunes turned in the Battle of Midway, I knew the senator's wisdom had been at work; I detected it too, as US troops pushed further into the Pacific, beating back the enemy from island after island.

One evening in a newsreel theatre, I watched an item about Japanese Americans. Herded from their houses, they were corralled into trucks and taken to internment camps; then, filling the screen, came the big-necked, porcine head of Senator B. F. Pinkerton (Democrat, New York), the policy's architect and most ardent supporter. With astonishment, I thought of Trouble's role in this, working coolly at his father's side.

The great man introduced me to the party surrounding him: this one, General Somebody; that one, Professor Someone; Miss Something – had I met Miss Something?

'And Bob,' he said, turning to a lean man on the fringe of the group, who appeared, I thought, a little out of place. 'That son of mine's introduced you to Bob, surely?'

'Oppenheimer,' said the lean man, and I shook his hand.

'Bob's the sultan of this desert kingdom,' said the senator.

Yes, I thought, and isn't happy that you're taking it over.

I said to Oppenheimer, 'So you're the man who's made the ultimate weapon?'

'He's making it,' said the senator. 'And he's nearly there. We'd better hope so, anyway!'

'Big test any day now,' said Trouble. '*Boom!*'

Oppenheimer eyed them both disdainfully.

'I wouldn't say *ultimate*, Major.' He drew on his cigarette. He had the sort of ascetic beauty one finds in a certain type of thin Jewish man. Cropped hair and prominent cheekbones provided the frame for eyes of a piercing blue, incongruous in a face so Semitic. 'Let's say it's the best we can do for now. Do you know anything about atomic physics?'

'Nothing,' I said. 'But I hear it'll change the world.'

'It's changed it,' he said. 'It's already changed it.'

'And this,' said the senator, slapping me on the back, 'is the fellow who'll explain it all to the American people. Major Sharpless here is our new chief of propaganda.'

'Public relations, sir,' said Miss Something in a motherly voice.

'And why,' I asked, 'does a secret project need public relations?'

'It will,' said the senator, winking at me. 'It will soon enough.'

* * *

'So what do you think?'

It was early next morning and Trouble had insisted, against my protests, on driving me back to the airfield himself. I had half-expected to be told I was not allowed to leave Los Alamos, but it seemed that – like Colonel B. F. Pinkerton II – I was under the senator's protection and afforded special privileges. I had been given a week to tie up my affairs before returning to New Mexico, more or less for ever, or until the world was obliterated.

'Quite an opportunity,' Trouble burbled on. 'History in the making, and you'll write the first draft.'

'Tell lies, more like it. Was it your idea, getting me this job?'

'You're the best man, everybody says so. Besides, I don't think you'll end up like McKenna.'

'My predecessor? Did he really go crazy?'

'Me, I blame Dr Atomic.'

'Oppenheimer?'

'He'd turn anyone's wits. We're winning the war, that's all we need to know.'

Trouble's words seemed hollow to me. The night before, I had watched him undress for bed, laying out his things neatly for morning; he stripped to his shorts and, though I could have stretched my hand between our cots and touched him, I felt as distant from him as if he were still in Japan.

That afternoon I had seen him play baseball. Miller pitched; Trouble hit a home run and pelted around the bases; all was as it had been at Blaze, yet all was not. After the cocktail party we took in a movie show, a rowdy affair of hurled popcorn and squeaky folding chairs. Trouble seemed happy enough, laughing when the others laughed, groaning when they groaned, but his mind, I felt sure, was not really on the trials of Rita Hayworth.

'Aren't you worried about the sniper?' I said as we rounded a rocky corner. I should have been frightened, but Trouble had enfolded me in his magic again. He could do it so easily. All he had to do was look at me and I lost all my strength. I might almost have believed we were still young, setting off on another reckless spree. 'You never said why they'd want to kill you,' I added, but my voice was light. 'Why you? Who are *they*, anyway?'

'Jap agents. Maybe they're getting at the senator through me.'

'Japs, running around in the desert up here?' It was too fantastic. 'And you're not worried?'

'About dying? Wouldn't it solve a few dilemmas?'

Shadows cut across the twisting road.

'You can't support all this, can you?' I said after a moment. 'One bomb that wipes out a city! It's wrong. It's evil.'

'It'll win the war, Sharpless.'

'Tokyo's flattened. What more can we do?'

'Complete and utter destruction.'

'Sink the islands into the sea? The Japs will surrender soon. They have to – they're finished.'

'Tell that to the kamikaze pilots.' By now the mesa lay far above us, and Trouble swung the wheel sharply, trundling off the road on to a rugged track. The jeep jolted violently over potholes.

'What's the idea?' I said. 'I've a plane to catch.'

'One of the sights – well, one I like to see.'

A sign ahead of us read RYAN RANCH, but this was no ranch, or was a ranch no longer. We drew up before a chain-link fence topped with barbed wire. Inside, across a tussocky field, was a line of barracks.

'There's a good view from here,' said Trouble.

'View of what?' I said, but in a moment more I knew. A siren sounded, and lines of bowed, ragged-looking figures shuffled towards a parade ground. They were far away, and only slowly did I register that all of them had black, sleek hair and Oriental faces.

'Japs,' I said, as if I werer surprised.

'Americans' – Trouble tore open a pack of Lucky Strikes – 'of Japanese descent. Up at Los Alamos there are rumours we'll use them for radiation research. Of course, we wouldn't do a thing like that. We're Americans. But you see why we need public relations.'

Gazing at the prisoners, I thought of Nagasaki. How strange they had seemed, the days I spent there! I thought of Trouble as he was then and as he was now. I looked at the track behind us: red earth, rocks, scrubby vegetation. My mind made a jump and I said, 'You don't want to be here.'

Trouble lit a Lucky and tossed the packet to me.

'I have to be somewhere.' He looped the fingers of one hand through the chain-link fence. 'There's an expression in Japan: *Shikata ga nai*. It can't be helped. Oh, well. Too bad.'

I said softly, 'What are you saying?'

'Only the senator protects me, you know.' Trouble's grip on the fence tightened – painfully, I thought. Many times he had perplexed me, but I thought I was on the brink of revelation as he turned to me in that red morning and said, 'What would you say if you never saw me again?'

My heart plummeted. I was frightened, but only said again, 'What are you saying?'

He grinned. 'Just kidding. Come on, slowpoke! We've a plane to catch.'

'*I* have, you mean.'

'Me too. I'm coming to Carmel! It'll be like old times.'

* * *

200

'Hey – Sophie Tucker.'

I nudged Trouble. The radio was low under the clamour of the bus. It was crowded: up front, a party of soldiers on leave sprawled at odd angles over several seats, guzzled beer, and played cards with many a guffaw, many a scuffle. Girls at the back shrieked and laughed and encouraged the soldiers if they came that way. A college boy, earnest behind horn-rimmed spectacles, read Karl Marx until a GI told him to lighten up and flung the book from the window. The summer afternoon was deep and long, and Sophie Tucker foghorned out the one about the blue river, blue river... did it hold the memory of a vanished dream?

Trouble had not stirred. His head had fallen against my shoulder. The night before, in Los Angeles, we had reeled from bar to bar. It had been like the old days: I hadn't laughed so much in years. I almost suggested we didn't come to Carmel, but I couldn't let Aunt Toolie down.

Heat shimmered from the road and beat through the bus's metal roof as we wound our way up the California coast. On one side was a vista of powdery, pale rocks; on the other, the blue Pacific, foaming whitely.

I thought of all the time that had passed – thirty years, since we were boys at Blaze; for me, thirty years largely wasted. What had I done? First I had thought I would be a poet, then a novelist; I was over forty and was neither. There are those, I suppose, who seize life early, who see at once what they should become and how to become it. For others, all is hazy. Perhaps we are empty: still, we feel there is a core in us we can never quite grasp.

I closed my eyes. Again I was a boy at Blaze: I would always be a boy at Blaze. But not Woodley Sharpless, bookish Woodley with his bad leg. I was one of the Townsend twins, sprawling in the hay with Trouble in the back of a farmer's truck as we trundled down a road that led from Burlington, Vermont. Wild exploits had filled the night before, but never mind, it was another day; the sun shone and the boys were coming home.

'Uncle Grover?'

I tapped my uncle's arm and he started. In bright sunshine, the little man had been sitting at the wheel of a red Cadillac Series 62 convertible, plump fingers laced across his paunch. 'Dear me, I am sorry! Rather too much wine at luncheon.'

'And our bus was late. This is Colonel Pinkerton.'

'My friends call me Trouble. I don't think we've met, Mr...'

'Grayson – Grover Grayson the Third. I say, you're not related to that senator, are you? But, no, you don't look a *bit* like him.' Uncle Grover adjusted his spotted bow tie in the rear-view mirror. 'Tallulah would have met you both,' he explained, 'but she's frightfully busy. Theatricals! Tonight we'll see the premiere production of the Tallulah Grayson Players.'

I clambered into the convertible beside him. Trouble flung our knapsacks into the trunk and hoisted himself into the rumble seat.

'Nice auto,' he said to Uncle Grover. 'What does she do?'

'Do? What can't she do!' Hunching forward, Uncle Grover started the ignition. With his goggle-like spectacles, he had about him the air of a racing ace on the starting block. If, at first sight, Grover Grayson III seemed an unlikely mate for Aunt Toolie, it was only at first sight. Many times she had told me how lucky she had been to find him. I believed her.

We tore along the coast, a red streak, the Pacific glittering below us in the afternoon sun.

Wobblewood West lay a mile or so out of Carmel. The house was a modernist castle of plate glass and concrete rising from lush, windblown gardens. Built in the twenties by an eccentric millionaire who had later been ruined in the Crash, the place made me uneasy, as if its very fabric embodied my anxieties. It was too close to the cliff; one day, I feared, the rocky edge would shake, shrugging the house into the sea in a powdery cascade.

'Usual room, Woodley. Your friend can have the one next door.' Uncle Grover pulled up with a jerk in the wide, gravelled drive. Four or five other cars, some rather shabby, had parked there already. 'Tallulah's down at the amphitheatre. I'd better check on her. Join us when you're ready.'

The house was silent. In my room I dropped my knapsack, loosened my tie. I went to the window. The sea glittered sharply, and I screwed up my eyes. Trouble moved in the next room. Bedsprings squealed. Had he flung himself down? All through our drive with Uncle Grover he had been animated, but I knew something was wrong. I should speak to him. But I could not think where to begin.

The afternoon's heat was at its height as I stumped out across the terrace. Carefully, I negotiated steps cut in rock. Voices drifted up from below, rising over swishing waves.

The millionaire who built Wobblewood West had been nothing if not determined. Developing a passion for Greek drama, he ordered the construction of an amphitheatre in the cliffs below; modelled in miniature on the ancient theatre at Epidaurus, it had kept several dozen explosives experts and sculptors in work for years, according to the locals.

Today, the amphitheatre provided a fitting stage for Aunt Toolie. She was not acting, but directing. Swishing back and forth, red hair stuck up at angles, beads and scarves dishevelled, half-moon spectacles halfway down her nose, she barked imperious orders to two masked actresses robed in white. Further masked figures, evidently a chorus, stood up on the *proskenion*, and several others sat off to one side. One old fellow, who had removed his mask, smoked a cigarette. I recognized him from somewhere, but was not sure where.

'Darling, it's like *this*,' cried Aunt Toolie, and read from a ring binder in a passionate voice:

> O sister mine! Beloved of my blood,
> Must trouble still descend on its dark flood?
> Dead Oedipus, our father, left us cursed.
> By now, I had supposed, we'd seen the worst:
> Yet still dishonour, infamy, and shame
> Must fall on thee and me. Who is to blame?

High in the semicircle of tiered seats, I slipped in beside Uncle Grover, who explained to me that the old fellow with the cigarette was Mr Foster from the filling station up the road. 'Quite a good Creon, actually. Eurydice, that plump matron next to him, is the local Sunday-school teacher – dubious about the Greeks on moral grounds, but Tallulah talked her around. Did you know we did the translation ourselves? Well, with a few cribs. Antigone? Oh, she's the daughter of the local real estate agent – Miss Hoity-Toity, but brave, I'll grant her that. In three hours' time, these tiers will be filled with all the local worthies for miles around. *And* a few unworthies—'

Aunt Toolie saw me. 'Woodley, is that you?'

'The same!' I made my way down the steps, meeting her halfway.

Fulsomely, she enfolded me in her clattering embrace. 'But where's your friend? I haven't seen that naughty boy for years.'

'Trouble's resting,' I said. 'He'll be down soon.'

'I hope Grover put you boys in the same room. This *is* Wobble-wood. Even if the floors don't wobble.'

'That won't be necessary,' I assured her.

'Hah! The army's rife with it, isn't it? Quite a shock for the Kansas farm boys. Still, broadens their horizons – among other things.' She clapped her hands. 'Come on, everybody – one more time!'

The rehearsal had reached a stormy point. Here was Antigone facing Creon's wrath, pleading that her dead brother had to be buried; here was Ismene, desperate to share in her sister's wrong, proclaiming that the blame was hers too – and here was the real estate agent's daughter, stepping on a corn on the garage proprietor's foot, while Aunt Toolie's cleaner, in the part of Ismene, stumbled over her robes and fell against Antigone, forcing her to step down even harder. The garage proprietor bellowed like a wounded bull and the chorus shook with mirth.

Delicately, Uncle Grover suggested that perhaps they had rehearsed enough. I feared Aunt Toolie would be furious, but she dismissed the actors cheerily, only calling after them:

'Curtain up, six o'clock sharp!'

'Knock knock?'

'Sharpless? I was dreaming.'

The door was ajar. Trouble lay on his bed, face towards the ceiling. If, as I thought, he was suffering, I had to find out why. Sunlight, still bright on the summer's day, angled through the drawn curtains, giving the room a burnished glow.

'I'm worried about you.' Uncertainly, I sat beside him.

'Oh? I thought we'd been having a fine old time.'

'Like the old days. Sure,' I said.

We might have been speaking through a pane of glass.

'Why Los Alamos?' I asked him. 'Why me?'

'The senator needs you.'

'There are a thousand propaganda men.'

'Not just for that. They've always been fond of you, haven't they – Kate and the senator? You help them. With me.'

'If that's my job,' I said, 'I've been an abject failure.'

'You talk about me, I suppose, behind my back.'

'Oh, Trouble! Wasn't I always on your side? I'm your second.'

'We're not fighting Eddie Scranway now. Give me a cigarette.'

My hand trembled as I lit it for him. Smoke wound up, bluegrey, from his small fingers, and he said abruptly, 'They're trying to kill me. They think they know things. And they don't, they can't.'

He stood abruptly. He paced the carpet.

'What *are* you saying?'

'Snipers on the road. Among other things.'

'You're Colonel Pinkerton. You're the senator's son. Who'd want to kill you? Tell the senator. If you don't, I will.'

'Poor Sharpless,' said Trouble. 'Ever the innocent.'

'I hate you sometimes.' I went to the window. With a jerk, I pulled back the curtains. I had to see the sea: I had to see the sun. The glare burned my eyes. 'I'm your second,' I said. 'And all you do is play games with me.'

'You've always wanted too much.'

'I wanted nothing.'

'You expected nothing. That's different.'

'Boys!' Aunt Toolie had appeared in the doorway. 'Do close the door if you want an intimate moment.'

How much she had heard, I had no idea.

'But Benjy, how marvellous to see you! I declare, you haven't changed! What's your secret?'

At once they were embracing.

'He keeps a painting in the attic,' I said.

Trouble smirked. 'Oh boy, you should see that painting! But I hear we're off to the theatre tonight.'

'Expect disaster. You boys lead the applause, all right? Whatever happens, applaud. Throw flowers. Oh Benjy, Benjy! Come, let me show you around Wobblewood West.' And linking her arm in his, Aunt Toolie hauled him from the room, adding, as they vanished, 'You'll never guess! Grover's invited a hundred servicemen from the base down the coast. Simple soldier boys! What they'll make of Sophocles I dread to think. Disaster, disaster!'

'Never mind – we'll have a *fun* disaster,' I heard Trouble say.

I lay on Trouble's bed, hearing the throb of my blood like the tide. After some time I stirred; reluctantly, I made my way downstairs. From the drawing room came talk in a steady ebb and flow, and a woman in a golden gown whinnied like a horse, tossing back her head. I could not see Trouble. The sun, sinking sharply, speared through the wide windows. The guests, for the most part, were local business types, plump men in tuxedoes with their wives – none of them, I surmised, much interested in classical theatre.

I consumed several Scotches in quick succession. The evening took on a mellow glow, and I went to the edge of the terrace. Deeply, I breathed the sea air and swivelled back to watch as Aunt Toolie, lynx-thin, with her cigarette holder, mink stole, and trailing gown, luxuriated in the attentions of an elderly professorial type and several attractive youngish men in uniform. *Our lady director* and *Our classical scholar*, I heard the professor call her. She had pinned up her hair, exposing the long curve of her neck; her make-up was light, and though her features were awkward – the jaw too heavy, the nose too beaky – she looked beautiful. She turned, speaking enthusiastically to the youngish men, just as I became aware of Uncle Grover eyeing me with concern. I smiled, as if to say there was nothing wrong.

A spoon clinked the side of a glass, and Aunt Toolie declared it was time for the play. I made for a bathroom and pissed copiously. I doused my face with water. When I emerged, most of the guests had disappeared down the steep steps towards the amphitheatre.

Uncle Grover, in the rear, waited for me.

'Bearing up, Woodley?' He took my arm.

'Oh, you know.' Gesturing airily, I lost my footing; he steadied me and I wished he had not, but he was determined to be generous, patiently helping the drunkard, the cripple.

'You know I've always been grateful to you,' he said.

'To me?' I wondered what he was talking about.

'Wasn't it on some jape of yours that Tallulah turned up at that Jap's penthouse that night? I'd never normally meet anybody like her. Do you think I'd have dared go to Greenwich Village? You see, if it hadn't been for you, I'd never have married Tallulah.'

'I'm glad,' I said. 'She's quite a lady.'

In the amphitheatre, GIs filled the upper tiers. They were noisy and drunk.

'You're sure the soldiers were a good idea?' I said.

'But that's precisely the purpose of the theatre! Culture for the masses, Tallulah says.'

In the front row, Trouble leaned forward and twisted his hands. Uneasily, I took my place beside him, while Uncle Grover went to check on Aunt Toolie. The sun, framed in the *proskenion*, had almost set; arc lights, attached to a generator, bathed the acting area in a lurid glow.

I asked Trouble where he had been.

'A walk. Along the cliffs.' His face was tight.

Aunt Toolie introduced the play with a speech that might have been a little too erudite, making much of developments in the drama between Aeschylus and Sophocles and quoting classical scholars. I hoped she could not hear the sniggering from the tiers further up. At last, to scattered applause, she took her seat with a proud Uncle Grover, while a boy with rabbity teeth strummed chords on a ukulele (a lyre being unavailable) and Real Estate Agent Antigone and Cleaning Lady Ismene emerged to declaim their lines.

Soldiers wolf-whistled; some clapped for each speech.

The play had proceeded only so far as the first chorus when I became aware of Trouble gripping my thigh. I looked down, startled. His fingers were white-knuckled, his nails digging sharply. The thought came to me of a rubber band, stretching tighter and tighter, and terror thrummed inside me. I whispered urgently, 'Trouble! What's wrong?'

Sweat stood out on his upper lip, and he gestured with a jerk of his head towards the upper tiers. 'You know, don't you?'

'Know what?' I turned to where he was looking. The audience, behind the arc lights, was deep in shadow.

'The soldiers,' he said. 'They've come for me.'

'What are you *saying*?' I said, too loudly.

I had no thought for the actors, the words, the embarrassed local worthies, or the jostling, whistling soldiers; all I could see was Trouble, now twisting back towards darkness; now hunching forward, head in hands. My pulse beat at my temples like a drum. I should have led him from the amphitheatre. I should have said he was sick. I should have known that, like a rubber band stretched too far, he would snap.

During the chanting of an antistrophe, he leaped up, turned to the audience, and screamed.

Startled, the chorus fell silent. So did the soldiers.

Trouble cried, 'Stop these games! If you've come for me, come!'

Murmurs broke out all around the amphitheatre: 'The guy's flipped' and 'Who is he? He's crazy!' and 'Is this part of the play?'

Aunt Toolie went to him, but Trouble shrugged her aside, stabbing an accusing finger into the darkness.

'I know who's sent you! I know why you're here!'

His shouts were for the soldiers.

His voice cracked. 'It wasn't my choice! I can't help what I am! You've no right to hold me and you won't!'

'Darling, please!' Aunt Toolie cried.

Could I intervene? I was rooted in place. Beneath the arc lights Trouble was unearthly, his pale exotic beauty transfixing, tormenting, like the vision of a god that might never come again.

He taunted the GIs, calling them cowards, weaklings, and, though he wore his colonel's uniform, there was more than one drunkard ready to hurl himself down the steps, fists at the ready, to challenge him.

A lumbering farm boy weighed in first.

Trouble ducked as the fist swung, then he stuck out a leg, tripped the boy up, and danced around him in triumph.

A second opponent appeared, then a third.

Uncle Grover was frantic, waving his little hands like a conductor in the grip of an epileptic fit.

'Out, out!' he cried. 'Out of my house!'

His gestures took in actors and audience alike, but it was too late. Some complied, scrambling up the stone steps, but most stayed, staring in wonderment – and not a little delight – as Trouble took on the enraged GIs. Possessed of powers beyond his slight frame, he punched one in the stomach, sending him reeling back; one flew through the air, landing heavily; one leaped on Trouble, tore back his hair, and would have slammed his face into the rock, but Trouble flipped him over, kicked him, and slapped him about the face. Cries ricocheted around the stony tiers. Aunt Toolie, like a mad thing, rushed back and forth, but for once the Queen of Bohemia was powerless. She tried again to intervene, just as Trouble veered from an oncoming punch.

It connected, but not with Trouble. She dropped to the stony floor.

'Tallulah!' Uncle Grover's cry was piteous.

Motionless, she lay under the fizzing arc lights. Uncle Grover fought his way towards her; GIs fell back, abashed.

Aunt Toolie moaned. 'Grover!… Grover!'

Trouble stood, breathing heavily. He had lost his cap, and his uniform was torn. Blood ran from a cut on his face.

He gazed up at the tiered rows.

'I didn't mean it,' he declared, his voice ringing, as if it were he who had struck Aunt Toolie; but no, he meant more than that. Such pain filled his voice that I believed then, as I believe now, that he never meant any of it: never meant to be what he was, never meant to become what he became.

Suddenly, as if shocked back into life, he pounded up the stone steps, and no one tried to stop him. Or rather, only I did, but I could hardly match his speed. By the time I reached the top, it was too late. I rounded a corner of the house, calling his name, just as he leaped into Uncle Grover's Cadillac, gunned it into life, and vanished into the night.

* * *

211

'Twenty miles! Twenty fucking miles!'

Two weeks later I sat in a long, low observation hut in the desert with Miller-Meyer-Maybee. Surrounding us were perhaps a hundred other pressmen, writers, and photographers. It was not yet dawn. We were crowded, cold, and had been there most of the night.

Meyer, the Robert Mitchum fellow, was increasingly restless.

'Have another beer,' said Miller, and tossed him a dripping bottle from the ice bucket.

'We won't see a thing. Not a fucking thing.' Meyer ripped off the bottle cap with his teeth and spat it to the floor. Our position underscored our lowly status. Base camp was ten miles closer to the blast site; for the VIPs, there were special shelters only five miles away. 'Say, Sharpless, how long did it take us to get to this godforsaken place?'

'Too long.' Leaving Los Alamos the day before, our party had rattled in a convoy of buses for some three hundred miles across the New Mexico desert, ending up in a corner of the Air Force's Alamogordo Bombing Range. History, we had been assured, was about to be made. Oppenheimer had given the bomb test the code name 'Trinity'. Later I read that he had intended this as a reference to Donne's 'Holy Sonnets': *Batter my heart, three-person'd God...* Oppenheimer had a way with literary allusions. He also had a way with blasphemy.

'Don't worry, Meyer.' Maybee, the Boston Brahmin, spectacles glinting in lamplight, looked up from his book. 'If the bang's as big as they say, we'll see it perfectly well. Even from twenty miles.'

'In this weather?' said Miller. 'The firecracker's damp, I tell you! What time is it now, Sharpless?'

'Nearly five.' I huddled into my coat.

212

Shame consumed me. I should never have been there. Why see history? I should turn my back on it. History was Oppenheimer blowing up the world. All the day before and all that night, fellows had been taking bets on the bomb and what it would do. Some, with a bravado I did not quite believe, insisted it would never work. Some wondered how many thousand tons of TNT the blast would equal; there were numerous rival estimates. Some said the blast would ignite the earth's atmosphere. Some said it would rain down radioactive dust, infecting us all. Psychiatrists were on hand in case any of us went mad.

Trinity had been scheduled for more than an hour ago, but deep in the night a storm had broken over the desert, pelting the roof like a rain of rocks. God, Maybee observed, was doing His best to upstage us. Lightning split the sky; thunder boomed and cracked. Only now, with daybreak, was the storm easing. Word had come that the test would go ahead.

'Potsdam,' announced a lean Englishman in an RAF uniform, swaying over to our little group. His moustache disturbed me; it was matchstick thin, a dark line above his upper lip. I imagined him shaving around it and wondered if his hand ever wavered. Mine would.

Miller moaned, 'Not Potsdam again!'

The Englishman blinked. 'It's still true,' he said. 'Why do you think Truman delayed meeting the other leaders until now, two months after victory in Europe? I'll tell you why. He wants a big stick to beat Stalin with, and he's hoping this bomb is it.'

'Stalin?' said Meyer. 'Stalin's our ally.'

'Shows how much you know.' The Englishman jabbed a Camel into a long holder. 'Enemies, that's what you Yanks need. Do you really think you'll shut down all this – this funfair of yours – after the war's over? You'll need a good excuse to keep it going.'

There was a blast of cold, and Meyer yelled for somebody to close the fucking door.

'Major Sharpless? Major Sharpless, sir?'

A young man, a corporal with a prominent Adam's apple, peered with curiosity through the crowd.

'The cripple,' said Miller, pointing in my direction.

'I'm Sharpless.' I rose. 'Who wants him?'

'Orders from Senator Pinkerton, sir,' said the corporal, saluting me. 'I'm to take you to him.'

Meyer goggled at me, outraged. 'Him? The fucking cripple's going to get a ringside seat?'

I made a rude gesture at him as I left.

'So what's this all about?' I asked the corporal, following him from the hut. I had tried to see the senator for days. He had ignored me. Why summon me now, out of all these observers gathered in Alamogordo?

'This way, sir.' The corporal held a groundsheet over me as I struggled towards his jeep. The jeep's cover was up, but rain seeped through, and a flap of canvas, torn half free, billowed beside me as we churned off through the mud.

I watched the windshield wipers slap back and forth. 'It's base camp we're headed for?'

'Closer. Senator Pinkerton's in one of the VIP shelters, sir.'

Rain had ceased by the time we arrived. Our destination was a concrete bunker barely visible in a rise of scrubby hillside. Far off, in the purplish dawn, a steel tower rose like a rocket ship one hundred feet tall.

The corporal led me down concrete steps.

Inside, the bunker was bleak as a locker room, but for the desert scene, like an artist's impression of Venus or Mars, that flickered behind an oblong of toughened glass. I half-expected

Oppenheimer to be there – poised over a detonator, grimly exultant – but, of course, he was at base camp. This was only an observation point, where Senator Pinkerton, his wide back towards me as I entered, conversed heartily with a congressman I recognized from the papers. A famous general and several other top brass pored over a map or chart; the base chaplain from Los Alamos clutched a prayer book with a harried air; scientists hovered, white-coated, over meters and dials. In one corner, a radio operator with cans over his ears yelled into a bulky microphone. The walls were grey untreated concrete, stained copiously by intrusive rain. 'Zero minus five minutes, gentlemen,' called the radio operator, exchanging a thumbs-up with the famous general.

'You sent for me, sir?' I had to interrupt the senator.

'Ah, Sharpless. One of you press fellows had to see it up close. Did you bring your black specs?'

I patted my breast pocket and listened respectfully as the fat congressman expatiated on the project as if it had been his own idea and the senator nodded, wryly perhaps, in agreement. He offered me a cigar, and I let him light it. I despised myself. I had never wanted to be in Los Alamos; I had never wanted to be in Alamogordo. Something was dying inside me and I was powerless to resist it. Impassively, I gazed into the senator's bland, broad face. We could have been businessmen at a Rotary meeting, gathered in the bar.

'Zero minus four minutes,' said the radio operator.

'A stiff shot, that's what we need,' said the congressman, indicating the drinks tray in the corner.

I moved to assist him, but the senator drew me back. Through the window, the steel tower flamed like a beacon in the rising sun. He draped an arm about me. 'You thought I never cared for my son, I suppose.'

'He isn't in Washington, is he?' I said. The arm was heavy across my neck, like a yoke.

I had stayed at Wobblewood West for four days after Trouble left. Aunt Toolie, unhurt, seemed pleased to have been at the centre of a drama that, undoubtedly, was a bigger hit than *Antigone*. With admirable panache, she applied steaks to her black eye and worried about Trouble. Uncle Grover's red convertible had been found abandoned, some ways down the coast.

When I got back to Los Alamos, Trouble had not returned. Fearing the worst, I said to one of the senator's staff, 'He's AWOL, isn't he?'

'AWOL?' The fellow shook his head. 'He's back in DC.'

Even then, I knew this was a lie.

Now, in the bunker, the senator rubbed his eyes as if with fatigue, and I almost laughed; for the first time I saw him as an old man, pathetic and defeated. I drew back on my cigar. I felt sick.

'You don't know where he's gone,' I said.

'Of course I know. He's been spotted in Mexico. Lying low, the little fool! The only question is how to handle things delicately.'

'You're thinking of publicity.'

'Damn right I am! But I'd gladly have him court-martialled.'

'He's cracked up. He needs help, not punishment.'

'Mr Sharpless! Are you really so naive?'

I flushed and wanted to ask him what he meant, but the radio operator gave the three-minute warning, the congressman returned with the drinks, and we clinked glasses together, toasting the detonation.

'Those Russkies won't know what hit 'em,' said the congressman.

'We're not at war with the Russians,' I said.

The senator stared out at the desert. He sipped his bourbon and swilled it around his teeth like mouthwash. 'Strange, isn't it,' he said, 'the way time passes? Fifty years ago I sailed from San Francisco. It was the first time I'd left the States. The world seemed so wide – stretched before me, all there for the taking! So long ago, but sometimes I think no time has passed at all; other times, it seems that everything I knew then is gone, crumbled like a collapsing wall.'

The congressman, looking uneasy, shifted his attention to the chaplain, who had opened his little book and was intoning prayers. The general and other top brass bowed their heads; the scientists continued with their instruments; the radio operator said, 'Zero minus two minutes,' and the senator pulled me close. 'I love my son,' he said. 'And all you've ever done is poison him against me.'

Uneasily, I looked around. No one had turned to watch us.

'You're hurting me,' I said. Still the heavy arm bore down on my neck.

'You've got to make him understand, I love him.'

'What can *I* make him do?' I dropped my cigar to the concrete floor and ground it out with my lame foot. Desolately, as if knowing it for the first time, I said, 'I'm nothing to him.'

The senator might not have heard me. He was muttering, talking to himself, and I was mortified, though still nobody saw. 'Ben, Ben!' he said. 'You'll do anything to disgrace me. Am I to forgive you? Perhaps I should take the blame. Why did you have to see too much? You saw through me like an X-ray. You knew I was guilty. Always.'

Desert dawn flared before us, blood-red through the glass. Softly, I shifted his arm from my neck as the countdown came again: 'Zero minus one minute.' Warning sirens, muffled through the concrete walls, rang across the firing range. Heavy doors shuddered into place. There was nothing to do except watch the blast. I would not. I turned away, but the senator, with barely a touch, propelled me back to face it. He drew the dark glasses from my breast pocket and calmly held them before my eyes.

'Watch,' he said, in a hollow voice. 'Watch and tell the world.'

Could I resist him? I donned the glasses, accepting my fate, as the countdown reached 'Zero minus thirty seconds' and Voice of America, caught on the same frequency as the base radio, crackled through the loudspeakers, filling the air with the anthem that began the day's broadcasts; as a scientist in a lab coat, taking his place beside me, brought long, pondering fingers to his chin; as the numbers clicked down, 'Minus fifteen', then 'Ten... nine... eight...' and the chaplain, murmurously, as if presiding over a deathbed, continued with his prayers, and the top brass stood, hands clasped before them like embarrassed mourners, uncertain what was required of them – and the senator, just before the countdown ended, reached up in a strangely casual gesture, smudged the black glasses from his face, and gazed, like a man bravely facing death, into sudden, searing fire.

'*O say, can you see, by the dawn's early light...*'

What happened next was the work of moments, but to me it unfolded in a timeless realm: as if time split into fragments when the count reached zero and part of me and part of the world would be there ever afterwards in that bunker at Alamogordo at five-thirty in the morning on July 16, 1945.

A new sun consumed the sky. The flash, silent and immense, was brighter than any lightning that had scourged the night, brighter than the desert in the midday heat. First it was white, then all colours and none: golden, purple, violet, grey, and blue, lighting the arid plain and the mountains behind with a clarity and power never seen before on earth. Never in my life have I known such awe.

Only later, hours later or so it seemed, came the sound, at once impossibly deep and high, shrieking through the bunker's walls and toughened glass like an express train passing and passing, as if eternally, just inches from our ears. *And I am witness*, I thought, *to a death that has no ending. The death of air. The death of earth. The death of water and fire. I have witnessed this and I am Death.*

Tears blurred my eyes. My heart was hushed, suspended between beats; the world I had known all my life was gone, annihilated in an instant; but when, impossibly, I found myself returned to the stream of time, I was the first to go to Senator Pinkerton, who stood, trembling, in the centre of the floor, hands covering his eyes. I reached for his wrists and pulled them down.

Voices said, 'What is it? What's happened?'

'He's blind,' I said. 'He's blind.'

Escape, to my surprise, was easy.

In the chaos, I forced back the blast doors, found the jeep that had brought me, and reversed on to the road before I even considered what I was doing. Checkpoint guards saluted me as I passed: Major Sharpless, VIP. What had the senator said? He could have Trouble court-martialled – imagine that! Now he could do the same to me: Major Sharpless, AWOL.

As in a dream, I sped past arid mountains. The scholarly Maybee, with patrician drollery, had said that the Conquistadores had dubbed this desert the *Jornada del Muerto*: the Journey of Death.

The sun was high and the heat burning by the time the rough road crossed Route 66 at Albuquerque. I turned westwards, drove until Route 66 was a blur, then stopped at the first motel I could find. It was the middle of the afternoon, but I fell on the bed, fully clothed and slept.

When I woke it was morning; raging hunger possessed me, and in the diner next to the motel I amazed the waitress by devouring plate after plate of greasy sausages, potato waffles, buttered toast, and eggs over easy, washed down with several pots of strong black coffee. I left her a tip worth more than the meal, staggered out to my stolen jeep, and drove on.

That night, in another motel, I wondered if the military police might be on my trail; I thought of them pounding on the door, ripping me from my bed, and was not afraid. But what crime had I committed worse than the explosion called Trinity? I dreamed of it: sometimes all I did was close my eyes and the memory rushed upon me. Again I felt that shuddering through the ground, that rolling heat; on and on went the express-train roar, on and on the searing brightness. What thoughts possessed the senator in that last moment I would never know; I imagined that his self-immolation revealed a longing to be redeemed.

Two days passed before I reached the coast. On a bright afternoon, a Wednesday, I pulled into the drive at Wobblewood West. The house was quiet and the blinds were drawn, but I found the door unlocked.

'Aunt Toolie?' I entered the flagstoned hall; I passed through the broad, open rooms. How empty this house seemed! Low chairs on spindly legs, flowers in brushed-steel vases, and bright abstract paintings loomed out at me, but none of it had anything to do with me, or the world, or what might happen next. Everyday life was the merest façade, a brittle shell that a shout could crack. I peeled back slats in a blind and peered out at the sunlit terrace. How long had it been since that evening of *Antigone*? I climbed the stairs.

'Aunt Toolie?' I longed to see her; she might have been the last link that tethered me to the world. In the upstairs corridor

I heard a radio playing low. Caressingly, a song curled towards me – the one about taking a sentimental journey, the one about putting your heart at ease – and I crept forward to meet it. At the end of the corridor, a door stood ajar, and I pushed it open to find a room in shadow. There, marooned on a sea of soft carpet, was a big bed with Aunt Toolie sitting by it. She turned towards me, unsurprised, as I entered.

Again I said her name, fearful now as I saw the inert figure in the bed, the head deep in the pillows, the hand in Aunt Toolie's hand. Her tongue moved over her lips, moistening them as if after a long silence. There was sadness in her eyes, but a strange happiness too.

In the bed, skeleton-thin, was Le Vol.

'Tallulah, I'm back!'

Hours might have passed, though perhaps it was only minutes, before the automobile pulled up in the drive. When I went to greet Uncle Grover, he shook my hand with what might have been relief and I asked him when Le Vol had arrived at Wobblewood West.

'Three days ago, four. We tried to call you, but that base of yours said you were off somewhere.' He clattered about the kitchen, putting groceries in cupboards. 'Your friend collapsed on the doorstep. To think, they'd let him out of a military hospital! Well, that's military hospitals for you.'

'But what was he doing here?'

'Why, looking for you, Woodley! That was all he could think to do, to come looking for you.'

Le Vol, after all these years! 'It's like a ghost coming back.'

'No ghost.' Uncle Grover held up cans of Campbell's soup: one cream of chicken, one pea and ham. 'He sleeps, but that's not all he does. We'll have that young fellow on roast beef and mashed potatoes, apple pie and ice cream before the week's out, mark my words.'

'But missing so long! Has he said where he's been?'

'They picked him up in the Pacific, that's all we know. Some nasty foreign island, Okin-something – is that what they call it? God knows what those Jap monsters have done to him.'

'He's said no more – nothing?'

'He will, Woodley. He's been waiting for you.'

Earnestly I joined the vigil at Le Vol's bedside, delighted when he stirred, offered desultory words, or sipped from spoons we held to his lips. What sufferings he had endured we dared not imagine; his eyes were haunted and his skin was yellow, clinging like parchment to his hollowed face. The doctor said he was undernourished, that was all, and would rally soon. Only one thing was certain: when Le Vol smiled at me, grasped my hand, and said he was glad to see me, I knew it was true.

After some days he was well enough to sit up. He said he missed the sun, so we took him down to the terrace, where he reclined on a wicker chaise longue and I read him stories by Somerset Maugham. Whether he listened I could not be sure, but perhaps the lulling, elegant words were enough; the words and the wash of the sea and the summer laving the cliffs and the blue Pacific, as if there were nothing wrong in the world and never could be.

That night Le Vol ate with us in the dining room. Uncle Grover, in his excitement, had prepared too much; Le Vol took only a little; but within days, as my uncle had predicted, we had him on roast beef and mashed potatoes, apple pie and ice cream. The hollows left Le Vol's face: the ghost was alive again. We began to take walks on the cliff paths. At first Le Vol used a stick, like me,

222

but soon discarded it. He would stride ahead of us as if he were our leader.

Our days fell into a dreamy rhythm. News barked from the radio, but I paid it little heed. The war dragged on in the Pacific. There was something called the Potsdam Declaration: some ultimatum to Japan. It meant nothing to me. My world was Wobblewood West.

I must have been home for ten days before Le Vol told his story. We were all on the beach with a bottle of Scotch and a pack of Pall Malls. Le Vol, as I recall, wore a pair of ragged shorts and a Hawaiian shirt – forced on him by Uncle Grover – that hung open over his bony chest. He had drawn up his knees and leaned forward, hugging them; he pulled back, hard, on his Pall Mall and, all at once, as if the time had come, began.

Much that he said was shocking; often, it was all the rest of us could do not to exclaim, but we did not exclaim.

All that mattered was the story he was telling.

Le Vol's Story

'I guess I owe you an apology, Sharpless,' he began. 'You must have wondered what happened to me after they threw me out of Nagasaki. I meant to write to you but never did. The tramp steamer that took me away could have been bound for Cloud Cuckoo Land or Timbuktu, I didn't care; those days in a cell at Yamadori's pleasure had left me shaken and ashamed. The place was a dungeon, a medieval dungeon. Christ knows what they would have done if I'd been there for keeps; as it was, I'd been stripped and beaten and doused in cold water so many times I thought my teeth would never stop chattering.

'So there I was on the tramp steamer, looking out morosely on the East China Sea, when a shabby fellow with a red nose offered me a cigarette.

'"Wainwright," he said, and held out his hand.

'I was hardly in the mood to talk, but didn't need to; Wainwright could talk enough for both of us. Quite a voice he had too: that dreadful, snide bray of the upper-class Englishman, except there was nothing snide about Wainwright. He was an "old China hand", or that's what he called himself. Been in the war, the first one, when he wasn't much more than a boy. Came back from the Somme an invalid. Lucky to be in one piece, but did he appreciate his luck? Don't bet on it. Fell apart. Couldn't settle to anything. There was a girl he was going to marry – Cousin Essie, he called her. If the Garden of Eden were in Aldershot, Essie would be Eve, or so Wainwright said. But, before he married her, he wanted to be worthy. And there lay the rub.

'His next years were a nightmare. Sent down from Oxford. Drinking, gambling. Job in finance, arranged by Essie's father. The firm was a family one, which was just as well, because when Wainwright was caught embezzling the father said, "Did you know we've got a branch in Hong Kong? I think you're going to get itchy feet, my boy, because that's where you're headed. Last chance. Make good and we'll take you back; you can even marry my daughter. Disgrace yourself and we never want to see you in England again."

'Of course, he never went back. Wainwright lasted three months in that Hong Kong office before the demons claimed him. Don't think he hadn't gone with good intentions. There'd been solemn, tearful promises to Cousin Essie; to himself too. He said he'd end it all if Hong Kong didn't work out.

224

'But Hong Kong didn't work out and Wainwright didn't end it. He picked up work as a stringer for Reuters, enough to keep body and soul together. Over the years that followed he rattled around China and Japan and Indochina. Sometimes he told himself he'd go back to England, but another year slipped by, then another, until he realized that something had happened he'd never expected: he'd fallen in love with the Far East. This filthy hole he'd been sent to in shame had gotten under his skin. Oh, his dreams wouldn't let up; sometimes in his cups, or in the arms of some almond-eyed whore, he'd sob for Cousin Essie, but for all that, Wainwright was happy, or as happy as he could be.

'Needless to say, I didn't learn all this on that first morning; still, I discovered enough to know there was a connection between Wainwright and me, something broken in me that responded to what was broken in him. By the end of that voyage we were fast friends, and when he learned I was a photographer, he said I was the man of the hour. Reuters would be more than interested in the snaps I could take in China. Wainwright could do the words and I could do the pictures. What a team we'd make! Suffice to say he was on the money.

'We ended up in Peking. For Wainwright this was an old stomping ground, and as spring turned to summer that year he initiated me thoroughly into its bars, its brothels, its opium dens; if it's true that every man has one special talent, Wainwright's was for immersing himself in the lowlife of any place he visited and dragging any half-willing accomplice down with him.

'But our pleasures were short-lived. Just over the border in Manchuria – Manchukuo, as its Jap masters called it now – the drums of war were beating. The Tosei-ha faction, wresting control of the government in Tokyo, was intent on fresh hostilities in China.

'When the "incident" happened at Marco Polo Bridge, just outside Peking, I don't think Wainwright turned a hair, but war had never come so close to me, and I was frightened. A minor skirmish, that's all it was: Jap troops, there to protect their embassy, firing on a party of Chiang Kai-shek's Chinese Nationalists. But we knew what was really going on. For the Japs to conquer Korea was one thing, but how could they hold Manchuria? Chiang Kai-shek would never stand for it. For the Japs, there was no going back. There was nothing to do but defeat him utterly. They couldn't stop until they possessed the whole of China. Now the "incident" gave them a pretext for new incursions. It was the Chinese! The Chinese had started it!

'Wainwright was in his element. There's something fearless about a fellow like that; I suppose if you've lost so much, you don't care if you lose the rest. The next few years saw us knocking around China as the Japs continued their relentless advance. Reuters got more than their money's worth. We were there when Shanghai fell; we were there when the Japs stormed into Nanking, taking possession of the city in an orgy of pillage and plunder.

'They say the Rape of Nanking shocked the world, but only if you'd been there could you understand the horror of those days. Who cared if you were a civilian? Who cared if you were a POW? The Japs had turned into monsters, driven by primitive hatreds. Their savagery knew no bounds – and I took the pictures. Remember that little pigtailed girl screaming and cowering as the Jap's bayonet lunges towards her? That was one of mine.

'Wainwright and I were lucky to escape with our lives. How many times did we fling ourselves on the last train out of a city that burned behind us? How many times did we trudge with refugees over devastated fields, always just one step ahead of the Japs? On and on they came, like locusts. Soon, pretty much all of

China was in Jap hands, except the provinces of Szechwan and Yunnan, but there was no end in sight to the war. Chiang Kai-shek wasn't giving up, and the Japs became more determined to bring him to his knees.

'Strange, how war changes time! China seemed like the world to me then; I barely seemed to have had another life, and if I had, it was so far away there was no going back. If you'd told me I'd be sitting one day on a beach in California, I'd never have believed you. America was unreal to me, as unreal as Wainwright married to Cousin Essie. We heard there was war in Europe and shrugged. We had enough going on in China, but never dreamed that the Chinese war would fan out to consume the whole Pacific.

'By the end of 1941 we'd holed up in Hong Kong. It was a relief to be in a British colony. We needed a rest and Wainwright's talents had found a new outlet. I'd always known that Oxford accent of his was worth its weight in gold, but never quite how much until he infiltrated the finest club in town. He'd put it out that he was Lord Somebody, a relative of the British royals. There wasn't a member of that club he didn't fleece blind. Our plan was to rake in as much as we could, then take a little vacation. Wainwright said he fancied a nice Pacific cruise. Well, I hardly need tell you what happened next.

'I'd be lying if I said Pearl Harbor took us by surprise. Oh, I've heard how they painted it over here – bolt from the blue et cetera – but if you'd had your ear to the ground in East Asia, you wouldn't see it that way. Things had turned sour between us and the Japs. Hardly a surprise. Let the white man storm about the world all he likes, throwing his weight around with the natives; that's in the natural order. Let the yellow man do the same, and the white man gets on his high horse. Ultimatums flew back and forth: the Japs must do this, the Japs must do that. Here's Roosevelt cutting off exports; meanwhile, here's the Japs, desperate to expand their new empire. How could they keep the show on the road without oil, minerals, rice fields? And how could they seize what they wanted with the American fleet so close? "Told you so," said Wainwright, when we heard news of the attack. But we were amazed at how quickly the Japs moved after that.

'It was only a day – one day! – after Pearl Harbor when they swept into Hong Kong. Thank God one of Wainwright's club cronies got his lordship and his loyal factotum – that's me – on a ship bound for Singapore. Surely we'd be safe there, back in the arms of the British? Well, maybe for a month or two. I got some of my best pictures during the fall of Singapore, but Christ knows what happened to them; I think they ended up at the bottom of the sea, coiled inside a Leica of which, alas, I had grown inordinately fond.

'We made it to Manila. In the Philippines, we thought, we'd be on American soil. Hah! Even before we docked, we could see the fires raging. Desperate days followed. We fell in with a party of GIs, hiding out in foxholes on the outskirts of the city. Wainwright and I had stolen uniforms from a couple of dead soldiers – he was a colonel, I was a corporal. If we were captured, he reasoned, we would be POWs and at least have some rights.

'I'm not sure the GIs agreed. To be taken prisoner by the Japs, they said, was a fate worse than death. I didn't need convincing. The GIs said that General MacArthur had evacuated to Australia, and when a chance came for us to do the same, we seized it. A Chinese captain said he'd take us all to Darwin, if only we gave him everything we owned and then some. Wainwright grumbled, but his ill-gotten gains from Hong Kong came in useful now.

'We set out, deep in the night, from a shabby fishing village on the Luzon coast. We were jubilant. Rumour had reached us of a big battle somewhere out in the ocean – the Midway, it must have been – where at last we'd got the Japs on the run.

'So the tide had turned: but not for us. The Chinese captain made us keep belowdecks. I lost count of how many days we spent in that stinking hold, ten or twelve men squashed in like sardines, with nothing to eat but weevily biscuits and the occasional smoked fish. I'd look at sunlight seeping through cracks in the deck above and feel like the Count of Monte Cristo.

'I was worried for Wainwright. For more than twenty years, ever since the Somme, he'd not gone a day without a drink – hell, he'd not gone a waking hour. Keeping him quiet was the hardest thing. He'd cry out in his sleep as if the devils were chasing him, and then the Chinese captain was upon us, threatening to chuck poor Wainwright overboard if we didn't shut him up. "Just let me take him on deck, let me get him some air," I pleaded, but that slitty-eyed bastard was immovable.

'I cursed him, but not as much as I did when we docked. Down he came, beating a baton against the hull, telling us to get up, get up, and go ashore; and though I thought I'd lost track of time, I was surprised – Darwin, already? Had we been at sea so long?

'When I staggered up to the deck, the light was so bright I was blinded; besides, I was doing my best to hold up Wainwright. But the GIs cried out, horror-struck. Then there were bayonets all around us, the Chinese captain threw back his head and laughed, and, as the glare faded, I saw the familiar harbour with its junks and sampans, saw the coolies and rickshaws on the quay and the Jap guards who surrounded us.

'Next thing I knew, our hands were bound and all of us, tied together, had to march ashore. The last I saw of that Chinese captain, he was licking his index finger, ready to count the wad of bills he'd received as his reward.

'The bastard had taken us back to Hong Kong.

'They say the Japs think you're a dead man once you're a POW. Well, Wainwright and I were dead. Whatever we'd been before didn't matter now. They sent us to Sham Shui Po Camp. We were starved, beaten, humiliated at every turn.

'Some of the torments would be funny if they weren't so ghastly. Wainwright and I hadn't been there long when three British officers managed to escape. After they'd gone, details of their scheme were all over camp: swim across Laichikoh Bay, scud through the occupied territories, hook up with Chiang Kai-shek's crowd before making it to India and freedom. Christ knows if the poor devils got that far, or any farther than the other side of the bay, but from the way the Japs carried on you'd think it was an escape worthy of Houdini.

'They decided we all had to sign a statement: *I, the undersigned, hereby swear solemnly on my honour that I shall not under any circumstances attempt to escape.* Would you believe it? Me, I'd have been all for signing if only they'd keep our pathetic rations coming, but some of the Brit officers got it into their heads that this just wasn't cricket – Geneva Conventions and all that – and Wainwright was with them all the way. The guards lined us all up on the parade ground for days, wilting in summer heat, while the CO virtually begged us to sign, sign, sign. We did in the end. Next thing we knew, a couple of Australians tried to break out. They were dragged back in chains and we all had to watch as they stood before the firing squad. *Bam! Bam!*

'Those months in Sham Shui Po seem like halcyon days now, given what happened later. I'd worried about Wainwright, but he thrived; something about the man seemed immune to adversity, or that's what I thought then. Perhaps it was his sense of humour. Absurdity piled on absurdity: here were Wainwright and I, not even soldiers, lumped in with men who were; here was Wainwright up to his old tricks, inventing one amazing story after another to explain how he, with that royal family voice, happened to be wearing an American colonel's uniform – and meanwhile doing his best to gamble his way to happiness, POW-camp style. In all this, I was his eager assistant.

'It must have been 1943, around Easter-time I suppose, when Wainwright and I and hundreds of others were informed that we were being moved. For what? We couldn't fathom it. But before we knew it we'd been marched down to the harbour and herded on to the decks of a Jap freighter.

'The voyage was a long one. The sun beat down, tropical rains fell, but we had no protection from either. Rations were *piffling*, as Wainwright used to say, and often rotten; there was never enough water to go around and what there was stank like piss. Soon half the fellows were sick and more than a few had died. I'll spare you details of the diarrhoea and dysentery, of the brimming latrine buckets, of the rats that scampered over our faces as we lay in sunburned stupor on the decks.

'Days and weeks went by. We stopped twice – at Manila, I think, and somewhere else, Saigon perhaps, where they took on more prisoners, crowding the ship even more intolerably. Finally, we docked in Singapore. We still didn't know why they had brought us so far. Had they taken us from Sham Shui Po all the way to Changi – one prison camp to another – only to torment us? Why didn't the devils shoot us and be done with it? But Wainwright said the Japs did nothing without reason. He was right.

'We'd been in the Changi camp no more than a night and a day before the guards formed us into battalions, several hundred men in each. Singapore was just a staging post. They shipped us off by railroad, in cattle trucks, packed so tight we could neither lie nor sit, while equatorial sun beat down on us. How many men died in those trucks, I wouldn't like to guess.

'For the first time in my long travails, I'd been separated from Wainwright; I was desperate to know what had become of him, but there was no way I could find out. The trains headed north, scything up through the Malay peninsula.

'The journey took a week; then there was no railroad any more and those of us who could still stand were forced to march, mile after mile every day over slithery jungle tracks as warm rain beat down. If you fell behind, the guards thrashed you; if you died, they left your body to rot in the jungle. There was only the relentless trek: onwards, onwards, ever north.

'We must have crossed from Malaya into Burma. For a time we were taken by barge up a broad, sluggish river, between green hills of jungle; at first we thought we were fortunate, welcoming the respite from our endless march, until we realized we would be given no rations for all the days of our voyage. More men died, and the guards kicked the corpses into the river.

'We had been sent to build a railroad. Only later did I figure out why. The Japs needed it to back up their forces in the Burma campaign. When completed, the thing would run between Bangkok in Siam and Rangoon in Burma – two hundred and fifty miles of jungle, hills, and rivers. Already thousands had gone before us, POWs and coolies alike, slave labour all of us, living in bamboo huts, toiling away from dawn till dusk and beyond to fell trees, make embankments, lay sleepers and rails. There were cuttings to be dug, bridges to be built, and always the hideous cruelties of the Japs and the jungle.

'Which was worse was hard to say. When it was dry, the heat was a furnace, and dust whirled up from the railroad banks, filling our eyes and noses and mouths; then came the monsoon, month after month of plummeting rains, turning the jungle into a slithery labyrinth.

'How I survived, I can't say. I had no courage. I had no shame. A Jap could sneer at me and I'd cringe like a dog. When the workday was done, I trudged the long miles to my hut and fell into oblivion for the few permitted hours. I can barely remember eating, though I must have swallowed my share of the maggoty rice and rotting fish and vegetables.

'Two years passed. Two years in hell.

'And what had happened to Wainwright? He had survived the Somme, but I hardly imagined he could survive this. Most likely he had died in the cattle trucks in Malaya or on our march through the Burmese jungle. There must have been ten thousand men or more, strung down mile after mile of the railroad's route.

'I fell sick. One morning as a guard passed through camp, ringing his bell, I flickered open my eyes to see only a haze in front of me. A crushing heaviness, like an anvil, pressed on my forehead. Shivery heat coursed up my limbs. The guard struck me with his baton, demanding that I rise. I feared he would kill me there and then, but he only turned away.

'Later, though at the time it seemed a fond dream, two fellows I had never seen before picked me up on a stretcher and carried me out of the camp. I was too bleary to understand what was happening, but I remember jolting in the back of a truck over mile after muddy mile, while fellows close by bellowed out dirty songs in accents I thought were Australian.

'Not until the fever had subsided did I realize I had been taken to a base hospital in Siam with POW medical staff. I found myself on a cot in a sea of cots, beneath a ceiling of billowing canvas. Groans and jabberings of fever sounded around me; once or twice I heard a scream, but there was laughter too, and even the brassy blarings of a phonograph, somewhere far away.

'"I thought they'd kill me," I said, when I could speak. "I thought they'd kill me."

'"They're bad, but not that bad," said the Australian nurse who tended me.

'She jabbed a thermometer into my mouth.

'"Lucky bugger, you are. This place is just overcrowded and understocked with medicines, as opposed to so hopelessly unsanitary that it spreads more disease than it cures. The prize exhibit, this one – one for the history books."

'I offered what I hoped was a questioning look.

'"Well, maybe not the history books, but the papers back in Nip-land. Some big wheel from Tokyo's coming by this afternoon to pose for pics with all of us. Our happy POWs! Who says we treat 'em rough?" She snatched the thermometer from my mouth. "You'll live. Think you'll be able to stand?"

'"So soon? Oh, please!"

'"Parade! And you blokes better look as healthy as you can or we're all up shit creek without a paddle."

'I promised to do my best.

'There must have been a hundred fellows that afternoon, lined in two rows down a dusty asphalt strip. They'd found fresh uniforms for a few of us – dead men's laundry, I dare say – but we must have looked like a shabby bunch, hardly capable of winning a war. How the Japs would laugh when they saw us in the papers!

'For a long time there was no sign of the VIPs. The photographers got to work all the same. One came and let off his flash in my face; it was as much as I could do not to snatch his camera and fling it to the asphalt, but after all it was a Seiki-Kogaku, and I respect a Seiki-Kogaku. Guards patrolled between us, guns at the ready; the POW doctors and nurses, also under armed guard, stood on a podium at one end. I inspected my fellow captives.

'That's when I saw him: Wainwright.

'There was no doubting it: the fellow across the tarmac was skinny as a rake like me and dressed in a different uniform – Australian, for Christ's sake, slouch hat and all – but I'd have known him anywhere. I almost laughed. How could I doubt that Wainwright would come through it all? He was a cat with nine lives. What stories he must have to tell! And if Wainwright could survive, so could I. But had he seen me yet? He'd made no sign.

'The VIPs arrived at last. We heard the whip of mighty blades and a roar; a shadow passed over us, and a Mitsubishi carrier fighter came bumpily to its rest in fields beyond the tents. The guards, on their mettle now, patrolled between us, guns cocked, bellowing at us in Jap. I could hardly believe anyone too important would visit this far-flung corner, but it seemed we would pretend. Crackly loudspeakers blasted out the Jap national anthem.

'Now came the official party: a fat general, decked with ribbons; a bearded admiral; a doddering old man in a scarlet sash – and a younger fellow, upright and handsome, who walked ahead of the others. For a crazed moment I thought he might be Emperor Hirohito himself, but whoever he was, he was important.

'As the VIPs passed between us, we were supposed to salute. I raised a hand to my temple: Wainwright did the same. I winked at him and grinned. I don't think he saw me, so I tell myself that what happened next wasn't my fault.

'We'd been in the sun a long time. Wainwright must have been light-headed; years in hellholes had done their worst. Either way, his brain was addled, though I think his last gesture had a touch of Wainwright about it all the same. He stepped out of line, turned on his heels – and thumbed his nose at Hirohito.

'There were gasps, cries. A guard struck Wainwright with a rifle butt. His slouch hat rolled across the tarmac, and he slumped to his knees and swayed.

'Now Hirohito stood before him. He pulled up Wainwright's head by the hair, slapped his face, then turned away, barking out an order. A shot rang out.

'They left the body, face down, where it fell.

'I trembled, as if in a fever again. To think that Wainwright had been through so much! To think that all of it should end like this! The heat was fierce. Already, insects would clamour for his blood, swarming in black rivers over his eyelids, nose, and lips. The VIPs proceeded towards me. I didn't care what happened to me now. They'd killed Wainwright and they could kill me. Hirohito's eyes flickered, wryly I thought, over the faces next to mine.

'Then he stood before me.

'"Murderer," I said, and spat in his face.

'The moment that followed seemed suspended, unreal. Blackness welled before me. I had so expected to be shot that I almost believed it had happened already, but when my vision came back I was alive, a guard pinched the back of my neck in the one truly vice-like grip I've ever felt, and Hirohito, with the same supercilious eyes, dabbed his face with a handkerchief and issued quiet orders to his retinue.

'I would have cursed him if the words would leave my lips. How could it be that I was not yet dead? It was cruel, for at once, like a scene change at the opera, everything was altered: no VIPs, no band, no guards, no prisoners ranged in shabby lines; only Wainwright, lying dead where he had fallen, and the man who had spat at Hirohito shackled to a flagpole, six feet away, in the full glare of the tropical sun.

'No one watched me. Night fell, as it falls in those latitudes, with the quickness of a theatre curtain coming down. Rain, in syrupy drops, soaked me to the skin. Hours passed. I shivered; I raged with hunger; I pissed and shitted myself, but still nobody came. Perhaps, I thought deliriously, I had died after all. I talked to Wainwright: "Can you hear me, old pal? No need to lie doggo now! Here we are in the afterlife, and the Japs can't get us."

'The rain eased, though the sky kept dripping; the moon, like a round rancid cheese, insisted its way through the clouds, and in the sickly light I saw Wainwright's corpse dance towards me, flesh falling already from its face, taunting me that Yanks were bastards and I was a bastard more than most, abandoning an English gentleman to die like this. I called out: "But I didn't! Wainwright, I didn't, I swear. They separated us. I wanted to find you."

'Then it was gone; the corpse lay unmoving again, but I feared it would rear up a second time, then a third, capering around me in dizzying derangement. But the ghost was nowhere in sight when I felt the knife at my neck.

'"Don't move." The voice was a whisper. "Move your head and I cut your jugular."

'I didn't need more persuading.

'"I wondered what happened to you, and now I know. Not so cocky these days are we, Mr Le Vol?"

'The urge to gulp came upon me and I struggled to hold it back, picturing my Adam's apple sliced open by the blade. My new companion edged around to face me. The moon was behind him; his features were in shadow, but I knew him now. Eight years had passed since the first time I saw him; he had lost a certain boyishness, but still I should have recognized him at once. How many times had he stood over me in that dungeon in Nagasaki? He had ordered my tortures. He wasn't

Hirohito. His name was Isamu, Prince Yamadori's nephew.

'I said, "The funny thing is, I'm not even a soldier. I'm a civilian."

'"You're a propagandist for the enemy's cause. Do you think I care how you got here? You're where you deserve to be."

'"And you? I've heard things, you know. In this camp, we're not so cut off as in Burma. There are fellows here from all over; some of them got here recently. The tide's turned against you Japs, hasn't it? You thought you'd conquer the world. Now you're fighting to hang on to your own paltry islands. Your cities are ruined. Your pilots smash themselves into American warships. You're desperate. It's over. Just a matter of time, and not much now."

'I thought I had said too much, but Isamu made no move to drive the blade into my neck. To my surprise, he sheathed it. He smiled at me. "Over, you say? Americans like everything to be so decisive. This war is just one turning of a wheel, Mr Le Vol, and the wheel shall turn again. Nothing begins; nothing ends; your victories of today shall be paid for in the defeats of the morrow."

'"Why didn't you have me killed?" I said. "Like Wainwright?"

'He looked down, then up, and I saw his face more clearly, smooth and radiant as a mask in the moonlight. "Permit me, your barbarian enemy, to display a little sentiment. There is no love lost between us, Mr Le Vol. Part of me should like to see you dead. But think how grievously I should upset Mr Sharpless. And I shouldn't like him to live without a friend."

'I could barely credit what I was hearing. "I don't understand. What do you care about Sharpless?"

'"It's complicated. And not your business."

'"So what do you propose to do with me?" I said.

'He stepped close. "I have informed my staff," he whispered, "that you are a valuable prisoner, a man it behooves us to keep alive. While I am not obliged to offer explanations, I have

238

intimated that my uncle has been attempting for some time to track you down. Tomorrow, after I am gone, you shall be taken to Bangkok and thence to Nagasaki, where you shall be kept in whatever safety we can provide until the end of the war. Don't look alarmed, Mr Le Vol. Behave yourself and you shall be treated with the utmost respect."

'I could have laughed at him. "What makes you think I want this? Do you have any idea what I've been through, while you've been swanning about East Asia on royal tours?"

"'I too have been through things, Mr Le Vol. We've all been through things. I don't pretend to know you, but I suspect you won't hold out for some absurd martyrdom. Shall you throw back my offer in my face – say you'd rather die? I don't think so."

"'Why are you doing this? You mentioned Sharpless, but—"

"'Do you know what love is, Mr Le Vol?"

'Now I really didn't know what he was talking about. He stepped forward; then, to my astonishment, he kissed me on the lips.

"'Perhaps one day you'll understand," he said. "All that I do, all that I've done, is motivated by love."

'Only now did some glimmering come to me. "You're talking about Trouble, aren't you? This Sharpless thing, it's something to do with Trouble."

"'They say, my enemy's enemy is my friend. Who, then, is my friend's friend? There's such a thing as loyalty, Mr Le Vol. There's such a thing as karma."

"'I thought you were loyal only to the emperor – and your codes."

"'Don't give me codes! I am a prince of my country. But I am not my country."

"'You're talking in riddles again," I said.

'"And you're failing to solve them. I'm tired of you, Mr Le Vol. I've done all I can for you. Just remember, when you're living high on my generosity in Japan, that we all betray our countries. But sometimes, if we're lucky, we don't betray our friends."

'Then he was gone, and, as if to signal that the scene was over, a cloud moved over the moon and I stood in darkness again.

'Next day, everything happened as Isamu had promised. The guards cut me down; I was permitted to wash, given a change of clothes, fed the heartiest breakfast I'd had in years, and put on a transport to Bangkok, where I stayed in a fine hotel on the river. I won't pretend I didn't feel compromised, cheapened, but I was alive – and for now that was all that mattered.

'The sea voyage that followed wasn't quite so pleasant. Allied planes cut relentlessly through the skies over the South China Sea. The war was going our way and sometimes I feared I'd be a casualty of our victory, as once I'd been a victim of our defeat. Several times I thought we'd be sunk. We ended up running aground on Okinawa, just as our side invaded the Jap homeland at last. I was there through the worst of the fighting, but to me it was glorious. I was back in American hands. The rest you know.'

We were silent for some moments after Le Vol finished. Gulls rode above the high, pale cliffs; the sea, blue and impassive, rolled against rocks and sand. The Pacific: turn the globe and it is half the world. I thought of explorers – Magellan, Drake, Cook – setting out intrepidly across the unknown. I thought of Perry and his black ships sliding into Edo Bay, cannon at the ready for some gunboat diplomacy. I looked at Le Vol with his downcast tousled

240

head. His shirt flapped about his bony chest; Aunt Toolie, sad-eyed, held his hand in hers.

Something welled in my diaphragm and I said, 'Isamu was always such a strange boy. I thought I detested him. But I can't.'

Uncle Grover asked, 'What did he mean about betraying our countries? We *all* do? But how?'

Le Vol stood, stretched: how tall he was! 'There's Wainwright, for a start. Turned his back on country, class, and Cousin Essie to slum it in the Far East. Never happier than in a Shanghai brothel. Never met another Englishman and didn't want to fleece him. Does that count?'

Aunt Toolie said, 'He was shell-shocked, wasn't he – from the Somme?'

'Isamu was talking about himself,' I said. 'Giving aid and succour to the enemy!'

'And I accepted it.' Le Vol paced down to the sea. Kicking up mounds of powdery sand, he called back, 'What about other traitors? I only impersonated a soldier. Isn't there a real one here who's gone AWOL? If anyone's in trouble, Sharpless, it's you. And who's been harbouring you?'

He picked up a stone and pitched it into the waves.

Good old Le Vol! Let the past go, I told myself. The future, let it take care of itself. There was only this moment on the beach. Aunt Toolie helped me to my feet. With Uncle Grover, we joined Le Vol at the ocean's edge. Solemnly, we faced the wide Pacific.

We did not hear Aunt Toolie's cleaner until she was almost upon us. Red-faced, breathless from the stone steps, she staggered towards us, turning a heel in the sand, and tremblingly pointed to me.

'Mr Woodley,' she said, 'I think you'd better come.'

***

Kate Pinkerton waited for me in the drawing room. To see her here – in this Californian castle with its blond wood, tubular steel furniture, paintings by Klee and Kandinsky – seemed a violation of the natural order. Many times during the war I had watched her on newsreels, earnestly addressing gatherings of charitable ladies or comporting herself dutifully at her husband's side. Here, standing by the unlit fireplace, she appeared no different from that image on the screen. Her bearing had always been regal. Queen of England? No: Queen of America. On a low glass table she had laid her hat: charcoal grey, almost military, suggesting wartime austerities, yet elegantly sculptural like her grey jacket, grey pleated skirt, black low-heeled shoes. My steep climb from the beach had left me breathless. Flustered, I asked her if the senator was with her.

Her voice was toneless. 'Don't speak to me of my husband.'

Many times since that morning in Alamogordo I had pictured his hands slipping from his eyes and the moment when I knew that, like Oedipus, he had blinded himself. I said, too quickly, 'If only I could have saved him! Please believe me – if I could have saved him, I would.'

She looked at the painting above the fireplace, pondering, perhaps, its black curving lines and bright splotches, and what meaning they might hold. At the neck of her blouse she had fixed the reddish brooch I had seen before; it glowed a little as she faced me again. 'Don't,' she said. 'It's over.'

A fear jumped in my chest. 'He can't be dead.'

'No, he's very much alive. And has orders for you. You'll receive them soon.' She touched the brooch, as if to press it in place, though it was perfectly in place. 'I suppose you're wondering why I'm here in California. Do you think I've come for you? My old friend, Mr Sharpless! You've aged,' she added, as if saying that the weather that day was warm.

She had barely aged at all. She was sixty-four. I gestured to a sofa, but she made no move to sit. She reached into a pocket of her jacket and drew forth a cigarette case. I was surprised: I had never seen her smoke. Flame flicked up from her lighter. She had not offered the case to me.

'You always seemed such a boy,' she said, and I felt I should protest, but knew I never could. 'Still, all men are boys. I suppose I told you about my brother. President Manville! That was his destiny, laid before him like a railroad track. And what did the boy do? He went and died in Cuba.' Smoke wreathed her face like a veil. 'You'll tell me he was a solider. It was war.' She snorted. She shook her head. 'Boys like to play at war.'

Her manner alarmed me. I summoned the courage to ask her why she had come. I sounded harsher than I had intended.

'We *are* old friends, aren't we? Allies?' She smiled at me. 'Well, we were. That's why I wanted to see you.' Her voice remained level though it hardened a little. 'I wanted you to look me in the eyes while you told me what you'd done to my son.'

'I couldn't…' I began. What would come next, I didn't know.

'You were always so sensible.' She paced in a wide arc. Was she describing a circle around me, like a magic spell? 'Solid. Stolid. Poor Mr Sharpless and his walking cane! I'm not naive, like some women. How could I be? There's nothing about men I don't know. There's nothing about my son I don't know. I only wanted to protect him. I was pleased when he brought you home. How fast a life could he be leading if his friend was that bookish cripple? We made a pact, didn't we? You'd look after my son for me. But you never did.'

Was all this true? Something in her certainty made it true. I whispered that I was sorry. I stepped closer to her, even moved to take her hand, but she shifted towards the wide glass doors that stood open to the terrace. Bleakly, she looked at the bright sea. The sun, sinking in the late afternoon, fell across her like a spotlight. Her eyes were not squinting.

'He wouldn't see me,' she said at last.

I took this in. 'They've found Trouble?'

A column of ash fell from her cigarette. 'What did I have to do, get down on my knees and beg? You'll tell me he was never mine. But he was. My son. And I let him go. I don't know how. It was as if I turned, just for a moment, and he was gone.'

Again I went to her. Delicately I touched her grey sleeve, and asked her – for there was nothing more I could say – whether she would stay for tea. She seemed not to hear.

'Tell me, Mr Sharpless, do you think me a cruel woman? Some say I am. Calculating, they call me – ambitious, as if that were a fault! Perhaps you share those views. But all I ever wanted was a husband I could love – a husband and a child. I believed you *were* my ally.'

'I am,' I said. 'I've always been.'

I could have told her that I loved her: I had always loved her. Instead I said, though I wasn't sure I meant it, that none of us could have saved Trouble. *Shikata ga nai.* It can't be helped. Too bad.

'You must want to know about your orders,' she said.

I had forgotten about the senator's orders.

'Our agents arrested my son in Mexico,' she said simply. 'He's in a cell in San Diego. He'll always be in a cell now, of course. Always, until he dies. You know what that means, I suppose?'

I felt cold, as if the sun had dimmed suddenly, sinking the room into shadow. I had wanted to see Kate Pinkerton as a statue, adamantine, unyielding. Was she now crumbling before me?

Counterclockwise this time, she retraced the steps she had made in the wide arc around me.

'I'll wear him down,' she said. 'One day, he'll see me.'

On the day the atomic bomb fell on Hiroshima (though I didn't know that yet), I stood in a cool corridor in San Diego, waiting for a young captain to unlock a door. The door was heavy and the lock was stiff. He was having difficulties and cursed beneath his breath. I had flustered him, no doubt. 'You're sure, sir?' and 'From Senator Pinkerton?' he had said as I showed him my papers. Yes, I agreed, it was most irregular. Yes, it was authorized in the highest places. No, I would not wait while he made a call. I thought I put on a good show: sighing, rolling my eyes, rapping my ashplant on the edge of his desk.

Uncertainly, he had looked through the venetian blind. My vehicle stood waiting, gleaming on the tarmac; my two guards leaned against the hood, smoking cigarettes. Those fellows! Before today I had never met them, but they treated me with a familiarity bordering on insolence. It was not my place to complain. They had arrived along with the senator's orders.

The captain opened the dungeon at last. But *dungeon*, of course, was not the word: the place was an airfield lock-up, the cinder-block walls neither dank nor dripping, the concrete floor free of straw and rats, the barred window surprisingly large. There were even touches of luxury: a bookcase piled with copies of *Photoplay*, a table on which lay the remains of breakfast, a silvery steel toilet bowl and sink, and two bunks made up with grey blankets.

Trouble sat hunched on the lower bunk, not looking up, leafing through a *Photoplay*.

I asked the captain to leave us.

'You're sure, sir?'

'Don't worry. I'll call if I need you.'

The door clanged shut and the key turned again, this time with a smooth, authoritative thud. Trouble did not look up. I stepped towards him. I had expected him to be changed, dishevelled at the least, cowed, chastened, but he seemed the same as he had always been. What about the hands, any nervous twitch? No. What about the eyes, were they circled darkly? No.

He licked a finger, turned a page.

'Did you know, Sharpless, that Howard Hughes designed a special brassiere for Jane Russell in *The Outlaw*? Remarkable. All his skills in aerodynamics, all that engineering genius that designed revolutionary aircraft, bent now to this task: lift up, push out.' He held up her picture in the magazine. 'Talented girl.'

Wearily, I sat on the cell's only chair.

'I've been AWOL,' I said.

'Back now, by the looks. And nobody cared?'

'You and me, we're not real soldiers, are we? We answer to the senator. Quite a privilege, all told. I never thanked you for getting me my job in Los Alamos. Smoke?' I held out my pack.

'Time can hang heavy on a fellow's hands, can't it? And sometimes a tattered *Photoplay* can't quite do the trick. I suppose you know Mama tried to visit me. I refused to see her. Made quite a scene, she did.' He sounded unconcerned, as if he were talking about a bit of bad weather, since passed. I lit his cigarette and he said, exhaling smoke, 'I already knew that about Jane's brassiere, didn't you? Christ, everyone knew that. That news is years old.'

I could abide his flippancy for only so long. 'What do you think's going to happen?' I said.

He stood and stretched, reaching towards the ceiling. His shirt pulled free from his trousers and I glimpsed his bare torso, still boyishly taut. 'Well, I'd guess the senator and Truman are clustered around the conference table right about now, debating what to do with the ultimate weapon. Kyoto? Yokohama? Or straight to Moscow and cut out the middleman?'

'Truman's in Potsdam. Or on his way home.'

'Oh? I'm so out of touch. On the run, you know.'

'Damn you, Trouble! What have you done?'

He had gone to the window and stood there, looking out, smoke curling above his head in an airy blue river. 'I never meant what happened to happen,' he said, his voice thick. 'You can't believe I meant it, can you?'

I perched uncomfortably on the grey metal chair.

'I suppose Yamadori put you up to it,' I said. 'Or Isamu. Everything was all a front. Senator Pinkerton's right-hand man! All just a distraction from what Trouble was really doing. But why run now?'

'Remember the sniper? Things were getting tough in Los Alamos.' He stood against the sunlight from the window. Darkness gathered in his eyes, and it came to me that he was a ghost already: flickering, vanishing.

'Kate said I'd let you down. She was right. I could have saved you.'

'You, save me? You can't even save yourself.'

I pushed back the chair. 'All I've ever wanted is to bring you back from the brink.'

He laughed. 'Is that what you honestly believe?'

'You're American, whether you like it or not: your father's son. And for the sake of some fantasy you abandon everything that matters and everyone who loves you. How can you betray your country, your father, your friends? This is wartime – life and death! Did you succeed? Come on, tell me all about it. Did you sell our secrets to the enemy?'

'Sell?' He shrugged. 'I gave them for free.'

'Traitor!' What happened next happened so fast I barely believed it was real. How, when, had I raised my arm? How, when, had my ashplant battered down? One moment I stood close to Trouble, close enough to have kissed him; another, and my ashplant cracked against his head.

He lay on the floor, face down.

Time stopped. A sob escaped my throat.

As he fell, he had struck the side of the sink. Blood pooled in his hair, while the captain rattled at the door ('Sir, sir!') and would have burst in, had I not shouted savagely that it was all right, everything was all right. I lowered myself to the floor. There was no way to sit that was easy for me, so I stretched beside Trouble as if he were my lover.

I touched his hair. I felt the blood and winced. Carefully, I turned his face towards mine.

His eyelids flickered. 'They'll be waiting for me, you know.'

'Waiting?' I said.

'I was almost there. The message had come and I was on my way. But you don't think they'd leave without me, do you? Isamu would kill them if they left without me.'

I thought I understood. 'A plane? A boat?'

'I've stayed too long here. I miss Nagasaki.'

'And they're over the border, these friends of yours?'

He smiled dreamily. 'Now you're just trying to get information out of me.' From the window, thick rectangles of light fell over us, honeyed and warm, patterned like the bars. 'Got your number, don't I? Kiss and tell.'

'Me, tell?' I kissed him, and his lips returned the pressure of mine. The moment seemed at once unreal and more real than any other I had experienced before. I felt myself sinking into a warm darkness, and all I wanted to do was sink and sink, never rising again.

What did I care if he was a traitor?

'But am I really a traitor?' he said, as if he had read my thoughts. 'What does that mean, anyway? I've been two things all my life. Be this, be that – always these voices in my head, pushing me this way, pulling me that. Believe me, if I could make everything all right, I would. But I never will, will I? I never will.'

'I love you,' I said.

'And I love you. Don't think I don't.'

'But there was always something else. Or someone. Isamu. Do you think you can stand?' I added after a moment. 'Senator's orders – I have a van outside and two guards, ready to take you.'

'They're going to kill me, I suppose. Oh, I don't mean right away. This is America. There'll be a trial, and witnesses, even a few caring liberal types – maybe you, Sharpless – who'll do all they can. But it'll be no good. I'm a dead man. You know what they say about golden lads.'

'Oh, Trouble!' There were tears in my eyes: '*Golden lads and girls all must…*'

He finished it for me: '*…As chimney-sweepers, come to dust.*'

We helped each other stand. I crossed to the door, thumped on it, and we heard the captain clatter with his keys. Trouble leaned towards the mirror over the sink. He dabbed his hair with a handkerchief. He splashed his face. As the door opened he took more movie magazines from the bookcase and cried, 'Did I ever tell you I *adore* Jane Russell?'

The captain advanced with a set of handcuffs.

'I don't think that's necessary, do you?' I said, but regulations were regulations.

I tucked Trouble's magazines under my arm and we made our way out to the van, where my guards, squashing out their cigarettes, assumed a military demeanour. Both were large, thickset fellows, but one, called McPherson, was freckled and fair, while the other, Mendoza, was Latin-dark. Trouble eyed them appraisingly as we approached.

'Not a particularly *armoured* van,' he complained, climbing into the back. 'Aren't I more dangerous than this? Where are we going, anyway – Alcatraz, like the Birdman? If only this thing had windows, I could look out at the coast of Big Sur on the way. De-lovely.'

'Look at Jane.' I handed him his magazines.

McPherson, revolver at the ready, climbed in beside Trouble; Mendoza gestured to me to sit in front with him. I was not pleased; he was surly, and my efforts at conversation met with little success.

San Diego, I observed as we moved off, was surprisingly pretty. His face remained stony. Lovely day, I tried again – *de*-lovely, even. You're from Mendoza, Mexico – I mean Mexico, Mendoza? Ha-ha. Silly me. Funny, to think it's just a few miles away.

Only when I offered Mendoza a cigarette did I get more than a grunt out of him. Smoothly, we swung around the curving coast; the wheel spun through his dextrous, dark hands and I grew sleepy. The cabin was stifling. My shirt stuck to the seat. A fly buzzed between dashboard and windshield, stopped for a while, crawled, and buzzed again. Through the panel behind us, Trouble and McPherson murmured, sometimes exclaimed. I think they were playing cards.

I woke suddenly, as if someone had jolted me. No one had. The sun glared blindingly through the windshield. We had stopped. Still the fly buzzed, but the driver's seat was empty and the door was ajar.

'Mendoza?' I said.

He stood by the roadside, pissing; the thick stream gurgled into the sand. Casually, he buttoned his fly, then mooched around the hood to the passenger side, yanked open my door, and jerked his head for me to get out.

The revolver flashed as he jabbed it towards me. 'Mendoza, what is this?'

'Hands up.' He waved me away from the van. 'Further; that's right.'

I had failed to retrieve my ashplant and lurched, stumbled. Sand, rocks, and scrubby desert plants stretched in all directions. Mendoza must have veered some way from our route. Buzzards hovered in the cloudless sky.

'Are we over the border, Mendoza? What do you want?'

He thumped the side of the van. 'McPherson!'

A lazy bellowing came from within.

'Radiator's blown!' Mendoza called. 'Wake up!'

Perhaps I should have warned McPherson, but I did not understand what was happening until it was too late. I assumed that the pair of them were in on this. I was wrong. Curses sounded from within; the van rocked on its springs; McPherson stepped out, scratching his head—

The shot cracked against the bright day. Buzzards scattered.

'Sorry, friend. Had to be done.' Mendoza tucked the revolver into his belt, crossed himself, then dragged McPherson from the road. Nearby rose a shelf of rock with green-blue scrubby vegetation sprouting up behind: a convenient place to conceal a corpse. I eyed the buzzards. After taking McPherson's gun and the money from his wallet, Mendoza returned to the van and ushered a bewildered Trouble, blinking, into the sun.

'Mendoza, why?' I said.

He gave no answer, only digging into his pocket, producing a key and releasing Trouble's cuffs. Blankly, I watched as he told the astonished Trouble that the van was now his. 'The keys are in the ignition. And those friends of yours must be getting impatient.'

'Sharpless, did you plan this?' Trouble said.

I shook my head. 'Who are you, Mendoza? Tell us!'

He spat in the dust. 'You don't know me,' he said, 'but I've seen you both before. I've done a bit of work for Senator Pinkerton over the years.' He mimed the action of a man with a rifle, lining up a target in his sights. 'Damned uncomfortable, crouching among those rocks.'

'You're the sniper?' said Trouble. 'I don't understand.'

'You don't need to, my friend.' He clapped Trouble on the back. 'Go. You're free.'

'What? We're way out in the desert! I'm just supposed to drive off? Which way?'

Mendoza waved a hand along the road. 'The border. Quickly. Don't worry about us. This gentleman and I will be quite safe.'

I swallowed hard. 'Do as he says, Trouble – senator's orders.'

Senator's orders. The thought was startling: Mendoza, the murderer, was only obeying orders. Trouble would have his freedom. And suddenly I realized how much his father loved him: loved him, with a love that humbled me. I tried to tell Trouble this, but my voice cracked.

He squinted into the sun. 'Sharpless, I—'

'Go!' I shouted.

The words shook my frame; I thought I would collapse, but Trouble, stepping forward, gripped me tightly. I clutched him, balled my hands into fists, and dug my knuckles into his back, hard enough to hurt. We had been through so much together. Now everything was over.

'Nagasaki,' I said. 'Think of Nagasaki.'

'I'm sorry, Sharpless.'

He climbed into the cabin, turned the key, and I stood with Mendoza, watching as Trouble disappeared in clouds of dust. Only when it was too late did I realize I had left my ashplant in the van. It would go where Trouble was going, and I could not call it back.

Just off the roadside the buzzards had descended, shrieking and scrabbling around the shelf of rock.

'Now what?' I looked at Mendoza.

He stuck out a thumb. 'What do you think?'

Hours passed before a shabby truck rattled to a halt beside us. In the back were chickens, squawking and flurrying in teetering crates. The driver blinked down at us: a chubby, incurious Mexican with an unruly grey moustache. Mendoza spoke to him in Spanish, and the fellow grinned and nodded, holding up a bottle of tequila. The chickens stank abominably.

As I limped after Mendoza to the passenger door, I half feared he would push me away and drive off, laughing, with his new friend. But Mendoza was honourable; his behaviour to me, indeed, was remarkably solicitous all the way back to San Diego, where he slipped away near the market where the Mexican left us. One minute Mendoza was there, then he was gone.

A cab crawled by and I hailed it. I had drunk too much tequila. By the time I made it downtown, the sun was setting. I checked in to the first hotel I could find and flopped on to the bed.

I slept. I had no dreams.

What time could it be? Pain, worse than I had felt for years, throbbed in my damaged leg. How long had I stood, how far had I walked, without my ashplant? I looked at my watch. It had stopped. I had not drawn the blind, but the light was dim, seeping down a well between window and wall. I heaved myself from the bed. The room was dirty: cracked linoleum, cracked plaster, cracked glass in the window. I pissed in the sink.

Downstairs, I asked the desk clerk the way to the railroad station. I'd go back to Aunt Toolie's: that was it, go home and wait. Should I consider myself a wanted man? Had I aided and abetted Trouble's escape? Perhaps this was part of the senator's plan: Woodley Sharpless, scapegoat. My head ached, and sadness clenched in my chest like a newspaper crumpled tightly, all its words in zigzag disarray. I would accept my fate.

The station lobby was crowded. Heat rose like marsh gas, and there was noise all around: automobile horns, dogs barking, a train whistle, a newsboy's reedy cry. What was he saying? Japan: something about Japan. I snatched a paper from him as I passed, but not until I was on the eight-fifteen to Los Angeles, sinking into my upholstered seat, did I dare unfold it.

They had dropped the bomb the day before: eight-fifteen in the morning, Hiroshima time. Later, every detail would be branded on my brain: the predawn takeoff from Tinian Island, just north of Guam, sixteen hundred miles from Hiroshima; the crew of twelve men; the B-29 called *Enola Gay*, after the pilot's mother. Over Iwo Jima, two other B-29s joined the first, their tasks to take photographs and make scientific records. On and on they flew through the gathering dawn. When they reached Hiroshima, no sirens sounded, no anti-aircraft fire boomed out, no Japanese fighter planes took to the air. The bomb, code-named Little Boy, had been scrawled on by playful crew-members, with messages for the enemy that the enemy would never read: obscenities, taunts, curses.

Gravity had done its work. Down dropped Little Boy through the placid morning. Seconds passed: forty-three seconds before the explosion, 1,900 feet in the air above Hiroshima. How precisely the scientists measured it all! It was a matter of mathematics: the 350,000 people in the city; the 4.4 square miles around ground zero devastated almost completely; the thousands or tens of thousands killed at once, blitzed out of existence like insects in a flame – and this was to reckon without the thousands more blinded, burned, or slashed by flying glass, stumbling through field after field of blackened corpses for hours, even days, after the explosion. Many had skin hanging from their faces in strips. Many would die later in agonies of the damned, eaten from within by atomic radiation.

President Truman heard about the bombing as he sailed home from the Potsdam Conference. He was elated – this, he declared to a group of sailors, was the greatest thing in history.

The official statement from the White House was simple and direct. The Japanese, said Truman, had been repaid for their attack on Pearl Harbor. Now they must surrender or the bombing would be ceaseless, blasting their islands into oblivion: *a rain of ruin from the air, the like of which has never been seen on the earth*.

The story continued on the inside pages. Senator B. F. Pinkerton (Democrat, New York) was to address both houses on the President's behalf on the morning of Thursday, August 9.

A pulse leaped in my neck. Could I talk to the senator – make him see reason? Might he not speak out against further attacks? For years his rhetorical gifts had been the envy of the Senate.

I could stop nothing. I knew that. But I had to try.

* * *

That afternoon I bought a plane ticket to Washington, DC. Flights across the continent were a long business in those days. We would put down in Salt Lake City and Des Moines, then change planes in Chicago.

In the air I drank whisky, ate nothing, and did my best to sleep. On the Chicago plane I sat next to a businessman from Baltimore. He wanted to talk about the bomb. 'Can you believe it?' he kept saying. 'Can you believe it?' – overjoyed, it seemed, at this latest revelation of American know-how, as if Oppenheimer were Thomas Edison and had just invented the light bulb. When the fellow asked me what I did in the army, I slapped my bad leg and told him I had been at Iwo Jima. He demanded to shake my hand. Later, at Washington National Airport, I saw him in the distance, staring across the concourse, amazed, as three military policemen approached me with rifles trained, arrested me, handcuffed me, and led me away.

I said to them, 'You're going to explain this?'

The oldest one looked at me warily. The youngest twitched his mouth. The one in the middle seemed about to say something, but glances from the others made him hold off – for a time, at least.

'Traitor,' he whispered to me, as our armoured car drew up outside the lock-up, a grim, red-brick building on a base outside Washington.

Blankly, I let them lead me to my cell. 'Do I get to call my lawyer?' I asked as the door slammed behind me.

I slumped on my cot. The cell was like Trouble's a continent away, give or take a touch or two. No toilet bowl, only a chamber pot. No movie magazines, only a Bible. I curled on the cot, face towards the wall, and did not much care what happened to me next.

It was morning. Breakfast came on a tray: toast, sausages, eggs over easy.

It was afternoon. Lunch came: lamb, potatoes, minted peas.

It was night. Dinner: chicken, potatoes, minted peas.

Morning again. I stood by the window. Swampily, greenly, the Potomac crawled by, and I thought of other rivers, harbours, seas. My spirit was a paper boat, buffeted on the tide.

Questions now: '*Major, could you confirm… ?*' and '*Major, could you clarify… ?*' and, ominously, '*Major, you're sure there isn't more… ?*' The military policemen were not the ones who had arrested me, but might as well have been: disguised a little, that was all. The middle one, the one who had called me traitor, had turned into an earnest, bespectacled type, taking down my answers like a clerk of the court; the older one, heavier of frame now, led the questioning in a Voice of America voice, while his young assistant, flush-faced, made stammering, supplementary offerings when prompted by his superior.

I told them everything. But everything was not enough.

When they came again, I could not think what to say. I was tired of minted peas, and said so; I wanted something to read other than the Bible, and said so; I wished the window in my cell were lower: such a pleasant view, I said.

'*But tell me, Major…* ' Questions again – and again, I told them about Mendoza. No, I had not known Mendoza before. Yes, I had been startled by what Mendoza had done.

Voice of America took another tack.

'In San Diego, you were alone with Colonel Pinkerton in his cell for some time – and keen not to be interrupted, I gather. Would you like to tell me why? What did you *do* with Colonel Pinkerton?'

'Do?' I said. 'Talked to him. What else?'

Voice of America arched an eyebrow. 'Just talked?'

'Of course. He's an old friend.'

'Or lover?' said the young man, more flushed than ever.

The question hung in the air like incense.

Had Trouble been my lover? I smiled. I laughed.

'Shut up!' cried Voice of America.

Still I laughed. And laughed and laughed, even as he struck my face and I jerked back, almost falling from my chair. Perhaps there would be another blow, and another; blood, tasting like rust, pooled beneath my tongue and I laughed again, splattering droplets down the front of my uniform. Oh, let him hit me again: I wanted him to hit me. Yes, I should have denied the ruinous charge, denied it vehemently. But I could not: I would not. I wanted it to be true.

Fearing nothing, I looked up into the glowering, disgusted face.

Afternoons in August never end. When days are long and heat coils around us, sticky as molasses, we enter an eternal realm where it seems that nothing will happen, yet everything could happen. Like phantoms, we pass through a dreamy haze, and I thought Voice of America was a phantom too, when he stood over my cot as that afternoon declined at last. His fingers touched my forehead. Ruefully, he smiled. I should have been puzzled, but in the fog that consumed me I registered no surprise as he crossed to the sink, wet a washcloth, bathed my lips, and helped me stand. I thought there would be handcuffs, but there were none. Calmly, he led me along grey corridors, down grey steps out to a waiting jeep.

Guards saluted as we passed through a checkpoint, and only as we ran along the Potomac did I become aware that Voice of

America was apologizing to me: I'd understand, wouldn't I, that they could never be too careful? Explore every avenue. Leave no stone unturned. And if, from time to time, an innocent man was caught up in the fray, it was greatly to be regretted but, but... Senator Pinkerton had explained everything. Now he wanted to see me.

We passed Arlington Cemetery, then crossed the bridge. Sunlight fell around us, golden in the late-gathering summer evening. Here, the Lincoln Memorial; here, the Washington Monument; here, the White House, where the Pinkertons had hoped to live, and never would. Familiar phrases jangled through my mind like fragments of a poem I might write one day, if only I were a poet.

O Great Republic... Land of the free... Home of the brave! One nation indivisible, with liberty and justice for all! How many years have passed since this nation was brought forth? Your star-spangled banner, how long has it waved? There are truths, you tell yourself, that are self-evident: Life... Liberty... Pursuit of happiness. Government of the people, by the people, for the people. But it is you, America, not God, who tramps the vintage where the grapes of wrath are stored. Where is there an end of it, the red glare of rockets, the bombs that burst in air? Why have you practised so long to learn to read? You have read a fiery gospel. You have heard the sounds of trumpets that will never call retreat... And we pledge allegiance to the flag of the United States of America and ask ourselves when this nation under God shall have a new birth of freedom.

The Mall stretched towards the Capitol, with its many-pillared dome. Never, until this moment, had I felt American. Love and hatred, pride and shame, swelled in my helpless heart.

'The centre of the world,' I said, and meant it.

'Yes,' said Voice of America, 'I like to think that too.'

We arrived, as I had expected, at Constitution Avenue. As Voice of America accompanied me from the jeep, I looked at him fondly; he held my arm, but only to make sure my steps were steady. He flourished a pass. I had never been to the Senate offices before. Trouble must have been a thousand times, and I realized, with a plunge of sadness, that he would never come again: never again through this wide lobby; never again up these broad stairs; never again to this set of double doors with this serviceman on guard and this brass plate, polished brightly, bearing the legend: SEN. B. F. PINKERTON (D–NY).

Before I entered, Voice of America shook my hand. I wanted to protest: Have you come so far with me, only to abandon me? I'm sick, Voice of America: stay with me, guide my steps. But all I could do was smile and watch as he retreated. Ten paces away, he raised a hand, not turning, waggled the backs of his fingers in the air, and whistled 'Avalon' by Al Jolson.

I looked at the guard by the door. A child: just a child.

Carefully, he opened the doors for me.

'Sharpless, is that you?'

The office was vast. Through tall windows, open in the heat, thick golden light disclosed acres of Turkey carpet; high walls, lined with stately volumes, supported a ceiling with elaborate carved cornices and a wide, mandalic rose, from which impended an immense unlit chandelier. A flagpole, with a draping Stars and Stripes, jutted up next to a kingly desk – and behind the desk, propped there like an enormous, bulky mannequin, sat Senator Pinkerton in a quilted smoking jacket, bandages covering his eyes.

'How long has it been?' he said. 'You've grown lax in your duties, I fear.' His hands toyed with an object that flashed, catching the setting sun; approaching, I saw it was a dagger in a jewelled scabbard. I had seen that dagger before.

'Senator, how did all this happen?' Sadly, I looked at the clutter before him: the legislative papers, the letters from constituents, the dossiers marked TOP SECRET that he could no longer read. Perhaps, in my next words, there was something mad, but no madness of mine could matter when all the world was mad. 'I've wandered in a mist,' I said, 'and so, I'm certain, have you. But everything's come clear. Don't you see better, now that you're blind?'

Three telephones squatted on his desk: one red, one white, one blue. The red one shrilled, a light flashing under its dial, and he reached for it unerringly. What was that? The mission on its way? They must keep him informed. No, no change of plan: the authorization remained. He spoke as if he were a machine, a mechanical man emitting lines someone else had written.

Gently, he replaced the receiver. 'Turn on the radio, Sharpless.'

Darkness gathered in the corners of the room, but I made out a large hunched curve of burnished cedar. I switched it on. It hummed and whirred, faceplate glowing like a tiny sun.

News, perhaps?

The senator shook his head.

A soap opera?

'Music,' he said, and I sought it out.

Tommy Dorsey was not to his taste. Nor was Benny Goodman. Only when opera swelled around us did he seem content. I knew the work: *Tartarin*, that curious mock epic, at once hilarious and sad, which Puccini had composed between *Tosca* and *The Girl of the Golden West*. Curling around us came the great leave-taking duet, '*Il mio amore puro, sarò sempre costante*' – my pure love, I shall be constant always. What gorgeous swirls of emotion Puccini conjured from the air, at once noble and decadent, elevating and absurd! 'They say that emotionalism is a sign of weakness,' the composer said once. 'But I like to be weak.'

I turned the sound low and asked the senator why he had sent for me.

His voice was hoarse. 'You loved him, didn't you? A fine irony. To think, that you – you! – should be the one who understands me! Woodley Sharpless. You were a baby in Japan when I first saw you. We all said, *Such a pretty baby! What will become of him?* The possibilities seemed wide open, though funnily enough no one thought to say, *The boy will grow up to be a cripple, a degenerate, and a traitor to his country.* Call us unimaginative! Back then, so much had yet to happen. We hadn't even had the Great War.'

'Then you understand,' I said, 'that we've come too far? This bomb, how could you let it happen? What was the argument – that we've spent two billion in Los Alamos, so we can't waste taxpayers' money? Let's just drop the damned thing and see what happens? Frighten the Russians? Because you sure as hell know we've beaten the Japs already.'

'Will you lock the door for me, Sharpless?' He touched his bandaged temples. 'Don't want anyone bursting in, do we?'

Why I obeyed him, I could not be sure. For too long the Pinkertons had held me in their power. But their power was fading, almost gone. The lock shut with a satisfying thud, and I recalled the prison cells of these last days: Trouble's, then mine. Then this, the greatest cell of all.

'That dagger,' I said, 'how did you get it?'

'My wife brought it back from California. They confiscated it from my son when he was arrested. Did you know there are words on the blade in Japanese? Something about dying with honour.'

'Yes, when you can no longer live with honour,' I said.

The senator withdrew the blade, held it up before his face as if he could see it, then sheathed it again.

'Did I ever tell you I was happiest in Japan?' he said. 'Not the sort of thing I say to the voters, of course. I suppose you think I didn't love that girl. No: I treated love lightly, but when I was with her in that house on Higashi Hill, I knew a contentment I'd never know again. She didn't understand I was just a naval lieutenant. She thought I'd bring her back to America with me, to live in my castle... strange, to think I spent the rest of my life becoming the great man she thought I already was! And she wasn't here to see it. The man who could have been president. Can't you see us in the White House? President Pinkerton and his Jap First Lady! Would there have been a war if that had happened?' His words rose, absurdly now, to their old oratorical pitch. In every great statesman there is something of the preacher. But this was a sermon no one wanted to hear.

He went on: 'What's the good of thinking of worlds that never were? Down the river of life we toss and tumble, and if we lodge for just a short time – a year, a month, a minute – on an island called Contentment, we should count ourselves lucky. Do you think I'm a lucky man, Sharpless? Oh, the luckiest! Because once, between sailings of the *Abraham Lincoln*, I lived in Nagasaki in a house on Higashi Hill.'

He faltered, slumping forward over his desk. I went to him; I embraced him, and his shoulders shook. I smoothed his head. Over the years the sleek grooves of his hair had grown sparser; he was almost entirely bald. Fat, in a thick roll like meat loaf, bulged from the back of his neck.

'It's over for us,' I said. 'For you and me, there's nothing left. But are we to say the world is ruined, because our lives are ruined? You'll never go back to Nagasaki. But your son's there, and has a chance of something neither of us will have again. Call Truman. Which one of these telephones is the hotline? Tell me: I'll get him for you. Talk like a great man one more time. Say there'll be no more bombings. The telephone, Senator – the telephone.'

Then came another voice: 'You're wasting your time.'

Deep in shadow, far from the desk, a black high-backed swivel chair had been turned away from the room. Slowly it swung around and the voice went on, bleakly wry: 'You've been entertaining me, Mr Sharpless. A little diversion to ease a lonely vigil! But I fear you're becoming boring.'

Kate Pinkerton stood. Long strands of hair hung dishevelled over her cheeks, and the jewel had vanished from the open neck of her blouse. She wore no jacket. She wore no shoes. The sky had grown red, and her face as she moved towards us was illumined weirdly in spectral light. Something cracked in my heart. The world had been ruined after all.

I stepped away from her husband. 'Is it so bad, what I've said?'

'Oh, Mr Sharpless! You destroy my life, then say to me, *Is it so bad?* Those Orientals you're fond of have the right idea, haven't they? Face ruin, die, but never mind, it's only one life and you'll have another. The wheel turns and one day, if your number comes up, you reach Nirvana. I dare say being suddenly obliterated is of little moment to the Oriental. I'd guess we've done the good burghers of Hiroshima a favour – wouldn't you suppose, my dear? After all, we've sped them on their way.'

She stood close to me, too close. I smelled her sweat. Appalled, I looked into her sagging face.

'It was your idea,' I said to her. 'The bombing.'

My words, I thought at once, were as mad as her own, but terrible certainty shook me as if the ground had rocked. Lightly, she touched my cheek. She might have been placating a child. I

264

almost sobbed. 'Really, Mr Sharpless!' she said. 'Does anyone listen to a weak woman?'

'When she controls her weak husband? Maybe,' I said.

She shook her head. 'When have I ever controlled that big mewling baby? Don't think I wouldn't have – I'm a Manville, aren't I? I could have been a senator like *that*.' She snapped her fingers. 'And why just a senator? I could have been president. But no, my duty was to preside over parties for campaign donors; my duty, to smile at VIP receptions and dance in the arms of fat foreign diplomats who reeked of garlic, and to assure them what fine fellows they were. Control him! Do you think he gave me a moment's thought? I covered up his every mistake, I supported his every decision, I worked for him like a slave, and he rewarded me by carousing with his whores. Do you think I let him know he was killing me? Think of it: everything I'd worked for, everything I'd lived for, a lifetime of duty and sacrifice – all of it, to be ruined by a half-caste bastard, son of a slant-eyed whore! Yes, I told my husband what to say to Truman: I told him what to say about the first attack and I've written his memo about the second one too. We'll save ourselves, I said. We'll root out the cancer that's gnawed at us all these years. But he had to spoil it. He had to be weak, weak to the last.'

Desperately, I said, 'I don't know what you're talking about.'

'Oh? I thought you'd met our friend Mr Mendoza. The sniper.'

The senator stood. 'Ben, Ben!' He clutched the back of his big leathery chair. 'That son of mine's a foolish boy. Always has been, always will be. He thought he was so clever! Of course we knew what he was up to at Los Alamos. I only wanted to warn him off, then cover the traces. Naturally, my wife wanted him punished. How she longed to stand over him in his cell, gloating at his disgrace!'

I said hotly, 'You know that isn't true.'

'Who are you to tell me what's true? She's my wife. He's my son. She never loved him. Everything that was real about the boy, everything that wasn't just an act, was a source of shame to her.'

'So you sent him back to Nagasaki.' Kate Pinkerton's voice choked. Horrified, I knew she was broken now: something in her had smashed, and would never be repaired. 'Nagasaki!' she repeated, expelling a sharp breath, as if the name contained all the sorrow of the world.

Fearfully, I would have asked her what she meant, but a telephone rang – the white – and she answered it, switching suddenly into calm, official tones; I thought she would pass the receiver to her husband, but she made no move to do so and he seemed not to expect it. He only stumbled towards the windows. I went to him. The evening was purple, with clouds fine as mist hanging in tattered scrims.

The senator spoke as if he could see the view, even pointing with the dagger. 'Now, take,' he said, 'the Library of Congress,' or 'Consider Capitol Hill,' or 'See that statue, Sharpless? Can you tell me who that is?' But more important than the sights was what they symbolized. Respectfully, I listened as he spoke of Life, Liberty, and the Pursuit of Happiness as if he really believed in them, but all the time I strained to hear Kate Pinkerton at the telephone.

Yes, they must come, she said. Yes, he was here.

Now I understood: I was too late. Until the last, the machine would grind on; Senator Pinkerton would command and be obeyed; there would be important calls; the guard at the door would imagine himself charged with a sacred trust; but the trust, like the senator's, was no more than a shell. The senator was a traitor, and the time had come to take him. We had all been traitors.

Kate Pinkerton replaced the receiver.

'Bitch. You bitch,' I said, but shame filled me as soon as I spat the words. All she did was look at me with implacable eyes. What else was there to be done? Nothing. We heard a siren, far away.

'They're coming, aren't they?' said the senator. He was staggering towards his wife.

'It's over, Ben. You've destroyed us, and for nothing.'

'Not nothing. There's my son, in Nagasaki.'

She shivered, as if feverish, and murmured: 'How I longed to see that place wiped from the earth – longed for it, all these years! Now, *a rain of ruin from the air, the like of which has never—*'

The senator clung to his wife; the dagger, still in his hand, glimmered against her crumpled blouse. For a moment she held back, then sank into his arms as if she were returning home at last, after a lifetime away. She moaned as soft words tumbled from his lips. 'Kate,' I heard him say, 'it's dark. Why is it so dark? You said you'd protect me from the dark.' On he babbled, a frightened child, until she calmed him with a kiss. I wished I were a thousand miles away. Still the siren sounded. Still the twilight faded: grey, almost black.

The blue telephone rang and I picked it up. 'Senator Pinkerton's office.'

A reporter. A leak, he said. Source reliable. No, he couldn't say from where (I hadn't asked), but could the senator comment? The senator, I said, had no comment. – None? None, when halfway around the world, where it's morning and tomorrow, a B-29 called *Bock's Car* is on its way home from its mission over Japan? None, when Truman's curse has come to pass and the rain of ruin is descending as we speak? They've done it, haven't they? Plutonium bomb! Crack in the clouds! Down, down, through the crack in the clouds…

'They've bombed Nagasaki.' I tried to replace the receiver but fumbled. It swung from the edge of the desk. 'Nagasaki.'

Blankly, I heard the siren; I heard the radio; I heard the Pinkertons sob when I repeated my announcement, louder this time; but as the senator pushed his wife away, then struck her, I could do nothing to intervene. The world lurched and I fell to the floor.

'Trouble,' I said like a prayer.

I felt the softness of the carpet beneath me; I fondled at the fibres and inhaled their rich aroma – so many cigars dropping ash, so many boots pressing down the gathered dust of years – before rolling on to my back and gazing up at the chandelier, ponderous as fate but still unlit, while the senator and Kate Pinkerton, in lurid shadow-play, ended their odyssey at last.

'You've killed my son.' Horror hung heavy in the senator's words.

'Ben, no! He was my son too.'

'You wanted this. You said so.'

Imploringly, she spread her hands. 'What does it matter what I wanted, what you wanted? The machine had been set in motion. Had the Japanese beaten us to the atomic bomb, they would have levelled Los Angeles. They aren't innocent. They aren't good. None of this could be helped. Not Hiroshima. Not Nagasaki. And not the world that lies ahead.'

'You've always hated him, and hated me.'

'Ben, I love you.' Her hands dropped. '*Ben, what are you doing?*'

I wonder still if I could have saved Kate Pinkerton. Time seemed to smash, like a plate on tiles. I might have been back in that bunker at Alamogordo; I would always be in that bunker in Alamogordo, dazzled by the beauty and terror of the three-person'd God, for all the years that I lived.

Half sobbing, I scrambled to my knees, but agony seared my injured right leg, and all I could do was watch as Kate Pinkerton backed away from her blind, blundering husband; as he ripped the sheath from the dagger and lunged at her; as she hurled one heavy statute book at him, then another, then crashed into the radio and brushed the bulky controls. The room filled with a deafening crescendo. It was Tartarin's great lament, '*Il mio sogno dei leoni è finito*' – my dream of the lions is over. For Kate Pinkerton, it marked the moment when all she had been, even the remnants of what she had been, fell from her at last.

The dream was over. Everything was over. She tore her hair. Like a crazed insect, she battered this way and that: against the windows, against a wall, against a map of the world, with pins and paper arrows marking the progress of the Pacific campaign. She rushed back to the telephones, grabbed one, then another, then swept them all from the desk; she doubled over, then gazed up in despairing rapture at the blind man with the dagger and stepped, ecstatic, into his embrace.

'I love you, Ben,' she cried, then slumped down.

The senator stepped away, raising the blood-dripping dagger like an offering to the night. He flung back his throat, as if to cry out to the gods, but the music was rising, bursting and cascading like the bomb that had blinded him. It filled the air, relentless as fire: that great despairing plea of Tartarin's that the world should be something other than what it had become.

There was nothing but the music: if telephones jangled, we would not hear them; if sirens wailed or snapped into silence, we would know nothing of it; if guardsmen's boots pounded across the marble hall below and up the stairs, we would remain oblivious – oblivious too, as fists, then shoulders, crashed against the locked doors like battering rams. There was no world outside, only this classical drama where a blind man, crazed and raving, staggered against a flagpole and made it topple; thudded to his knees, sank to his haunches, hunched his shoulders, then raised his torso, clutched the dagger in both hands, positioned it below his diaphragm, and thrust it abruptly upwards.

No, I thought to say, but I never wanted him to stop. The machinery had worked its way to the end; the ticktock motion begun in Nagasaki so many years before had at last achieved its rest.

When a guardsman splintered through the doors, he cuffed a light switch, disclosing in the dazzle of the chandelier two corpses, one collapsed across the other. Half draped over the senator's shoulders was the fallen Stars and Stripes.

Curtain

And that, I thought, was the end of my book. I pulled the last page from the typewriter with relief. Of all the books I had written, this had been the hardest. After the war I felt as if a curtain had come down, dividing me decisively from the world I used to know. There was so much I wanted to forget. I ignored articles about Hiroshima and Nagasaki. I appeared indifferent to campaigns against nuclear weapons, angering my students at the liberal arts college in Monterey where I taught for many years. Only a sense of duty compelled me to tell my story. Now I need never look at it again. My neat stack of pages, bound in twine, would lodge in a drawer of my filing cabinet, undisturbed until their author was dead. I was finished. I could forget.

Soon I received a letter that changed my mind. PEN, the writers' organization, was sending an American delegation to Japan to commemorate the fortieth anniversary of the atomic bombings. As arguably (I liked the 'arguably') America's most distinguished living biographer, would I… ? Would I! My first reaction was a rage I could neither control nor explain. I crumpled the letter and flung it across my study. But I knew it was a summons I would not be able to resist. Rage gave way and I retrieved the ball of paper, smoothing it flat with a sorrowful reverence, as if it were a love letter from long ago. Would I… ? Of course, though I told myself I was a fool. I was old. I expected to die soon. Perhaps I would die in Japan, overwhelmed by memories.

I need neither have feared nor hoped. The world of skyscrapers and neon, salarymen and pachinko parlours that confronted our delegation when we landed had nothing to do with me. Modern Japan has about it the quality of a stage set. The modernity so strenuously imitated seems likely at any moment to vanish, revealing the eternal country beneath. Nothing seems real.

In the days that followed, we travelled in a plush coach, a sort of movie star's Greyhound, from Tokyo to Kyoto, Kyoto to Hiroshima, Hiroshima to Nagasaki. Even when our travels provided us with visions more picturesque, I saw them unfold like a film, outside me: the toppling tiered rice fields, the temples and torii, the painted geishas, the Shinto shrines, the statues of the Buddha. This was Japan, and Japan was pictures.

Piously, my fellow delegates clicked their cameras. I suppose they found me remote. Arwin Janis Quirk, the prolific feminist novelist, made no attempt to interest me in her denunciations of patriarchy. Earl Rogers, a boozy literary lion some twenty years my junior, who had published a 'searing' war novel in 1948 and not much since, lost all respect for me when he learned I had spent the war as what he called a 'pen-pusher'; I resisted saying I had never respected him. Schneider Kipfer, the Beat poet, had few interests other than smoking marijuana and reading the I Ching. I had hopes of friendship with Hooper McGee, the Southern short-story writer, but while she warmed to me when she thought I was Southern, she cooled when I told her I had grown up in France. Chip Striker, the black activist playwright, whose political pronouncements had made him even more notorious than his taboo-defying plays, had too much to do in speechifying on race prejudice, war, and American imperialism to pay much attention to me. On the coach stereo, our Japanese driver played American country music. Chip Striker complained, to little effect, about 'redneck shit'. There was a song by Buck Owens about a man who left his heart with a girl made in Japan. The driver repeated it remorselessly.

The three days we spent in Hiroshima were – or were meant to be – the most important part of our itinerary. Dutifully, we trailed through exhibitions, stood through ceremonies, sat through speeches, and made speeches of our own, but the blankness in me remained. I was grateful for the kindness of our Japanese hosts, who treated me with a solicitude I felt I hardly deserved.

On the morning of August 6, at the commemoration of the bombing, I did my best to be moved by Peace Memorial Park, with its cenotaph and surmounting arch. Standing between a blissful Schneider Kipfer and the ostentatiously sobbing Arwin Janis Quirk, I gazed across the pool and lush gardens to the old Industrial Promotion Hall across the river, one of the few buildings left standing after the bombing, with the skeleton frame of its shattered dome. *This is life. This is death. This is what men do*, the dome seemed to say, but I did not want to hear.

There is a torch in the park called the Flame of Peace. It always burns.

'An eternal flame,' I said, when our Japanese lady guide had explained it to us the day before.

She shook her head. 'No, not eternal. When the last atomic weapon is destroyed, the flame shall be extinguished.'

The ceremony wore on. Voices spoke in Japanese and English, reciting familiar facts, but still I felt only numb: the destructive power of so many thousands of tons of TNT, the radioactive fireball, the heat so searing that only shadows of some of the dead remained, branded on the rubble like photographic negatives. I breathed slowly, as if I were sleeping. We build our memorials and make our speeches: what else are we to do? What had happened in this place was too great to comprehend, let alone allay. Had it been inevitable? It was no act of God: men had made decisions, bent their inventive arts towards this end, and this had happened. It is what men do: we kill one another, and invent our reasons why.

I looked away from the impassive arch and the faces all around me: towards the trees that stirred a little on a scented breeze; towards the blue, cloudless sky to which, forty years before, an indifferent gravity had reached up and pulled down the sun. Birds sang in the trees, and the speaker quoted lines from a thirteenth-century text: '*Ceaselessly, the river flows and yet the water is never the same, while in the still pools the shifting foam gathers and is gone, never staying for a moment. Even so is man and his habitation.*'

That evening I excused myself from a banquet and rested in my hotel room. There was something comforting in the anonymous plush decor. I could have been anywhere: Atlanta, Buenos Aires, Cairo, Delhi…

Next morning the movie-star Greyhound took us to Nagasaki. It was an afterthought of sorts, if a necessary one. Our mission was accomplished: the main business over, the main photographs taken, the main quotations recorded by reporters. I wished I could go home at once. I was weary of solemn, useless words; weary of floral tributes; weary of Earl Rogers and Chip Striker with their aggressive voices and confident simple certainties and competing never-resting efforts to go to bed with Arwin Janis Quirk.

When we reached Nagasaki I announced, to the consternation of our hosts, that I would attend only the memorial service on the morning of August 9. I pleaded tiredness and was believed; I was an old man, and frail – but not so frail as I made out. Liberated from a conference on nuclear weapons, I set out to explore the city.

Nagasaki had not been destroyed so thoroughly as Hiroshima. Hills and valleys had confined the worst of the blast to the north, where the harbour narrows into the river. Around the harbour, much of the old city I had known could still be made out, like scraps of a collage, papered over here and there with many a recent addition.

Renting a cab to drive me around, I surprised the driver by saying I had no wish to see Hypocentre Park or the Peace Statue or the Atomic Bomb Museum. I visited temples and browsed in stores. I looked at the view from Inasa-yama, across the harbour and over the sea. Whether my purpose was clear to me from the first, I cannot say. Can our intentions grow in us unknown, deep in our minds, before we become aware of them? Mine revealed itself to me with no surge of insight; I felt no surprise, unless at the fact that it had taken so long to come to light. But of course: I could avoid it no longer. On the afternoon of August 8, I asked my driver to take me to the top of Higashi Hill.

My heart beat hard as the cab climbed. How could so many years have passed? How could I have grown so old? I closed my eyes. The afternoon was hot. A fly buzzed against the back windshield, and I wanted to tell the driver to stop and let it out. The motion of the cab made me feel sick; but then the cab slowed, gravel crunched under the tyres and I let my eyes open.

That the house would still be there was more than I had dreamed. The place was neither dilapidated nor altered in ways that I could see; still it stood in its fecund gardens, gazing down to the harbour. I hauled myself from the cab, and looked back at my driver, who had alighted as well. He smiled, gestured for me to go ahead, then bent with a scooping hand into an open back door, endeavouring to release the trapped fly.

Summer caressed me and scents were strong as I moved through the gardens. Unreally, I ran a hand down the warm trunk of a cedar; I touched the flesh of ferns; light flickered over paving stones in a dance of shadows and sun; none of it was real, and nor was the man I saw when the path turned: an old Japanese man – a gardener, I assumed – hunching his coppery, naked back over a bed of azaleas. His hands were knotted and his head was bald. Trimming stalks, he hummed a little. I moved closer. The old man had not heard me, but my steps were slow and soft.

I wondered if I could make him understand me. I wanted to ask him who lived here now.

I cleared my throat and tried.

He did not turn.

I tried again.

'He's deaf,' came a voice behind me. 'He likes to say it was the bomb. Just old age, really.'

I turned, and was sure I was dreaming.

'Trouble,' I said. 'You're alive!'

I can hardly say he had not changed. He was an old man, like me; hooded folds half-concealed his eyes; his hair was white; when he smiled, as he did then, his face pleated into a thousand wrinkles and his teeth had acquired the brown-ivory patina of age. Yet somehow, strangely, he defied time. He was still what he had always been. He was still my Trouble.

'You aren't surprised to see me?' I said.

He shrugged. 'I've been waiting.'

'For forty years?'

'Don't flatter yourself. We get the papers even here, you know. I read about your delegation. Come into the house,' he added. 'Or doesn't a busy man like you have time for tea?'

As we passed the gardener, Trouble bent down, laying a hand on the old man's back. The face turned to look at his, and Trouble, enunciating clearly, said something in Japanese. The gardener nodded to him, then to me, and smiled, but I knew by then that he was not a gardener.

'Isamu,' I said.

Shaken, I let Trouble lead me up to the veranda. A sparse tatami room stood open to the outdoors. We sat on mats at a little low table. Isamu joined us, and a girl who looked like a young Suzuki served us green tea.

'Of course, hardly any of this is original,' said Trouble, gesturing around him. 'We've replaced so many walls and beams, it's a whole new house, really.'

'But still the old house,' said Isamu, whose deafness, I gathered, was not complete.

Much of our conversation that day was trivial. We were three old men whose lives had been and gone; there was little left for us but to enjoy the garden and wonder whether there would be rain soon. Yet I learned much. Isamu had married after the war, though his wife was dead now; the girl who served us tea was his daughter. Until his retirement, he had been a Mitsubishi executive; Trouble had given English lessons and translated business documents. In old age, the two men were comfortable, but not rich. Prince Yamadori, executed by the Americans as a war criminal, had left his nephew nothing; Yamadori's title had been stripped from him, his assets confiscated.

Still the war, and its bitter end, loomed over them. Vividly but calmly, Trouble spoke of those desperate days after the bombing, when thousands of dying refugees crowded the roads around the harbour, many of them blind or mutilated hideously, all of them struggling uselessly to flee.

'We cared for them,' he said, 'as best we could. But it was never enough.'

He looked into the distance, and I thought: he's changed. But of course he had changed. When I had last seen him he was over forty, but even then he remained in essence a callow boy.

Now, at last, Ben Pinkerton was a man.

I wondered if he regretted anything and was not sure he did. Life had been difficult for him during the years of the occupation. At all costs he could not be identified as Benjamin Franklin Pinkerton II. Lying low, he had kept out of sight of the Americans. He had changed his name and carried forged papers; to this day he was known in Nagasaki as Mr Glover.

'Hey, Sharpless, remember this?' Trouble said suddenly, leaping up like a man much younger. In a corner of the room stood an old-fashioned phonograph with a frilly, yawning horn, like the one the fellows at Blaze had smashed years before. He wound it up, let the needle drop – and the years fell away; it was 1914, and there I was, hearing that intemperate bellowing voice, rising startled from my dorm-room bed, moving down a line of curtained cubicles to meet a boy with the most extraordinary eyes I had ever seen.

A lifetime later, I looked into those eyes and wondered if I would weep – cast myself down and weep helplessly, abandoned to all dignity and shame. *Some of these days – oh, you'll miss me, honey*, sang Sophie Tucker. Good old Sophie Tucker! She had been right about everything.

When tea was over Isamu retired to rest, and Trouble and I took a turn about the garden. He praised Isamu's gardening skills, and I was keen in my admiration; I kept my voice light, but something was slipping inside me, ready to fall. Was there a lesson I must learn, too late? Trouble asked me about my books. One of them had won the Pulitzer and he said he had better read it; I doubted that he would. I told him about the PEN delegation and he murmured interest politely. We talked about Aunt Toolie, and the theatre company she still ran in Carmel – though by now she was well over ninety; we talked about Le Vol and his recent retrospective at the Museum of Modern Art. Trouble urged me to give them his best wishes. I said I would, and, of course, I would not. I would never tell them he was still alive. He would be my secret, locked inside my heart.

Sorrow filled me and I gazed at Trouble. I felt as if a wall had descended between us. Then I knew: Trouble was Trouble, and I was Woodley Sharpless. Hemispheres divided us and always had.

We stood at the foot of the garden, looking down to the harbour where the *Abraham Lincoln* had docked so long ago. A lifetime later, the ships still came, drawn as if by strange enchantments from the many corners of the world. I raised my eyes to the blue, distant hills that hovered above the city and its busy waterfront. I said to Trouble, 'Do you think Nirvana might be a place like this – the perfect lookout?'

He said, 'I think Nirvana's got no lookout at all.'

'Perhaps you're right,' I said, and turned away.

We were walking back up the garden when Trouble asked me, 'You were there when the senator died, weren't you?'

'Yes,' I said.

'And Mama,' he said. 'Poor Mama. I didn't let her see me in San Diego. I've regretted that. I believed we'd meet again. I thought she'd always be there.'

'She loved you,' I said. 'They both loved you.'

Trouble ran a hand through a spray of blossoms. 'I remembered too much. That was my problem all along, wasn't it? For years I had an image of a face that loomed in front of me, eyes wide and tearful. More has come back since. Even now. This house. This garden.' He gestured around him, as if a frail Japanese woman might linger nearby, a ghost among the trees. 'The wind blows, and she whispers in my ear. Sometimes she plays the samisen or we peer together through holes in a shoji screen. I remember once, perhaps the night before she died, she made me stay by her all night until dawn, waiting for my father to come. We waited and waited. And then he came. In the end, he came.'

Lightly, I touched Trouble's sleeve; it was the first time I had touched him that afternoon. I smiled and said it was time I was going. My cab was waiting.

He said, 'There's an expression here in Japan: *Shikata ga nai*.'

'I've heard it,' I said. 'It can't be helped. Too bad.'

'It was all bound to happen. Somehow or other, it was all bound to happen.'

'You'll thank Isamu for me, won't you?' I said.

'He'd rather be thanking you. He's always been grateful to you, Sharpless. If there's a hero of this story, he thinks it's you. After all, I wouldn't be here if it weren't for you.'

'Oh, you'd have found a way – a rascal like you!'

By the cab, Trouble hugged me, and I gripped him more tightly than perhaps I should have done. I never wanted to let him go; but all I could do, all I could ever do, was let him go.

'You'll be at the memorial service tomorrow, I suppose?' he said.

I asked him, too eagerly, 'Will I see you there?'

'All those Americans? I'd better lie low.'

'You flatter yourself, Mr Glover. Who'd know you now?'

'You did. Has your life been happy, Sharpless?'

What a thing to ask! I thought of my books. My students. My travels. Of Wobblewood West, of Aunt Toolie and Le Vol, waiting for my return. What was my life? Our three dogs, our Sunday drives, our friendly squabbles over the dinner table. None of it could last. Aunt Toolie would die soon – glad, perhaps, to join Uncle Grover; Le Vol, for all I knew, would die before me. Once we had been young. Now we were old and our world was ending.

Dear Trouble! Even now he was an enigma, an essence perpetually escaping me, as I looked at him and said, almost meaning it, 'I'm happier than I ever believed I could be.'

'Me too.' His eyes held mine and I studied him intently, as if I might understand him, might understand myself, if only I could fix his image in my mind.

As I climbed back into the cab, he called after me, 'Sharpless, wait! Where's your ashplant?'

'The walking stick? Oh, I lost it years ago,' I said. 'I always meant to get another. Then I learned to walk without it. That stick had just been keeping my leg weak, all those years.'

I waved from the window as the cab drove away.

The memorial service was early the next morning, but there was a final ceremony still to come. In the evening I gathered with many others by the river, where I lit a candle and set it drifting in a paper boat towards the harbour. Afterwards, I stepped back, anonymous in the crowd. There were thousands of candles, but not so many, not nearly so many, as the dead that they remembered.

Silently, I watched the little flaming pillar, tremulous in the wind, drifting away from me in its precarious vessel, until I could no longer be sure which one was mine. Darkness gathered; the waters, defiantly, were a sea of flame, but within a short time the paper boats were sinking, some taking on water, some burned through already by the candles that they carried.

Acknowledgements

Without Puccini's *Madama Butterfly* (1904), this book would not exist. As well as the opera and its libretto by Luigi Illica and Giuseppe Giacosa, I have drawn on earlier incarnations of the story: David Belasco's one-act play *Madame Butterfly* (1900), which inspired Puccini; John Luther Long's short story 'Madame Butterfly' (1898), on which Belasco's play was based; and Pierre Loti's novel *Madame Chrysanthème* (1888), which appears to have furnished Long with many details and was itself the basis of an 1894 opera by André Messager. Jan van Rij's *Madame Butterfly: Japonisme, Puccini, and the Search for the Real Cho-Cho-San* (2001) taught me much, and I recommend it to those wishing to explore further the origins, meanings, and permutations of the Butterfly story.

Many other sources leave traces in this novel. Several are of particular note: Ronald Takaki's *Hiroshima: Why America Dropped the Atomic Bomb* (1995) and J. Samuel Walker's *Prompt and Utter Destruction: Truman and the Use of Atomic Bombs Against Japan* (1997) offer brief and compelling investigations of why the bombings happened; Gar Alperovtiz's massive study *The Decision to Use the Atomic Bomb* (1995) is, I suspect, the definitive account. David C. Cassidy's *J. Robert Oppenheimer and the American Century* (2005) and Peter Goodchild's *J. Robert Oppenheimer: 'Shatterer of Worlds'* (1980) depict in detail the development of the bomb. *Doctor Atomic*, the 2005 opera about Oppenheimer by John Adams, helped me imagine the Trinity test.

Accounts of the bombings from the point of view of the victims include that classic of reportage, John Hersey's *Hiroshima* (1946; rev. ed. 1985), Takashi Nagai's memoir *The Bells of Nagasaki* (1949), and Masuji Ibuse's novel *Black Rain* (1969). *The Rise and Fall of Imperial Japan*, ed. S. L. Meyer (1976), proved of great value to me, not least because of the pictures. Ian Whitcomb's *After the Ball* (1972), a favourite book of mine for years, fuelled my interest in old (very old) pop music. Sir Hubert Parry's setting of 'Fear No More…' appears in Charles Vincent's anthology *Fifty Shakspere Songs* (1906). *Tartarin de Tarascon* (1872) by Alphonse Daudet was a novel Puccini planned to adapt as an opera, before scrapping the project in favour of *Madama Butterfly*.

Antony Heaven gave me the idea for this book. Roz Kaveney read it at just the right time. The London Library was, as ever, my best resource. I am grateful to Ravi Mirchandani, Margaret Stead, Orlando Whitfield, Richard Evans, and all at Atlantic Books in London, and Steve Rubin, Barbara Jones, Kenn Russell, Kathleen Lord, Rebecca Seltzer, Joanna Levine, and all at Henry Holt in New York. Thanks to Ian Pindar, Charlotte Webb, and Colin Tate. Special thanks to my agent, Sara Menguc, for her patience, persistence, and belief.

David Rain is an Australian writer who lives in London. He has taught literature and writing at Queen's University of Belfast, University of Brighton, and Middlesex University, London.